FOURTEEN NEW GHOST STORIES

First published in 2017 by DPN Books

Cover design by Marie Bussiere

For my mother

With thanks to the Velkys, Steven Lownds,
Marie Bussiere and everyone else who
has given their time and support to the
project over the years.

For exclusive content and audio stories, visit
www.newghoststories.com

CONTENTS

INTRODUCTION

It's been quite a journey. Over six years have past since I embarked on my quest to hunt down Britain's untold ghost stories. And even after all this time, I still find myself startled and terrified on a regular basis.

Sometimes the reaction is delayed. My confidence builds and I think I'm becoming immune to all the scares. Perform any action often enough and it becomes routine, regardless of how strange or unpleasant. I have spent countless hours sat behind my laptop, working with material that any normal person would find shocking and upsetting. These are events that have damaged people's lives, but have become just part of my everyday routine.

But that norm never really lasts. Something always breaks through. There's no predicting what it will be, no way to guess what will make one element extraordinary or more frightening than another. Something will just click. It can happen too easily if I've let my guard down, when I'm tired and working late, or when I've let my attention drift to something else. Suddenly, unexpectedly, my resistance drops. And I find my heart racing, my palms sweating, and goosebumps, breaking out on my head and down to my toes.

When it comes to the dark, the disturbing, the horrific, you can't stay detached for long. We're all afraid of the dark, the unknown. No matter how much we know, we can never really be sure what might be hiding out there, somewhere.

I used to joke about my book giving people nightmares. Well I've had plenty. When something gets under your skin, it doesn't go away very easy. The idea can linger and haunt you again.

For the uninitiated, let me explain how this all came about...

Years ago I was inspired by a chance encounter to reach out to people across the United Kingdom. I wanted to know if anyone had ever had a supernatural experience. I wasn't interested in the melodramatic fodder found in cheap magazines. What I wanted to know was whether anyone had experienced something that they had not shared before. A story that, for whatever reason, they had been afraid to share, or had just assumed no one would take seriously.

I would offer them the chance to tell their story with complete anonymity and without judgment. I would take them seriously, as long as they took me seriously. I had certain conditions that had to be met. I wanted to be open-minded, to listen and not to judge. But I also had no intention of being gullible. If they had claimed to live on a certain street, in a certain house, in a certain town, I wanted them to prove it. If they had met with so-and-so at such a time, I wanted confirmation from both parties. If they had travelled to this place or that, I wanted them to show me how they travelled there, how much they spent on petrol, how much the train cost, etc. It's hard to prove the paranormal, but it should be easy for honest people to provide simple circumstantial evidence. It's been a surprisingly effective test; tricksters don't usually like their own time being wasted.

I have spoken to several hundred people. Some were liars. Some had complex problems. Some had only a small story to relay – a strange shadow, a moving object or a weird voice. With these put to one side, there remained a small group of subjects with stories to tell that were genuinely compelling. Could these stories actually be the real thing? Actual encounters with the supernatural?

In 2014 I presented 11 of these cases in a book. I laid out my intentions clearly then as I do now; it was and is still not my intention to press upon the reader a belief that these stories are true, or that they prove the existence of the supernatural. I invited them on a journey towards the unknown and to consider what these stories might mean if they were true. Or what other sinister truth they might conceal if they were not.

I was content to allow my work to speak for itself. Once the first volume was published, I got back to writing. Enquiries were still coming in; there were more stories to tell and I already had several I wished to prepare for publication.

I had not really spent a lot of time considering what the reaction to my first book might be. There would be reviews of course, and they had the possibility of being positive or negative. But I was proud of what I'd achieved, and felt confident enough to shrug off any unconstructive commentary.

I had somehow forgotten just how divisive the subject of the supernatural can be. Sceptics, of course, wished to have their say. And they most certainly did. I received a lot of criticism, ranging from the ugly and abusive to the thought-provoking and intelligent. I wish I had received more of the latter, but alas, the internet doesn't behave like that.

What really had never occurred to me was that professional voices within the field of supernatural studies, everyone from parapsychologists to mediums, would wish to contact me, to share and discuss views, even to trade data and notes.

That professionals would take a serious interest in my work is flattering, but also rather intimidating. I had always assumed that my enthusiasm for the project, my empathy for my subjects, and my many good intentions were all that I needed. Suddenly I found myself being posed questions about project data and ethical conduct that had never even crossed my mind.

I'm obviously not a scientific or psychical research professional. I expected that by telling these stories, I would encourage discussion and evaluation, but it was not my intention to drive that conversation or present any thesis myself. I have always been clear that I was putting the task of interpreting these stories squarely in the hands of the reader. It was for them, as it now is for you, to make up your own mind.

So before we continue, I think it's worth responding to some of these issues. There have been a number of common threads that have featured time and time again in conversations and correspondence that are relevant to the first book and to this one. I will address each one, definitively, for the record:

1) The stories are obviously made up.

That's a valid perspective. I imagine many readers feel that way, although I hope they arrived at that opinion after reading the book rather than before reading it.

I do not present these stories as true accounts. I've been clear about that. I've not been uncritical, and as we've already covered, I have set certain criteria to establish the reliability of each subject. This criteria does not prove that what they say is true or not. It establishes only pieces of the puzzle. The full picture can only be provided by the subject. Whether or not the story they tell is accurate or false is unprovable.

In terms of truth, I will make only this claim: I do not believe that I am being lied too. I do believe that the subjects who feature in both books believe that what they say is true, that they have not deliberately set out to mislead. But this is just my personal view.

2) Oh come on! The stories are absurd, how can you possibly believe them?

If you look at the news you'll find that absurd things are happening all the time, even outside of election years. Yes, some of what you've read in the first volume is bizarre. What you'll read in this volume is even more so. But the subjects believe what they say. It is not absurd to them.

You are entitled to believe that the seemingly far-fetched nature of some accounts immediately marks them as being false. Personally, I prefer to keep an open mind.

3) Some of this stuff would have made the news? I can't find it mentioned anywhere – it must be false!

Some stories did make the news. But to maintain the anonymity of the subjects, a number of redactions and alterations have had to be made. Names, locations, dates and other small details have been altered to prevent readers from tracking the subjects down.

It's also worth noting that some of these stories took place decades ago. Google tends to only take you back so far.

4) So you've altered them too – that makes them even less trustworthy.

This is a standard journalistic practice. I've used the same techniques employed in the news profession. These have been implemented carefully to avoid changing the facts of a story while maintaining confidentiality. No story in either collection has been impacted in any significant way by the changes I have effected.

5) Why should we trust you?

It's really up to you. All you can do is read my statements, read the stories, and then make your own judgement.

6) Didn't I hear that someone had tracked one of the subjects down?

Perhaps you heard it. But I would never confirm or deny it. The subjects featured in both books have placed their trust in me. I will not betray that trust.

7) But someone you wrote about has accused you of being a liar, haven't they?

I can confirm this. But I can do little more than that because of the confidentiality agreement I am committed too. All accounts are either written by the subject or recorded to tape. Any subject is welcome to request an unexpurgated copy of any recording or statement – I will gladly share it with them. If they find that I have misquoted them, manipulated information or fabricated any information, they are welcome to pursue further action against me. I stand fully behind my work.

8) Has it occurred to you that these people have mental health problems?

There are subjects in both collections who have or are currently experiencing issues with mental health. But mental health problems are not uncommon, and they do not guarantee that a person's sense of reality is impaired. A mental health problem does not mean a person should not have their voice heard.

9) These are clearly vulnerable people and you're exploiting them for commercial gain.

Commercial gains are not quite what they used to be in the publishing market. But I do not believe that by publishing any of these stories that I have put anyone at any risk or left them vulnerable to exploitation.

I have been very clear about my intentions. While I am not an expert on mental heath, I have been careful to avoid subjects whose behaviour was noticeably erratic. I have always required subjects to relay their stories more than once. Those who were unable to do so consistently have not been included in either book.

10) You're just interested in sensationalism and only print the most gruesome or shocking stories.

Most people's encounters with ghosts are fairly mundane and consist of little more than a glance out of the corner of their eye. I could include all these stories, but they wouldn't make for a very interesting book.

I confess to prioritising for print the most thought-provoking and most exciting of the stories. I don't apologise for this; why would any author seek to hold back their most exciting material?

Strong material comes with it's own difficulties. It is safe to say that the stories in this volume are even more extraordinary than the first. The sequel must deliver more than the original. But this led to a real problem for me. Not only was I finding myself taken with occasional sensations of creeping dread, I was also starting to feel something else. And that was doubt.

I had challenged my readers to look at the stories I had presented, and to consider the possibility that they were true, or to reject them as false.

But the stories collected here, they reach new levels of strangeness and horror. This made them more enticing and more fascinating – hence the goosebumps, sweats and nightmares – but to consider these tales to be true, to be absolutely accurate, meant a great deal more than simply accepting that the subject was not a liar.

A fence is not an easy place to sit. If I present these stories as something that could be true, does that not mean on some level that I have to actually accept that they might be true?

Having gone to the effort of trying to prove the reliability of my subjects and talking to them with an open mind, I was giving them the benefit of the doubt. And if I was willing to do that, I had to be willing to accept that all they had said might be possible.

This was a problem. The even more bizarre nature of these stories meant that they could not be possible within the boundaries of what I would consider reality. To accept them as true represented a significant challenge to my very perception of what was real. It meant accepting that the universe was not the rational place that I thought it was. That there really were strange unknown forces that existed, that might be malign and dangerous to us in this life and perhaps even beyond that.

This is what I began to find most frightening of all. The chance that reality was nothing like I thought it was.

This conflict led to an emotional backlash. This was more serious than any creeping fear, this uncertainty had unexpected effects. I found it hard to work, hard to sleep, hard to relax. My work had not just got under my skin; it had undermined all that I took for granted in the world.

For a time, I ceased all work. It took months for me to collect my thoughts and re-assess my perspective. As a consequence to the questioning of reality, I rebounded and became drawn harder towards the opposite. If I could not accept what seemed to be impossible, then I had to believe that these stories were not true. Reality was just what I thought it to be, rationale, stable, predictable.

If that were then my view, I was faced with another dilemma. If I believed the stories were falsehoods, then I was indulging in the spreading of lies and fiction. My whole premise was a fraud.

I was confused and I was in turmoil. I won't go into any great detail regarding my naval-gazing. What happened to me was, in retrospect, inevitable. You can try to be open-minded, and stay impartial. But you can only act in these ways; you can't stay perpetually undecided. Ultimately you have to have an opinion. You can't run away from one. Not when a subject occupies so many of your waking hours.

I was in denial about my own feelings. What I was doing was affecting me. How could it not? These weren't everyday stories. I had sat and listened to people explain to me events that had devastating consequences. These stories are powerful. And if nothing else, the consequences were very real. You can have doubts about the causes of a crime, but you can clearly identify the impact.

Yes, I too am a reader. I have found myself in the same shoes that I have put my readers in. I left them to make up their own mind and I have been forced to make up my own. I could not continue without doing so.

So what do I think? What is my assessment of all that I have heard or seen? That alas, would be telling. The point of the project is not changed by my own developing opinions. Journalists and writers are called upon to deliver all kinds of stories from a balanced perspective, regardless of their own personal views. I am no different. My purpose was always to give the reader a chance to make their own judgement. I have made my own. But my views must not affect yours. You must make up your own mind. It is still not for me to tell you how to understand or interpret what is to come.

It only remains for me to thank all those who have helped and supported me in this endeavour. A special thank you must go to everyone who was brave enough to speak to me and trust me with their secrets. And for all the patience they have shown through my many questions and demands.

I sincerely hope that this book creates as much discussion and debate as the first. But don't come looking for my views on the subject. I must insist, at least for now, that they remain outside of the conversation.

THE GIRL ON THE BENCH

Me and my friends we all loved Lisa Ward – everyone did. She was a teenage boy's wet dream. She was just incredible; amazing body, and great tits. Proper full-handful tits. Cracking arse too. She was in the year above us, so she was that bit more experienced. And she wore these skirts; they always seemed shorter than everyone else's. And black underwear – you could see it under her school shirt.

She used to have this tight leather jacket too. She was so fit. Christ, even the teachers wanted to fuck her.

She was fit and she knew it. But she wasn't a bitch about it, you know? She didn't look down on you. I think she liked it, liked it when you looked at her. She wouldn't stick her nose up at you like some of them would. She'd sort of smile at you, cos she knew you were looking. I mean, if you dress like that you want them to look, don't you? Fucking sex on legs; no wonder her dad was shouting at her all the time, having a go at her on the front doorstep. Have a daughter like that and you know there are guys who are gonna crawl over broken glass to get their hands on her.

It wasn't just the looks, it's the way she carried herself. She had such attitude. She wasn't just fit-as, she was cool. Real rock chick. Smoked, yeah, but not a lot. She never stunk of fags. She was class. She had everything. She had it all.

There were other girls at school, but only one Lisa.

She went out with this guy, Craig Ashley. We hated his guts, course we did. They were proper all over each other, all the time, whenever you saw them. He was a biker; had his own leather jacket and slicked-back blonde hair. Proper James Dean wannabe. We hated him. But we didn't, not really. He was all-right; he was in the year above Lisa, so I'd known him at school too. And while some of the older kids would have goes at you, he'd be more like your mate. If he saw someone having a go, he'd tell them to lay off and leave you alone.

Loved himself though. Proper pretty boy. He looked like he wanted to be a model, or a rock star, but he was really working in a garage. He was into bikes. He used to ride this old fixed-up Triumph. We'd have probably thought he was cool if he wasn't touching Lisa up.

He used to come up the road on that bike and rev it up as he came so she'd know he was coming.

Forgot to mention that she lived up the end of my road didn't I? God that made me popular. I mean, we tried everything, me and my mates: binoculars, telescope, camcorder, mirrors... but you just couldn't get the right angle up the street to see anything. We'd hang out in front of the house, hoping just to catch a glimpse of her in the window. We never did though; she wasn't stupid. She wasn't going to just undress where we could all see her.

We all dreamed about Lisa Ward. But none of us ever came close to going with her. Except me. You'd think I'd want to boast about something like that wouldn't you? But I've never told anyone about it, ever.

It was fucked up. So unbelievably fucked up.

Her dad and her used to have these fights. And he didn't like Craig. But they never like the boyfriends do they? I don't know about the arguments, who said what, but at some point Craig stopped going to see her at the house. Instead, she'd walk to the park across the road and she'd sit on this bench and wait for him. So he'd come along on his motorbike, go straight off the road and into the park and pick her up.

Sometimes they'd start feeling each other up and disappear into the bushes. I had a good look, but I couldn't see anything that far. This bench – you could see it right from my bedroom window. There were a row of trees blocking the big open area of the park, but there was this gap where I could see right through to the bench and to where she used to meet him. I'd sit in my room and I'd watch her waiting for him. And then, when he'd come swanning along on his bike, right up to her, I'd watch and wish it were me over there and not him.

It went on like this for months; she'd be on the bench, he'd come and pick her up. Sometimes he'd bring her home, sometimes he wouldn't. I think he had a place of his own, but I didn't really know him that well.

Or what happened to him. Sometime around Easter – and this was when I was in year ten – we heard that Craig had been in an accident. Later we found out that he'd died. What we heard at the time was he'd tried to overtake on a country road but had to swerve out the way of some lorry and gone head-over-handlebars at the side of the road and broken his neck. But later the rumour was that he'd been in a bar fight and got stabbed. I dunno. I didn't really know him. My family didn't either; he wasn't part of the neighbourhood. They put a plaque up at the school, that's all I know. 17 years old. We didn't like him, but we were all a bit, you know, upset, maybe. We weren't close but you don't really think about that kind of stuff happening when you're kids, do you?

Of course we all wondered what was going to happen with Lisa. She wasn't at school; soon as it happened she was out of class, and it's GCSE year for her, so that was a big deal.

She just seemed to completely disappear for a while. The guys would ask me if I'd seen her, but I never saw her. Never saw her walk down the street. Never saw her in the window, or at school, or in their front garden. For weeks she was just... gone.

And then one night – it's late, I've been revising, cos I've got exams coming up too – I look up from my desk, about 10 o'clock at night, and I see her. First time in weeks, I see her and she's there on the bench again. Just sitting, like she used to. Foxy as ever; she didn't look any the worse for what had happened.

She just sits there. Doing nothing. Waiting.

I watch her for ages, just sitting with her hands crossed on her lap and her head hanging down. She must've been there for well over an hour. I don't know when she left, I looked away and she was just gone.

I felt sorry for her. I was glad to see her face again though. I didn't think it was so weird at first, because I just assumed she was still upset. But then the next night I was going to bed and just before I closed my curtains, I saw her again. She was sat in exactly the same spot, waiting for him just like she used to.

That's what she was doing: going back there night after night, waiting for him to come to her. Like he was never dead. It was always late, after dark. Wasn't every night, but it was most nights. Same spot every time, same position: head down, never looking up. I'd sit and watch her some nights. Sometimes I thought about going out to her, but of course I never had the guts to actually do it. But after a few weeks, it was clear she was going nuts.

People about the neighbourhood started to talk. People never saw her now, unless she was on the bench. She never left the house any other time. And she never went to school either. It was her GCSEs but she never went to any of them.

The girls at school used to gossip about her, but none of them knew anything. Not everyone had a mobile back then, or email. You couldn't just get hold of people like you can now. No one seemed to know anything about what was going on with her. It was like she'd dropped off the face of the earth. Except for at night, when she'd go out to that bench... and sit... and wait...

Months went by. I did my revising, night after night. And I'd turn off the lights and she'd still be there. I did all my exams. The year ended. And she was still out there, out on the bench, waiting.

Rumour at school was that she'd just dropped out; hadn't even arranged to do re-sits. She'd just given up. Seeing her there, outside in the park, it almost became normal. Just what you expected. Those odd nights when she wasn't there – they were the strange ones.

Then this one night – it was just after the holidays started – my mate Smithy: his brother was in a band, and they were having a gig above this pub, The Red Lion. We weren't that bothered about seeing his band – we'd seen them practice in their garage. But it was a private do, so Smithy thought we could get some drink on the quiet.

18

So this whole bunch of us went down there and got smashed, proper smashed. We'd all had a bit to drink before, even got a bit merry. But they were just serving anyone there; they didn't give a fuck. And we got wasted. My mate Daz chucked-up in the car park; Smithy's brother had to carry him home.

Me, I'd had a pretty good evening. I'd got pretty confident on a few pints of lager, got off with this girl, one of Smithy's brother's mates or something. I punched above my weight and got off with an older girl. I felt like a million quid, I can tell you. Cloud bloody nine.

I wasn't sick or anything, but I probably wasn't far off. I could walk back to mine from The Lion. Not too far. So I'm walking there and I take the shortcut across the park, which I would always do. And as I'm going, I spot her there, Lisa, out on the bench, as usual.

This has been going on for ages now; months I've been watching her out there. And I see her and I think, fuck it, I'm going to go talk to her.

I'd never have done it if I wasn't drunk. By this time she's lost some of her allure. I mean, sure, she's still drop-dead gorgeous, but she's also a nutter now. I wasn't just intimidated by her for being so hot; I was a bit scared of her now for being a bit mental. But, I've had a few, I've already won one contest that night, so I just decide to go for it and talk to her.

I just walk up to her and go "Y'all right darling?" – in a funny way. She knows me, even if she's never really paid me much attention.

She raises her head just a little, looks at me through her drooping hair. She doesn't say anything. So I walk over and sit right down beside her. Drunk and stupid, I just say, "So, how've you been?"

She still doesn't answer. So I just keep on talking.

"Last week of exams this week. So glad to get those over with." Still can't find a conversation starter. It's silent for a moment.

"What do you come out here for?" I blurt out. "Every night you're out here; why d'you do it?"

"Why shouldn't I?" she says, almost in a whisper.

This makes me a bit more nervous, but I still go on. "You're, you know, a good-looking lass. You've got your whole life ahead of you. You don't want to go and throw it all away on one..."

She turned her head towards me. I get the first good look at her face. I thought she was going to look a bit wrecked, all teary-eyed, mascara running down her face, like she'd been crying. But when she looked at me, she was totally made-up. She had all her stuff on like she was going out.

She looked right at me with her big chestnut eyes and froze me on the spot. Completely took the wind out of my sails. My confidence was just gone, like that.

She stared at me fiercely and then said "Go on, what were you saying?"

She had my tongue tied in knots.

"You were saying how I shouldn't waste my life all on one man."

I sort of babbled: "Well, I just meant."

"Should I get another man?"

Suddenly her hand was on my knee; she was walking her fingers up my leg. Almost made me jump.

"You up to the challenge? Hmm? Stud..."

She was taking the piss. She was going to wind me up and then brush me off. Give me a slap and walk off.

I was just about to bail; I was out of my depth. But she knew, noticed somehow, and she put her hand up my back, under my coat, and hissed in my ear "Don't be afraid." Then she moved in and put her tongue down my throat.

Fuck me, that was some kiss. It wasn't my first time, but I can't remember any of the other times now. She was proper going for it. I was trembling, but I was loving it. Got really into it. I put my hands on her, started to touch her.

A moment later she pulled away. She stood up and said, "Come with me". She pulled me up by my belt and dragged me into the trees. She ran ahead and I ran after her; we pushed our way through tree branches and bushes and weeds.

We eventually found this clearing. She stopped and let me run into her, so we both fell down. She locked her legs around mine and started to kiss me. She pulled off my jacket and started to undo my shirt. I did the same to her, took off her leather jacket and her top, clumsily and slowly. Not like her; she does it fast, like lightning, swift and smooth.

We're there rolling in the grass, together. Naked from the waist up and I'm feeling her all over, kissing her shoulders, licking her tits. She slips her hands down my trousers and I almost blow my load right there and then. But I keep it together, stay focused. She unbuttons the top of her trousers. I get up onto my knees and undo my belt. As she strips off, I undo my trousers and pull them down till they're round my ankles.

She's in front of me now – stark naked. And I'm kneeling before her in my boxers. She's there, glowing in the moonlight, most sexy, beautiful, dangerous thing I've ever seen. And she's looking right at me, gagging for it.

And all I can think of is that I don't have a condom. Fucking sex education has kicked in and I don't have any contraception.

"What's the matter?" she says, staring at me.

"I don't have a condom," I say back.

She glares at me with... cold, fire, anger. And she says to me "Just do it, you coward."

I know it was wrong, but I just couldn't say no. Without hesitating, I pulled down my boxers, and shuffled forward. I'm about to put it in, but I feel something move behind me. I don't notice it; try to ignore it. But as I look into her eyes, I see her look past me.

Something flashes past my eyes and then tightens around my throat. It forces all the air out of me – it was my belt. Someone had my belt; had it around my neck and they were choking me.

I couldn't scream. I could barely even breathe. They were dragging me backwards. I was forced onto my feet, but I couldn't put them flat. I was being pulled back on my heels. I

21

couldn't turn my head. I couldn't see who was doing it – they made no sound.

I fell on my back. They dragged me through the grass like I was nothing, like I was no effort. Just before I blacked out, I looked at her, saw her. She was still on the ground, but leaning up and looking at me. And smiling...

I passed out. But I wasn't out for very long.

I can't have been out for more than a minute. I wake up in a flash and she's still there in front of me, lying on the grass naked. Except now she's moving about.

I can't move my head. The belt is still round my neck and it's tying me to a tree. I'm sat leaning back against it, legs out in front of me. Trousers still around my ankles. The belt is tied so tight the back of my head is flat up against the tree. I can't move my neck. I can barely look upward.

But I can see her: she's there, moving about in the grass – writhing and moaning. Not miserable moaning, I mean sex moaning. She's naked in the moonlight and getting off.

She's not touching herself up; her hands are behind her head. And the way she's moving... she's getting fucked. She's moving in the grass likes someone's thrusting it in.

But there's no one there. She's getting fucked and there's no one there.

I try to move, but I can't. As soon as I try to lift my head the belt digs in and cuts off the air. I gasp and cough, and then I hear this voice.

The voice just says "Ssshhh."

It's then I realise – I'm not the only one watching.

There are people, people everywhere. Just standing, staring.

Ordinary people: men, women, all shapes and sizes. Some fat, some thin – there's even one there with a fucking walking stick.

They're all watching this girl get it on with a ghost. They've all got, like, hoods or bags or masks over their faces. You can't see who they are, but there's loads of them; I couldn't tell you how many – they're spread out. But spread as far back as I can see. And they just stand silently watching...

22

But she, she's not quiet. She's moving her head from side to side making a noise like a porn star putting it on. She's throwing her arms around, rubbing her tits, saying "God, yes! Yes!"

Christ almighty, I was so scared. I'm shaking so hard I'm starting to choke myself against the belt. I got my arms up and dug my fingers under it best I could. I try to stop myself gagging and try to pull. I pull really hard, my face going blue and my eyes watering.

Eventually the buckle breaks. I throw my head forward and I'm gasping for air. She's getting, louder and louder now. I don't waste any time; I get up and try to run. I do it so quickly I fall over my trousers, which are still round my ankles, and fall on my face in the grass. I get up again, quick, holding up my trousers. I ran like fuck out those woods.

If anyone saw me leave, I don't think they came after me. Probably too busy watching. As I'm leaving the woods, she comes. Climaxes – but with a scream. I swear, a real scream of fucking terror, not pleasure. It was a cry of pain, I'm sure. I sometimes still wake up at night sweating when I think of that night and that scream.

I ran back home, let myself in, bolted the backdoor and made sure all the other doors were locked. I then went to the front window, stuck my head through the curtains and looked out to see if anyone had come after me – they hadn't.

In the morning my parents found me with my head flat against the window ledge asleep. I had a real bad time trying to explain what had happened. I just pretended it was because I was drunk. I had been drinking and it was easier to admit to being pissed than to seeing whatever the fuck it was that I saw out there.

They didn't seem to mind. I think your parents just expect you to start some time. And the hangover gave me an excuse to stay inside all day. I didn't want to go out. I didn't know what was out there. Who were those people? Were they my neighbours? Did I know some of them? Christ, every time I saw a man with a stick I thought about pissing my pants.

I stayed away from the park after dark after that. Never took a shortcut through; never even went near it at night.

I'll always remember the night after, when tired, wrecked, feeling sick, I went to bed. But before I went, I just pulled apart the curtains a little, and I looked out to that bench. She was there, but this time, when I looked out, she saw me. She raised her head and looked right at me.

I let go of the curtains and dropped to the floor. I never dared look out of those curtains again; once it was dark, that was it. I didn't want to see into those eyes. I didn't want to look at that girl again.

And I didn't. At some point her family just moved. A For Sale sign appeared in their front garden one day and they were just gone. By that time it was final year and most of my friends were chasing other girls. But I still couldn't get Lisa out of my head. It was years before I went near another girl. I'd get close to doing it, but it would bring me out in a sweat. Like a full-on dripping-wet sweat.

I've never told anyone this before. It still brings me out in a sweat, sometimes. God knows what happened to that girl...

DAMP

It's always been a bit of joke in my family that I'm the clumsy, useless one. Couldn't organise a piss-up in a brewery without burning the place down first.

I've always been like that – stumbling about, knocking stuff over, dropping things. My brothers they were all athletic; me, I was always tripping and falling. I was hospitalised before I turned one year old for falling over a doorstep and cracking my head open. I was there again a year later for exactly the same thing – same doorstep too! Once I tripped and actually got a black eye from hitting a door. When I told my teachers at school, they phoned social services because they thought Dad had hit me. He used to tell me that he had to show them the dent in the door before they'd believe him.

I've just always been like that – a walking disaster. It's always been such a joke to everyone how clumsy and disaster-prone I am. People used to laugh at me all the time. Couldn't have a conversation with anyone without them rolling their eyes at me. Laura found it lovable at first. She's the type who likes to nurse a sick puppy.

Wasn't so lovable when I knocked her up though. My family said it: only I could get a girl pregnant while wearing a condom. We'd been going out six months, but that's way too early for something that serious.

Things did get pretty serious after that. She was angry at first. Furious. But I said to her that if she wanted to keep it, we'd sort it out. I'd leave uni, for just a bit, and start working full time. And we'd save up enough money and we'd be ok. She didn't want to get rid of it anyway; I don't think she could go through with it. But I wanted to make sure she was going feel right about keeping it.

She had doubts though, even then. I knew. I'm not really a prize catch. And she could've had other guys, of course she could. Good-looking girl, sweetest little face. She was built like a child, always looked like she was wearing her mother's clothes; she could never get anything that fit. And you should have seen her when she was pregnant. She was almost as wide as she was tall. You could've knocked her over with a push.

She found me funny at first. That's probably why we kept seeing each other, at least for so long. I'm pretty harmless – mostly just a danger to myself. I'm not a complete dick – I'm good to girls, I treat them right. But, you know, once she got pregnant, things needed to get serious and she looked at me and, well, she had doubts that she could ever be serious with me.

She never said anything, but I knew. I could see she wasn't sure whether we could have a kid together and be together, like a proper family, a real mum and dad. I did my best, like I said, tried to show her that we could make it work together. I might be a bit of an idiot, but you couldn't say that I didn't try. I've never been a quitter. And she went along with it. But the doubt, I could see it in her eyes in those moments. Those bad times when it all gets a bit real, at the NCT classes or when looking at the costs of childcare or trying to make sure you buy all the right stuff.

And when I'd get something wrong… that look of panic, like the walls were closing in.

I was determined; I wanted to prove that I was more than just some clumsy idiot. I was serious, and wanted to get serious. You know I… I loved her. She was the sweetest little thing. And I took my responsibilities totally seriously; it's the biggest responsibility in the world being a parent, isn't it?

I worked hard, totally hard. I was working in the call centre all day and doing two or three shifts at night delivering pizzas. She can say what she likes about me, but she can't say I didn't work hard or that I didn't try my best. She can't say that.

What we needed, what we really needed was a place to ourselves. I was sharing a flat and she was sharing a house and we really needed to share a place together where I could look after her. That's why I was working so hard.

But I couldn't get all the money together in time and when the baby was born we had to live for six months at her parents. They didn't like me much either. Always sticking their noses in – hold her like this, feed her likes this, don't put her down like that. I know I'm a little accident prone, but it's not like I'm a total disaster area. I was trying. But she, she'd always listen to them and never to me and that always really got under my skin.

Couldn't wait to get out of there. Couldn't wait. With the money we had, though, you couldn't afford much. Of course we had to get a fixer-upper. She agreed to it, she was there, she saw and she put her name on the dotted line like I did. But when we got there she's all teary-eyed and unhappy and screaming and shouting at me. What did she expect? All it needed was a lick of paint. Sure it was going to be hard work, but I'd do it, I said I'd do it.

She was just like up and down all the time. Emotional rollercoaster all day long. I got all the stick, but she was no picnic either. I suppose it was the hormones. But she was just laying into me all the time. I was doing my best. No matter what she said to me, I kept working. Kept on going, for her, and the kid.

It was tough looking after the kid and working and trying to make a nice home for them both. Didn't get any thanks for it. Not at all. No thanks at all, still.

Of course it's going to be hard work moving into a new place. Of course it is. But every little thing used to set her off. She was crying more than the baby was. Perhaps we should've waited longer to move in. But she wanted space from her parents as much as I did. And I did us up a room for us all to live in to begin with. It was cramped but I did it up nice before I started working on anything else. Don't know what she was getting so stressed about; it was me who had to go to work all day, me who had to do up the house for them both.

Then we found out about the damp. We knew we had some, sure. Our place is an upstairs flat, but with its own stairway and entrance and there was some down in the entrance hall just below where we would hang our coats, or where we would've hung our coats if there wasn't damp there. But then we found there was loads of damp under the wallpaper in one of the rooms. Managed to miss that on the survey, didn't they. So she goes off on one, storms out and goes back to her parents.

Couldn't believe it. But they said to me that she was just taking things a bit too hard and maybe it was best if we had just a couple of days apart so she could calm down and relax. They were much nicer than usual; perhaps they realised that just maybe – just maybe – I was trying my best.

So I stayed there a couple of nights, just by myself. Giving her some space or whatever. When I wasn't at work, I was trying to sort out the walls. I went at the damp, did my best to get rid of it. Hot water and soap at first, and then bleach. I thought the bleach seemed to do it, but it just seemed to come back after a few hours. Then I put this seal over it; that was supposed to stop it from getting worse. Then I painted over it and it seemed fine. I didn't want it to be there when she came back. Even though we weren't really working on that side of the flat yet, I just didn't want her to have to see it and get upset.

She came back the Saturday after. Actually apologised to me – that was a first. I'd worked hard while she was away – got some more carpets down so little Amy could play on the floor without risk of her getting a splinter or cutting herself on a nail. At least in the living room and small bedroom. It's hard enough keeping kids' hands to themselves, never mind when you've got DIY stuff all over the house. Baby Amy had the little bedroom; we were sleeping in the living room.

Those few days away seemed to really change Laura, she was a lot more chilled and understanding. Even when the damp came back, she didn't seem to get too upset.

I didn't understand it; it was like I'd never painted the wall. It just showed back through, it even looked worse. I thought that at the time; that it had somehow got worse. I thought it was a bit creepy-looking. There were spots and patches all over the wall, but there were these big four shapes, tall waves or shadows in the middle.

I just thought it must be my imagination, even when I started to hear noises coming from the room, late at night. I heard the floorboards creaking. Like there were people moving in there. I remember nudging Laura, but she said she couldn't hear nothing. And she was there more than I was, all day and night; she never heard anything from that room. I just thought it was me, stupid old me.

Her dad said I must've used the wrong kind of sealer; just assumes I must be wrong. Like he knows everything about DIY.

It was hard work, I can tell you. I could only work at the flat when I was at home and Laura had Amy to look after all the time, so she couldn't do much. Even when she was asleep, Laura had to be careful not to do anything that she might accidentally carry with her on her hands, or leave something out the baby might hurt herself on. We didn't want to wake her up either.

We used to leave the painting till the weekend, take Amy to Laura's parents so she wouldn't be breathing the fumes. We ended up leaving that other bedroom till last because of the damp. Couldn't explain it. We got this guy to come round – a mate of a mate of mine. We had to call in all the favours we could, by this time we were even more skint. He couldn't explain it, didn't know why there was damp there. He recommended this special damp-proof paint. It was expensive. Had to wait till I got paid before I could get some.

Maybe I should've got it sooner. Maybe that would've stopped it. Maybe it's my fault after all. I got home one day and there was this black footprint on the landing. First thing I thought was that I was gonna get the blame for that, even though it wasn't my fault. That's what happens when you're known to be a bit clumsy; people start to blame you for stuff they did cos they don't want to admit that they've made a mistake.

I was about to shout for Laura – that carpet was brand new! When, I don't know why, maybe instinct, but I looked at that damp; the door to that bedroom was wide open. And was it me, or was it different, like it had moved around a bit. The big shapes had shifted. I just thought I must be imagining it. I'd have forgotten if it wasn't for what happened, but I did honestly think that at that time.

What happened next was that some of Laura's friends were getting married down south. Laura said we couldn't go because of the kid; we wouldn't be able to enjoy ourselves, have a drink; and it was a really long way to go and we'd have to get a hotel and it was all too expensive. Her folks would be on holiday, and mine were no good. Mum had died a couple of years before and Dad was off his face most of the time; Laura didn't like Amy being near him at all and we were definitely not going to leave her alone with him.

So I said she should go down, have a good time and leave the baby with me.

Well, you can imagine the look I got when I said that. Leave the baby alone with me? Mr Disaster Area. Mr Clumsy. Mr Fuck-Up. She wouldn't admit it, but I knew – she was afraid to leave me alone with the baby. She was afraid!

I was so mad; so angry. I worked so hard for them both. Done the whole flat up practically single-handed and she couldn't trust me with a child? I mean, I'd hardly had any accidents. Only a few cuts and bruises, the only thing that hadn't gone right was that damn wall!

"You can't leave her alone; you got to watch her all the time" – yeah, as if I didn't know that by now. Jesus, she was almost a year old, I knew all about what to do. I knew about feeding and changing and naps and all the stuff. She didn't trust me; that's all it was. She didn't fucking trust me.

We had such a row. I was so mad. I don't normally get like that, but we just flat-out rowed. I told her that she had to let go; she couldn't be there all the time. She had to cut the, what's it called... umbilical cord.

She had no defence. Not really. She was just scared to leave the kid alone with me. After I stopped getting angry with her, I calmed down and tried my best to show her I could handle it all on my own. I'd done it all before anyway. She was just scared I'd fuck it up as usual.

It became a massive issue and in the end I made her go to her friend's wedding, shouted and yelled at her until she said she was going. Fucking idiot I was!

She still made me do a run-through the weekend before. She spent the day out with friends, and came back that night to make sure I'd not killed her by mistake.

Come the day, she struggled to even go out the door. I had to call the taxi for her and practically pushed her down the stairs. She left about 15 phone numbers I could call if anything went wrong while she was away. It was unbelievable.

But perhaps she'd had a premonition, some kind of female intuition. I remember that look as she left. That look of fear; she was almost in tears.

Everything seemed to go all right at first. That first day was fun. I felt a bit restless; there was still so much to do in the flat, but you can't really do anything with the kid around. Can't paint or sand or anything. But we had the TV on and I sat with her and played with her, cleaned her up, put her to bed on time. When it was time for me to go to bed, I actually pulled her crib back into the living room, where we were still sleeping. I was a bit nervous about having her on my own for the first time too I suppose.

She was always a good sleeper. Didn't often wake me and Laura up at night. But I was restless; don't know why. I couldn't really get to sleep. I'd wanted to get to work, get stuff done all day, but I just hadn't had chance.

I was lying in bed and I hear the floor creak. I don't make much of it because that happens; it's not a new flat. But I hear it again and I reckon it's from close by. And when I hear it right by the crib I roll over and suddenly see this shadow right over Amy.

I leap out of bed and accidentally knock the bedside lamp off the table. So I get up and run for the light. I switch it on and there's nothing there. The kid is stirring, moving about a bit, but there's nothing there.

I'm a bit freaked out, right. And when I go look at the kid, I notice there's this little black mark on her pillow. Might've been nothing. Could've been me earlier, maybe I put my hand in some dust or something. But it freaks me out and I've already been having strange thoughts about that other room. I get this

31

clothes chest and I put it in front of the door to keep it shut. I know my mind is playing tricks on me, but I thought I'd sleep better that way.

Didn't sleep hardly at all. That next day I decided I was going to sort out the damp once and for all. Just to put my mind at rest. I had the paint – I was going to put the kid down for a nap and paint the room. Keep the door closed and the windows open. It was a warm day; it should dry pretty quick.

So I wait – make breakfast for me, feed the kid. Play for a few hours, wear her out, put her down for the afternoon and then I got myself ready for work.

I put her cot back in her bedroom and closed the door. I got my paint tray ready, filled it with the cream-coloured paint, put on my work overalls and I got ready to paint that wall.

I didn't like it. Those shapes, those shadows. They creeped me out, and I wasn't sure why. But I was ready to get rid of them.

I was stood right in front of them with my roller, all ready to paint them over, when I hear the kid cough. I think whether or not to go in there, but it stops after a moment. Then I turn to look back at the wall.

It was a hand – it could only be a hand. It rubbed itself over my face; it was cold and clammy, but dusty. It rubbed the black damp dust over my eyes. I almost screamed. My whole body was, like, paralysed. I dropped the roller and started to fall backwards. Lost all my balance; I stumbled in to the wall at the other end of the room, knocking over all the paint and landing on the floor.

I was shaking – I rubbed my hands over my eyes. I couldn't see properly. And then when I tried to open them I saw it coming towards me. It peeled itself off the wall and was walking up to me. The biggest shadow; it was human and it was coming towards me. It was coming right up to me; it had this limp, it was dragging its leg behind him. And he was coming right for me. He had something in his hands, a club or a stick or something; he was coming right at me with it. He was gonna hit me; he was gonna kill me!

I fucking panicked. I was out of my mind with fear. You've got to believe me – I have never been so scared. I actually pissed myself. Pissed right down my trouser leg. When I saw that thing come out of the wall, and come towards me, I have never been so scared in my entire life.

I couldn't think straight; I was crazy with the fear. I jumped up off the floor and ran for my life. Pretty much fell down the stairs, bolted through the door and ran out into the street. Paint footprints all the way down the stairs and onto the pavement.

I was there, in the street, broad daylight, piss running down to my ankles. And I don't know what to do. I'm hysterical, totally hysterical. But there's no one around. No one to shout to, no one to yell to, no one to help me.

Christ, what are you supposed to do? Something comes alive, comes alive and comes out of your wall trying to murder you and what do you do? Call the police? What are they going to do? *What are they going to do?*

I could barely stand up. I could barely breathe. I was so out of my mind, so absolutely out of my mind with fear, otherwise I'd have never forgotten. You got to believe me: I was terrified, otherwise I'd have never... I'd never have left her alone.

I couldn't believe I'd left her alone. I screamed when I realised – it wasn't my fault! I looked at the flat and I could see into her window, her bedroom window. And in the window were shadows. Not just one, all of them. They were stood there and they were looking right at me. It was a family, two parents and two kids. They held hands and they stared at me. I couldn't see their eyes, they didn't have any eyes. But I knew they were looking right at me.

I bolted back for the door – charged through it and back up the stairs, tripping on the landing, smacking my chest against the floor...

And I was too late. They'd taken her. Her cot was empty, just sheets covered in black smears and dust.

They'd taken my baby.

I rushed back to the other bedroom. The damp was gone; I mean it was still there, but the shadows, the shapes – they were gone. There were still dots and patches of the black but that was all it was. They'd gone and they'd taken my baby.

What could I do? What could I say, what could I do? I get all the blame, but no one can tell me. What could I have done?

I don't even remember what I did next. I just sort of lost it. I just wandered around and around the flat. I wasn't even looking for her because I knew I wouldn't find her.

And then Laura came home...

She couldn't believe it at first. Thought I was playing some sick joke. Then she started screaming. Called the police... I hadn't called them cos I didn't even know what to say to them.

They didn't believe my story. I was arrested; thrown in the cells. But they couldn't prove I'd done anything. I told them the story over and over. They didn't believe me and they kept on at me and they kept blaming me and telling me to come clean, but they let me go in the end because they had nothing.

She's never forgiven me. She blames it all on me. And what did I do? I just tried my best for them both, did everything I could.

Can't be trusted for anything me. I always fuck everything up.

BLIND

Me and Kayla practically grew up together. We went to high school together, both native Aussies in a strange, and bloody cold, land. She's one of the nicest people you can ever meet Kayla. Seriously, she's so nice. Too nice, that's why she was such an easy target.

I didn't know Richard before I went travelling. I'd met him once or twice when I'd gone to see Kayla at work, and he seemed ok; not bad looking, friendly. It was only after I went away that I started to hear stories. Shila hated him and didn't mind saying it. The rest of the gang didn't like him either. But Kayla never said anything bad, never said anything was wrong when she emailed or Skyped. Although she's like that; she probably wouldn't.

And when I got off the plane and I was over an hour waiting at stupid Heathrow passport control, he seemed fine about it. He was chatting with me, asking me about the flight, my trip, what my plans were. He seemed fine. But I did notice Kayla was looking a bit stressed, and a bit pale. Thin too, but she's always been skinny. Lucky cow.

They said they'd had a crisis at home, that their boiler had started to leak and there was a bit of damage. So I thought that was probably why she was rattled. And in the car on the way back to theirs (or should I say his) there was a little bit of tension between them; stuff about shopping and who agreed to do what, where, when. Normal couple stuff; me and my boyfriend, we do the same. Shila and Emily made it sound like I was entering a bloody tiger's cage when I told them I was going to stay with them. But at the time I thought they must have been seriously over-reacting.

Shows how much I know.

I had dinner with the two of them; he did the cooking. That was fine, although I couldn't have a shower cos there was no hot water, which was a pain. Then we went out in the evening to get together with the whole gang, like old times.

He came along, which I thought was a bit weird; I thought it was going to be a girls' night out. He was the only guy there. And of course it was all girl talk. He kept trying to butt in. Like, take over the conversation. We'd be talking about one thing, and then suddenly he'd start talking about something he was doing, trying to find the most tenuous link to what we're talking about. But he couldn't keep control of what was going on that way. So when that failed, he took the first chance to move into Kayla's seat when she went to the john. So when she came back, he could cut her off and just talk to her. She was sat on the end, so she had to talk over him if she wanted to talk to us.

I don't know how much of this I noticed at the time; I still thought he was ok. It was when I went out for a cigarette with Shila that she started to tell me stories. She told me he hardly ever let her come out, and almost never on her own; he always insisted on tagging along. And she came out less and less because he only wanted to do things he wanted to do and if he didn't get his way when they were out he'd be a pain in the ass and snap at her and sometimes the other girls if he didn't like what was going on.

They hadn't actually seen Kayla in ages. A few months ago they'd got her to come out by herself and they'd decided they were going to make sure she had a good time.

He was texting her all night, so she was always on her phone. But they got her drunk, so she stopped answering. They stayed out really late and Emily missed her last train, so Kayla said she could stay at Richard's place – it was always Richard's home, never their home.

So when they got there, Richard is still awake and he's absolutely livid. Why didn't she call? Anything could've happened to her. He doesn't trust her friends to look after her. He's worried sick...

Emily's a bit of a shrinking violet too, but even she had a

massive go at Richard for being so bad to Kayla. He was really vile to her; made her cry, spoke to her like she was a child. This was the first time she'd gone out with them since, and that was months ago.

I still thought he seemed ok, but he soon showed his real colours.

When I got back inside, I heard him ask Kayla how long they were going to stay out. I heard Kayla say she wasn't sure. When I sat down I watched them at the bar for a while and he seemed to be getting a bit annoyed with her.

This was the first time I'd sat down with my friends for a year and a half; I really wanted to have a proper night out. But suddenly Kayla says they're gonna leave at half-ten. I mean, seriously, half-ten – that's not a night out, that's like when you're grounded.

Kayla said Richard had to be up early. I asked her why she couldn't stay out and she said she should go back with Richard so she wouldn't wake him later. And of course she didn't say it out loud exactly but it was implied that I should go back with them too.

So at ten-thirty on the dot, he was gathering up his coat and waiting for her and me. And we were saying our goodbyes and I was talking to the guys and making plans to catch up with them and this went on for a few minutes. Richard just stood in the doorway waiting. And then, while I was still saying goodbyes, I saw her look back at him. He made this face at her, saying, like, "What the fuck?" So that was supposed to be her signal to get going, and she goes after him and he slams his way through the pub door and doesn't even say goodbye to the girls.

So we're walking back to his and he's marching off and it's cold. I said we should get a taxi but he just ignores me. I've been getting tanned on the other side of the planet – I'm freezing my arse off.

I was dragging behind them, letting them argue and staying out of it.

"You know I've got to work early tomorrow," he snapped.

"I'm sorry. We were just saying goodbye."

"Taking as long as you could about it.

"I couldn't just walk off without saying goodbye."

"I'm already stressed with this leak stuff on top of all the shit at work. I don't need this."

"We were just talking. We've not been together in ages, and Annie's just got back."

"But she can talk to them any time she likes now. Perhaps they can take her out to get hammered too."

I was only walking three or four steps behind them and they were talking like I wasn't there. I had to bite my tongue. I get pretty gobby after a few, but I didn't want to get stuck in the middle of that.

When we got back, he went to bed quietly. Didn't even say goodnight. I asked Kayla "Is he all right?"

"He's just in a mood because of work," she said. I found out later there was a job opening for deputy manager at the branch of B&Q where he worked, but he had issues with some of the other guys there, so he was stressing out about whether they'd have it in for him.

She was always making excuses for him.

The next morning I was feeling pretty drowsy – a mix of the alcohol and the jet lag. Kayla was really sweet; she made me breakfast. She seemed much more relaxed now that he wasn't there.

While she was in the kitchen, I got a really good look around their place – it was a two-bedroom bungalow – and I started thinking to myself, this place couldn't be any less like Kayla. You know, I grew up with that girl. She was an artist, a really creative person. And not a tidy person; she used to be the most untidy, disorganised and lost-in-her-head girl I knew.

But this place, it looked like it had come out of an IKEA showroom. It was just so, ordinary, kinda boring... sterile! That's the word. It just didn't feel like Kayla at all.

Emily told me that Richard made her pay rent for the place. It was his home and not hers, even though they shared it together. He'd inherited it from his aunt, so it wasn't like he was even paying off a mortgage. But he still made her pay to stay there. Seriously unbelievable.

He'd set us a job that day. The plumber was coming over to fix the leak in the boiler. So we had to clear the attic out so he could get up there. I suppose that wasn't such a big deal.

There was all the usual crap up there. He hadn't cleaned it out since his aunt had lived there, so there was some seriously dusty old stuff to get rid of. I was dragging stuff to the hatch and Kayla was carrying it down the ladder. It was just old junk – broken furniture, old wallpaper roles and mouldy duvets.

Underneath it all though was this box. It was taped up so I had to use some scissors to get into it. I got a surprise when I opened it up – there was a head in there.

Not a real head, obviously. It was a bust, a phrenology head. You know, that dumb old science about different bumps on your head meaning something about who you are and why you behave the way you behave. I had a quick look at it and wondered whether Richard had a big bump on the section of the head marked 'dick'.

Kayla came up and looked at it. She said her Dad used to have one of these, and that's when I realised where I'd seen one before. There was one at her folks' house growing up; I remembered it.

It was her Dad's and she said he'd taken it back to Aus when her folks split. He'd died a few years ago, so she never knew what had happened to it after that.

We searched the box and it was mostly full of old paperbacks and cookbooks. But there was a photo album at the bottom.

It was half full with old family photos. Kayla figured it must've belonged to Richard's aunt. But she was surprised because there were family photos in there, and as far as she knew Richard's aunt had died alone, because otherwise why would the house get passed down to him?

But this was a young family. Cute new family: mum, dad and a little blonde girl; really pretty, really smiley. There were tons of pictures of her playing, right from being a baby to building sandcastles as a toddler, right up to her going to school.

"It must be from his aunt, look that's Richard there," Kayla pointed out to me.

There was a photo of a birthday party, with the little girl sitting waiting to blow the candles out on her cake. The boy sat next to her was obviously Richard – you could easily recognise the scowl.

"He's never mentioned having a cousin to me before," she said slowly. And it turned out there was a good reason why.

We finished clearing the stuff out and squeezed as much as possible into the bin, but kept the books and the album and the head.

Kayla liked the head. It reminded her of her father and it was a bit cool. She wanted to keep it, and I said she should. It was as if she never even thought that she could just have it in the house; she'd have to get permission.

"Go quite nice there wouldn't it?" I said pointing to this little table with just the telephone and nothing else on it except a note pad. Kayla went and put it there. She wasn't sure, but she looked at it and said, "Yeah, it does look nice."

A little act of defiance. There was hope for the girl yet.

We had a nice chat in the afternoon; had a goss about friends and talked about what my plans were for the future. Everything was really nice until the plumber found a second leak and said he was going to have to call someone to bring him some parts or something. He'd still get it done that day, but it was going to cost more.

From that point on Kayla was all nervous and stressed. She said she was worried about the cost, but she was really worried about what Richard's reaction was going to be. I tried to tell her it would be ok, but she was all on edge for the rest of the day

Shila had a spare room she was renting, but she'd said her tenant might be moving soon. I was hoping they would; this was already such a tense place. It had such a bad atmosphere. Poor Kayla, I don't know how she could stand it.

He came home around seven. I was prepared for a scene, and was anxious too when he came in through the door. He shouted that he was home, he walked to the living room and then he froze solid.

He was staring at the head. Right at it, not moving at all. His mouth was hung open; he was literally frozen in his tracks.

"Hey," said Kayla coming from the kitchen.

He didn't say anything for a moment. Then he said, "Where did you get that from?"

"We found it in the attic," I said.

"It was in a box of your aunt's stuff."

He still didn't seem to know what to say.

"Don't you like it?" I asked.

He said after a moment, "It just surprised me, that's all.'

That seemed to leave him pretty subdued. Even when Kayla told him about how much the repairs were going to cost, he didn't seem to take it very badly (she still had to pay half though). He was really distracted.

He definitely didn't like the head. He let me and Kay talk at dinner without saying much, until he said: "I'm not sure the head goes there, in the living room".

"I like it," I said quickly.

He stared at me really sharply, like I'd just trod on his toe. But he didn't snap at me. He wasn't going to bully a stranger; it was just ok to bully his girlfriend.

"I think it looks nice there on the table," said Kayla. "Brings character to the room."

"Good place to rest your hats," I joked.

"What I'm saying is I'm not sure I like it."

"Why not?"

He took a moment to answer and said: "I don't like the way it stares".

Both me and Kayla laughed at that; and that didn't go down well with him. He spent the rest of the meal scowling and sulking. I made sure the conversation kept going; I wasn't going to let him spoil our evening.

We watched a movie that night. Can't remember what it was, but I kept seeing him looking across at the head, which was close to where I was sitting. I thought at first he was staring at me, which made me feel pretty uncomfortable. I didn't like the idea of him eyeing me up.

When we went to bed I overheard him asking Kayla whether I'd started looking for work yet. I'd only just got there for Christ's sake. And already he was asking for rent, or more likely how long he'd have to put up with me.

Problem was that the next day Kayla was at work. Kayla was a legal secretary. I still don't know how she got into that, but she was doing really well. She's so smart; she's pretty good at anything she turns her hand to.

But it was his day off, so I was stuck at home with him. He was polite, I suppose, but he wasn't going to spend his day with me. It was up to me what I was doing; he was going to do his own thing. I found out later he had his job application to do. I mean, if he'd just said he needed peace and quiet, he could've just said that. But he didn't; he just kind of ignored me.

I was sat with him all day without much to do. So I did actually start to look at jobs and stuff. I wasn't planning to do that yet, but I was going to be really bored otherwise. He'd camped out in the living room, so it wasn't like I could watch the TV or anything.

It was pretty awkward. I thought about going for a walk or heading into town just to get away. I text a couple of friends, but they were all at work.

We got to lunchtime, and he must've decided to have a break because suddenly from nowhere he said he was going to make a sandwich and asked if I wanted one. I was like "Ok, sure." I wasn't expecting him to be nice.

He made us both a BLT and suddenly we were talking and having a chat. He was asking me about my travels about the places I visited. We were having a proper conversation. He was a human being again.

I remember he told me this really funny story about eating in this hotel in India. He was being served by this guy who looked just like Christopher Lee, but more Indian. But he'd already got the 'Delhi belly' so his stomach was already turning over. So whenever he ate it sounded like a bathtub emptying.

"This guy thought it was something I'd maybe eaten at his place. And he was really scared because my stomach was rumbling so loud people at the next table could hear it. So he was afraid other people would be afraid to eat there. So he was like 'I'm so sorry, are you ok?' But he also wanted us out really quickly. So the second we finished he had the dishes away and said 'No, no, it's on the house. I can see you are a little sick, it is no problem'.

"And this guy looks just like Christopher Lee, so he looks really intense and scary, so we weren't going to argue. But we still left a tip, just to be nice."

He was really funny. I suppose I could see why Kayla would fall for him. When he was being nice, he was charming. And he was good-looking, kinda fit basically.

We kept on talking and I started to talk about my brother who was thinking about travelling to America, but he was having visa issues.

While we were talking about siblings I suddenly thought about the mysterious photo album from yesterday.

"Did Kayla show you the photo album we found in the attic?"

It was like somebody had thrown a switch in him. Within a flash, he was all different – uncomfortable, irritated, offish.

"Yeah, she did," he said, shuffling in his seat and looking away from me.

"Was that your aunt's family?"

"What there was of it, yeah."

"Did something bad happen to them?" I could see he was upset, so I tried to be sympathetic.

"They died," he said. "Well, Sophie was drowned in the bath tub, probably by Uncle Bob."

"God," I said.

"My aunt came home and found the house smashed up and Sophie face down, floating in the tub. Bob disappeared at the same time. No one ever saw him again after that day."

"Holy shit!"

"She was disabled, blind. He wanted rid of her and just drowned her. No one knows why. I heard he was planning on leaving Auntie for another woman, but I dunno. Why not just go? Why do that to Sophie? She was just a kid."

"God, I'm so sorry."

43

"Yeah." he mumbled. He took our plates out and then I lost him for the rest of the afternoon. He went back to working on his application and didn't say a word.

I was helping Kayla do the washing up later and was asking her about it.

"Did you know?" I asked her.

"No, he never said before."

"No wonder, it's really horrible."

"He wasn't very old at the time. He doesn't remember that much. He doesn't hear much from that side of his family very often. Not these days anyway."

"Do you think that's why he didn't like the head? Stirred up some bad memories for him?"

"Maybe, I don't know what goes on in his head," she said.

Neither of us said anything for like a few seconds. Then I said, "He gets a bit intense doesn't he?"

"Sometimes," Kayla said.

It all went a bit quiet again after that.

"I think it all might be a bit much for me," I said slowly. I watched Kayla as I said it, but she didn't say anything back. She kept on washing up as if I'd said nothing.

"If it was me I think that..."

Something slammed down on the draining board – it made me jump bad.

Richard had brought a dirty mug into the kitchen and snuck up behind me without me noticing.

"Having a good chat are you?" he hissed. He turned around and went straight out.

Kayla rolled her eyes and sighed before going after him. I just stood there thinking, *fuuuck!*

We ate dinner in dead silence that evening.

Yes, we were talking about him and I get it that no one likes to hear people saying bad shit about them. But it's not like I was saying much. I didn't really say anything too bad; I just said he was a bit intense. He just flew off the handle. And he did this all the time, just flew off the handle about absolutely anything.

I tried making conversation that night; I really tried to

change the atmosphere. Kayla would answer me, but the conversation would never get very far, because he just said nothing. Not a word.

I got out of there and went straight to my room that night. As soon as I was gone they started rowing. I thought, fuck, what am I going to do? This was turning into a nightmare. This prick had me on edge now. He was pretty scary when he went off on one. He was a big guy and he would go insane.

I'd just have to try and get out of there as soon as I could. Find myself a new place, get a job. The sooner, the better. I was hoping to relax for a bit first, but it wasn't like I was going to relax much in this place. How could Kayla put up with it?

But things started to get really weird. I sort of fell asleep early while I was reading. I woke up quite late and had to go to the toilet. And when I left the room I got such a fright. Richard was just standing there in the hall. In the dark.

He was looking into the living room. He was looking right at the head. Staring at it. He didn't even notice I was there. Not at first.

After staring at him for a few seconds, I just said, "Are you all right?" He didn't even answer me. He just turned around and went back into his bedroom.

A fucking sleepwalker too. Just when I thought I couldn't have liked him less.

I had lunch with Shila the next day. Gave her an update on all the dramatics. She couldn't wait to have a bitch about Richard. She told me he checked Kayla's emails and phone messages all the time, so they had to be really careful what they said in them.

"He's never been violent has he?" I asked.

"There was this one time when I called round for Kayla and she had a black eye".

"Holy shit!"

"Kayla swore that she fell off her bike and hit herself on a fence post. I don't know if I believe her, but Mo" – that's Shila's husband – "he was threatening to go over there and hit him. It's never happened since so maybe she did just have an accident with her bike."

She said I could stay on her sofa if her tenant wasn't going to leave. I said I might take her up on the offer.

I told her all about the head and the photos and Richard's missing uncle and dead cousin. Shila said being a prick must run in the family. That did make me laugh.

I spent the evening having a long Skype conversation with my mum and only had a sandwich for tea, so I didn't really talk to either of them.

But that next night, I heard him whispering. The living room is right next to the room I was sleeping in. And I could hear his voice. I thought maybe he was talking to Kayla, but it was late. I didn't know why he would be whispering to her in the living room.

I couldn't really hear what he was saying, he was just kind of muttering. But he started to get louder. Then, I'm sure he said, "Just leave me alone". And then I heard his bedroom door close pretty hard. Not slammed, but you know, you could tell he wasn't happy about something.

I could barely sleep that night. I thought, fuck, this guy really is off his head.

I was spending time with Kayla the next day and thought I had to ask her about this. So I said to her, "Does he sleepwalk a lot?" But she didn't know what I was talking about.

I said I'd heard him wandering and talking in the night. But she didn't know anything about it.

Things were quiet between us, when she said "Richard was asking me again about how long you were thinking of staying?" I noticed the use of the word 'again'. Not that she'd ever brought it up with me, but obviously it had been mentioned a few times between them.

She was really awkward, the way she said it; but it got my back up right away because she was doing his dirty work. By this point I'd really just had enough of this prick.

"I hadn't thought about it."

"Richard just wanted to know that's all."

"Getting in the way am I?" I said bitterly. I shouldn't have had a go at Kayla, but I'd had enough of this.

"No, it's not that. He just wants to know."

"He did say I could stay as long as I needed to."

"I think he just wants to know what your plans are."

"But he couldn't ask me himself. He had to get you to do it?"

"What's wrong with you? I'm just asking."

"Why do you put up with this shit from him?" I just lost it. "Why'd you let him treat you like this?"

She was shocked for a second, and then I saw her start to cry and I was so sorry, straight away. But she got up and she just ran into the bedroom.

I thought, *fuuuuck.* I decided I'd wait a couple of minutes before going in after her. She was in there, head down on the bed, still shaking and crying.

I said to her "Kay, I'm sorry, I didn't mean to have a go."

She didn't say anything for a minute, but then she said, "He didn't use to be like this."

I sat on the bed and I hugged her. Let her cry out a bit longer.

"He used to be really sweet," she said. "He still is sometimes".

"He can still be nice, sometimes," I said. I couldn't stand his guts, but I couldn't just say I hated him.

"But he gets so stressed out. It's because of his work".

"That's no excuse for taking it out on you."

"He doesn't mean to. He does say sorry when he's done it."

"Sweetie, that's no excuse".

She cried a little longer.

"You can't let him do this to you. Look what a state he's got you in."

"But I love him. I really love him and care about him."

"I know sweetie," I said, thinking she'd lost her mind.

"He's all I've got."

"That's bullshit."

"I don't have anything else. I don't have anyone else."

"That's crap. You're a smart, beautiful, amazing person, Kay. Anyone would be lucky to have you and you don't deserve this. Look at me. You do not deserve this."

Her phone rang. It was his ring tone. She got up in a flash and went to answer. Turned out she was supposed to pick him up from work, but she'd forgot.

I tried to keep her talking, but she'd been summoned. I said she wasn't in the right state to drive, and she shouldn't be getting up at his beck and call. But she suddenly turns on me – *seriously* – and gets angry with me.

"You're just like the others. You all hate him. I don't know why. I don't know why you can't leave him alone, it only makes him worse."

"Kayla, he treats you like shit."

"I can't take this now. Just leave me alone."

And then she just left. She's still crying, she still has snot coming out her nose. But she went because his highness demanded it.

She was gone ages, which was fine with me. I wandered round the house getting angrier and angrier. What kind of fucked up mental gymnastics was this guy pulling on her? Why didn't she get it?

I hadn't even mentioned to her about the head, about him talking to it. I looked at it on the little table. It had a tea towel over it for some reason. I took it off. It was there with its blank, peaceful stare. As I looked at it, I wondered if it knew something I didn't. Richard had some problem with it. That's probably how the tea towel ended up there; he didn't like it being there and looking at him.

I thought about leaving it in his bed. Probably wouldn't help anything, but it would sure shit him up a lot. And make me smile.

She was away so long it got me worrying. He obviously had her wrapped around his little finger. He was probably with her now. Talking her out of it. Making excuses. Telling her that he loved her and he needed her and that it was all us lot trying to tear them apart.

I holed up in my bedroom until they got back later. She'd taken over two hours to pick him up. I didn't say anything when they got back and they didn't say anything either. No hello or hi, nothing.

I didn't know when to go out of my room. I didn't want go out and catch them. It was dead silent for hours. I didn't hear anything. I was so tense. It was so uncomfortable. I waited in that room for so long but eventually, I just had to take a piss. So I went out and I went to the bathroom and then I thought about getting some food. I walked into the kitchen without knowing he was there.

"Hey," he said, finishing some washing up.

"Hi," I answered. He seemed ok. Not angry. Kinda normal.

"I didn't know if you needed dinner, so I made you a sandwich."

"Ok, thank you," I said, as if he was setting a trap. But it looked fine. If he'd poisoned me, I couldn't tell.

"You working tonight?"

"Err, yeah," I said. Made up some bullshit about applying for a bar job. He said that was good and left me to it.

I stayed in my room watching episodes of Entourage on my tablet. Then quite late in the night there's a knock on my door and it's Kayla.

She comes in and says, "Look, me and Richard have been talking and we think it's best if you try and find your own place sooner rather than later."

"O-kay," I say.

"It's all a bit stressed right now and we're all getting in each other's hair and we think it'll just be better for all of us if we just all have a bit more space."

"Stressful time – Kayla he's applying for a job. Normal people have shit happen at work all the time."

"Look, I know you don't like him. And that's fine. He's having some issues right now. That's why it's better if you move on as soon as possible so we can all stay friends and get on. Ok?"

I didn't even know what to say, I just said "Fine Kay, whatever you want".

She said sorry and waited there for me to say something else but I just put my headphones in and kept watching my tablet.

I text Shila a few minutes later saying I might need her sofa after all. All my other friends didn't have their own places, so a sofa was the best I was going to get.

I fell asleep watching more TV and woke up after a few hours when the battery ran down. I start to get ready for bed when I hear the whispering again. Richard's back talking to the head in the living room.

I wonder if I can record it, but I'm not sure where I've left my phone and I don't want to make much noise searching for it. I creep up to the door and open it just a little. He's whispering but I can hear him.

He's talking to the head! And he's saying stuff like, "I could've got really angry, but I didn't".

Then he waits a moment and says, "I tried really hard, and I didn't get angry at all, like I promised. Not today, I was good."

Another moment goes by, and he says.

"It was really hard. It was, but I didn't get angry. I promised I'd try harder and I did try hard. You've got to stop going on at me. I'm doing my best. I'm doing my best."

They're having a conversation. The head is talking to him. Or he thinks the head's talking to him. At this point, I just thought he was crazy.

"It'll be easier when she's gone. Much easier. That was the best thing to do, just ask her to go. Best thing for everyone.

"You don't have to keep on at me. I told you I'm trying. Yes I did promise. I'm going to be nice. Going to be nice from now on. Now will you leave me alone?"

A few seconds later he gets up and goes quietly back to his bedroom.

I sat by my door for ages before I dared to sneak out. I crept out into the hallway and looked into the living room. The head was staring right back out at me. It was just the same, no different than before.

But now when I looked at its blank stare, it seemed smug, pleased with itself. I started to not like it.

It hadn't changed. It was just so blank; you could read anything in its expression. It was creepy. What the fuck was going on with Richard? What was I supposed to do about it? If

50

Kayla couldn't see what he was like, how was I supposed to show her?

And how was I supposed to tell her about this? She'd think I was the one who was crazy?

Then that next day. Jesus – that's when it totally went to shit.

I got up late and overslept. And I had no idea that Richard's mum was over. Christ, that made a lot of sense of things – she was a total bitch.

I came out of my room in just my nighty and she's standing in the hall. She was dressed all in black and peered down her glasses at me as if I were someone who'd just brought her coffee when she asked for tea.

"You must be Annie?"

"Err, yeah." I said back to her.

I went straight into the bathroom and swore at those two for not even telling me.

I washed and then planned to go back and hide in my room, but just as I was walking into the hallway I heard her say, "Where did you find this old thing?"

She was talking about the head! I glimpsed her lifting a scarf off the top of it. I wanted to hear this. So I went back into my room and really quickly put some clothes on and got back out there.

They'd stopped by then of course. She was asking Kayla about her job while Richard was sulking in the corner with his laptop.

Richard resented that Kayla was doing her law thing while he was working for a DIY store. That was just his part time job at university but now he did it full time while Kayla had moved on to bigger and better things.

Kayla went off to get us all some coffee and Richard's mum, Margot, started talking to me: "So you've been travelling?"

I began to tell her about all the places I'd visited. She'd been to many of them herself and wasn't short on opinions about where she liked and didn't. She liked Germany, couldn't stand the Italians, and thought Brussels was the most boring place on earth. Something we both agreed on.

"So what are you going to do now?" she asked. I noticed Richard glance up from his laptop.

"Oh, I'm not sure really. I might go back to uni and do my MA, might just do some part-time work. I haven't really made my mind up."

"Well Richard could always get you a little job at his DIY shop, couldn't you Richard?"

Richard pretended not to hear her.

"Kay tells me you've applied to be the manager there."

"Assistant Manager," he said with hostility.

"Well, if it's what you want dear."

Kayla came back with the coffee and it was all dead silent again. Someone had to say something to break through the tension. And I saw the head, looked at Richard to check he had no offensive weapons he could throw at me, and said "You remembered the head then? Me and Kayla found it in the attic."

Richard's eyes darted upward.

"Yes, I haven't seen that thing in years. Belonged to my sister. Never liked it myself."

"Did Kayla show you the photo album?" I could feel Richard twitch on the other side of the room. But I had to know what this was all about and it definitely had something to do with his dead cousin.

Margot took the photo album and stared at it.

"My goodness there we all are," she said flicking through them. "I haven't seen these in years. I didn't know there were any other photographs. Felicity stopped keeping them, after the accident.

"Oh my, little Sophie, she was so beautiful, wasn't she Richard?" He said nothing. "She really was the most beautiful little girl. Photographers loved her. They loved to take her picture. She was in magazines. She earned Felicity and Bob quite a bit of money before..."

She closed the photo album. "Oh, such a tragedy."

Richard got up and left the room in one of his huffs.

"He still doesn't like to talk about it," she said in a hushed tone. "He was there, he saw it all."

"What happened?" Finally I was getting somewhere.

"They were playing hide and seek. Richard and her, and one of Bob's little nephews. What was his name Richard, your second cousin?"

No answer came from the hall, so she just went on. "Well little Sophie, she tried to squeeze herself down behind the toilet, goodness knows how she thought she'd fit. In fact she didn't, she got herself stuck.

"But Felicity, she had been cleaning the toilet that day. And she had left the bleach on the shelf above the sink, and as she was wriggling about it fell over and the cap wasn't on properly and the bleach, it poured straight down on her eyes and over her face and she couldn't move when it landed all over her.

"Poor thing started to scream and Richard found her and we struggled to get her out and to wipe it all off because, well you've seen the bathroom you can see how little space there is between the sink and the toilet.

"The damage was done. She lost most of her vision. She could hardly see and it scarred her face and it was horrible. The poor, poor thing."

Richard came back in and threw himself back into his armchair. He didn't look at us; he just looked out the window.

"Felicity was distraught, and so was I. But the worst thing was that she actually blamed Richard. She said it was Richard that poured the bleach on her. Well, can you imagine?"

And you know what – I could. I tried to not look over at him. I did try to look at Kayla, see what her reaction was, but I couldn't tell what she was thinking. Did she know already?

"But Richard was hiding in the bedroom at the time, he was the one who found her first. It might've been worse if he hadn't found her."

"Do we have to talk about this," Richard snapped. "Aren't we supposed to be going for lunch?"

"It wasn't your fault dear," Margot was completely oblivious to his moods. She was probably used to ignoring them. "It was Felicity's fault, she should have been more careful. You can't leave things like that lying around with children in the house.

"Of course things were never the same with me and Felicity after that. I tried to forgive her for blaming Richard. Tried to talk to her many times. Especially after that animal Bob went berserk and killed her, drowned poor Sophie. I told her she should never have married him, but she never did listen.

"You'd think after she'd lost everything she'd want to get help from her sister. But that was always Felicity; headstrong and stubborn."

"Why did he do it?" I asked. "Why would he kill her?"

"Sophie had so many emotional problems afterwards and he just couldn't take it. The poor girl was distraught and he was weak and stupid and he just couldn't handle it."

"We're going to lose our table if we don't leave soon," Richard snapped.

"Of course dear," Margot said. She got up and went to fetch her handbag.

I was so shocked. Here was this totally fucked up story and here was this woman talking about it like it was something she'd seen on the TV. You wouldn't have known she was talking about her own sister and brother-in-law – and niece – who got murdered. She was so matter-of-fact it was sick.

"Honestly Richard," she said. "You're telling me to get a move on and you're not even ready."

Richard was searching for his shoes and Kayla was after her coat.

"Are you coming with us Annie?"

You could've heard a pin drop at that moment.

Me, Richard, Kayla – we all looked at each other. It was *soooo* awkward. I didn't want to go. God no. Wild dogs couldn't have dragged me.

"I think Annie's busy today aren't you?" said Richard, dropping his hint.

"I thought you said you had nothing to do?" Margot said. And it was true, and I'd told her without realising she'd use it against me.

"Well, not much..." I was going to say I needed to look for jobs, but she cut in too quick and said:

"Well come along then. I'm paying, you don't need to worry about the money and the food is very good."

And she went out of the room and I just didn't know what to say or how to refuse. I just ended up saying, "I'll need a moment to get ready."

It was horrible, the whole thing was just horrible. And I was sat next to Richard, and I just daren't look over at him for the whole lunch. Who was this guy? Did he burn out his own cousin's eyes with bleach? Could that be who this guy was? Could he be that much of a monster?

If Kayla was thinking what I was thinking, she didn't let it show. He must've hit her that one time, I was sure of it now.

But the whole lunch just got worse and worse. Margot was talking to Kayla about her job. She spent the whole time just going on and on about it. She was doing it to get under Richard's skin, it was so obvious, to rub it in. Her precious boy was too good to be working for B&Q.

I bet she was the kind of woman who never let anything shift her stiff upper lip. She knew what she was doing to him. Just tweaking him for not having such a good job.

And then he got brought the wrong main course. I thought he was going to explode. But his mother told him not to make a fuss when he snapped at the waiter.

I wish I knew how to take the wind out of his sails like that. He sat there like a pressure cooker. His eyes open wide like a bull about to charge. I kept having to go to the toilet just to get away from them, to take a breather, just to try and calm myself down.

It was a nightmare. Like waiting for a bomb to go off. I could feel the tension from my teeth down to my toes. I don't know what Kayla must have been thinking.

It seemed to drag on forever. Margot ignoring the foul atmosphere as if she didn't know it was there. She just talked and talked and talked. She drove us all back to the house, everything quiet unless she was talking.

And when we got back...

We all walked inside in silence. Richard leading the pack. And then as soon as the front door closed, he was up in arms:

"Well that was a fucking nice wasn't it? You enjoy that, did you? Talking about your job, how wonderful it is, how great your fucking job is."

"She was just asking me Richard."

"And you couldn't wait to rub it in. You loved it!"

"You need to calm down," I interrupted. I could feel my heart beat as I said it. After what I'd heard today, I didn't know what this guy was capable of.

"Why are you still here? At least I have a job!"

"No one here cares about your job."

"Oh fuck off, who even asked you?"

"If you want to get another job, get one. How many times have we got to have this argument?" Kayla started to cry.

"Well... she goes first!"

"What have I got to do with anything?" I shouted.

"I can't take it. All you fucking women. Always fucking having a go. Always on my back. Why you can't you leave me alone?"

He turned around to storm into the living room and there it was – the head, staring right at him.

"And I've fucking had enough of you too!" he yelled at it. He went for the head; he picked it up and spun around to smash it against the wall.

"Richard don't!"

Kayla came up behind him. He swung the head round... and hit her in the face with it.

It made a horrible thud sound. Kayla fell down hard.

The head landed miraculously without breaking.

It was all silent for a minute. No one could quite believe what had happened.

I stared at Richard, Richard stared at Kayla. Kayla was on her knees, clutching the side of her head.

He hadn't meant to hit her – not that time at least. But he didn't say, "Are you all right?" or "I'm so sorry." No. What he said was unforgiveable.

"Don't look at me like that. Serves you right for getting in my way, like you always do."

Kayla was shaking; she was terrified.

"You get the hell away from her!" He wasn't getting away with this. No fucking way.

"I told you to get out!"

He came towards me – "Don't you dare fucking touch me," I shouted, backing off.

"Get the fuck out of my house."

"Not without Kayla. She's coming with me."

"Fine, both of you fuck off. I don't need you. I don't want you. All you do is fuck me around."

Kayla was shell-shocked. She couldn't believe it. I helped her up off the floor.

We didn't stop for anything. I just took her straight out of there. Left all my things behind.

I only took one thing – and I don't even remember taking it. As I practically pulled Kayla out of there, at some point, and I don't even know when, I picked up the head. I found that I had it under my arm as we walked to Shila's, squeezing its neck under my arm.

Kayla kept breaking into tears. At one point she tried to go back to him. I told her she was out of her mind and made her come with me.

I managed to drag her to Shila's. I managed to call her and Mo before we got there. I was just glad to give her to someone else. I hate to say it, but I wanted to slap that girl too. What was wrong with her?

She wanted to go back to him. Said he needed her. That we didn't understand him like she did.

I told her I fucking understood him all too well. That she was the one who ought to get her head straight.

Shila glared at me, which really got at me. She hated him more than I did. But she said later I was coming on too strong.

This guy just smacked a porcelain head against her face – and she thought I was coming on too strong!

Part of Kayla knew we were right. Somewhere in her head she knew that she couldn't go on like this. That he'd no right to do these things to her.

Me and Shila went into the kitchen to strategise and said that we just had to keep them apart. If we could keep them separated, then maybe we could get through to her and get her to end it.

We did a lousy job. Part way into the afternoon Kayla went up to the toilet and she was gone for ages. It was a while before me and Shila realised that she had her mobile with her.

She'd locked herself into the bathroom and she was talking with him on the phone. I could barely tell what she was saying, she was crying so hard. We banged on the door but she ignored us. Her voice started to get louder; she was getting hysterical. She was apologising for something, but also saying it wasn't her fault. Asking him why he was being like this to her. She just wanted to help him – all that kind of shit.

The phone call stopped and she was crying for ages. Shila kept banging on the door. She was starting to worry she might hurt herself. I thought that was a bit much at first, but she started to get me worried to.

When Shila threatened to get Mo to kick the door in she eventually opened up and came out.

Richard hadn't got the job at B&Q – they'd called him that afternoon. Apparently that was her fault too, because she'd invited me over and I'd ruined it for him.

"That's such bullshit," I shouted.

"Leave him alone. He really wanted that job. If you weren't here none of this would've ever happened."

"Because of me!" I completely lost patience with that girl. "You're as crazy as he is. Do you know what he does when you're not there? When he thinks we're not looking!"

"Not now!" snapped Shila.

"What does he do?" Kayla asked.

I didn't say it. Me and Shila had agreed that I wasn't going to talk about the head and what I'd heard him say to it. She wouldn't believe me anyway. And she wasn't in the right state of mind to hear it.

58

Shila was annoyed with me too now. She took Kayla into her room. I went back downstairs to try and calm down. And guess what was waiting for me? I got into the living room and it was there, staring right at me again.

"Well, what do you think we should do?" I said to the head, wondering if it'd talk back to me. "This is your fault too. Both of us, we totally ruined his life, stopped him from getting his dream job."

The head decided not to confide in me. I pointed it to face the wall, because I was starting not to like the way it looked at me either.

That was one long evening...

Shila was with Kayla for hours and Mo was off on his evening shift. So I was just hanging around in someone else's house again. I asked Shila, when she went to get a drink, if she wanted me to take over. She said it was best to let her handle it. I wasn't sure if that was because Kayla hated me right now or whether it was because of my temper. I just let her go. I was worried about Kay, but honestly, I didn't really want to spend the evening with her crying on my shoulder.

It was dark by the time Shila came down and said Kayla was in bed sleeping, exhausted emotionally. We had a few drinks, but neither of us felt much like talking. We couldn't let her go back to him. We had to keep them apart.

We made a pact to go to Richard's tomorrow. All my stuff was there. Kayla's too. We were going to go without her. Leave without telling her if we had to.

I agreed. We watched a bit of television and then all went to bed.

I slept on the sofa in a sleeping bag. I didn't sleep well.

All night I felt freezing. It was spring, so the weather was ok. It was warm in the house. But I was freezing. Even in the sleeping bag, all night, I remember being absolutely freezing.

I dreamt I was outdoors. I was walking through the woods. Did I know this place? I did, but I couldn't quite remember. It was a beautiful sunny day, which made no sense because I was so cold.

I finally worked out where I was. I didn't know Shila's part of town well, but I'd been on walks there before. It was quiet; there was no one around. I was in a forest, walking along a path. I was barefoot. I came out of the woods and found myself by a river. It was wide with a little island in the middle. You could pay to take a boat out there, if the current wasn't strong; people would have picnics on the island.

But there was no one out today and no boats in sight. It was a beautiful day, and the park was empty. And as I walked along the river it was completely quiet. Until a rock skipped across the water, only just making a sound.

Someone was skimming stones. There was a little girl standing on a jetty. I walked to her slowly. I stood next to her and she turned to me. It was Sophie, and she smiled at me – her eyes were blank, white and empty. I felt frightened, I don't know why. She reached out and took my hand.

We stood there in silence until a shadow came over us. A man had walked on to the jetty. He wore a suit, but he was a total mess. His shirt was out of his trousers, his tie above his collar. He had a suitcase with him.

We all looked across the lake. He never said a word or even looked at us. He threw his suitcase in the water. Slowly, his other hand rose. There was a jagged rock in it. He stretched out his arm, then hit himself in head with it.

I screamed. He staggered around, he bent forward, but somehow stayed on his feet.

Sophie's grip tightened around my hand. "Again!" she shouted.

Half standing, he hit himself right across the temple. He fell down on the jetty and rolled into river.

I woke up with a start; almost jumped off the sofa. I was shocked and shaking and fucking cold, still.

I tried to calm myself down. It was really early. But I couldn't get back to sleep.

I went right upstairs to take a shower. I had to warm up. I wondered if I was sick, like I'd caught a fever or something. That hot water felt really good.

I noticed that the water at the bottom of the shower was really dirty. I thought for a second it was the water that was dirty, but it wasn't – it was my feet. My feet were filthy. There was dirt all over them.

I didn't get it at the time. I thought maybe there was filth in my shoes, or in the socks I was wearing the day before. And maybe I didn't want to connect it to the dream I'd had.

Shila heard me in the shower and got up too. She thought it was best to go to Richard's before Kayla was up, so she wouldn't insist on coming with us.

Just as I was getting ready I noticed the head was gone. It wasn't on the sideboard where I'd left it. I asked Shila if she'd moved it. She didn't know. She said maybe Mo had moved it when he got back last night. I didn't want to dwell on it. I could only deal with one fucked-up thing at a time.

We drove over to Richard's and left the car quietly. We had Kayla's keys, but we knocked on the door first. There was no answer.

We unlocked the door slowly and went in. I noticed straight away that there was something wrong. The place looked like it had been ransacked. That someone had gone around and trashed it up.

There were broken shards of pottery in the hall. I went to see what they were, and as I went to pick them up, I could see around the corner towards the bathroom.

The head was there. It was half smashed. Now only one side of the head was left. It was placed in the hall and was staring with its one remaining eye into the bathroom.

It was me – I'd taken it back during the night. I must've done. That's why I was so cold and why my feet were filthy. I'd walked it across town in my knickers and t-shirt. Sleepwalked it. I didn't remember a thing, but that must've been what happened.

And when I went to look at the head, I found Richard. He was in the bathroom, down on his knees, head on the floor, forehead resting on his hands. He was crouched down with his head between the sink and the toilet. Just where they must've found his cousin.

He was breathing heavily. And trembling. And sobbing.

Me and Shila were dumbstruck. "Richard," I said to him quietly.

"She made me do it," he said. His voice was croaky and dry. "She made me do it because I was bad. I had to be punished."

"Made you do what?"

"She said she was giving me one last chance. One last chance to be good. And I promised. And you must never break a promise. She said she'd forgive me if I was good. But I couldn't be good because I'm bad. I'm a naughty boy who does terrible things."

"What did you do Richard?" I was trembling now. Shila as well.

"I did it to her. You know I did. They all liked her better than me. Everyone did. She came along and nobody cared about me anymore. They loved her. They ignored me. They loved her. They didn't love me.

"So I ruined her lovely face," he said with a little laugh. "I saw her stuck just here and I poured the bleach all over her when she couldn't move. She didn't look so pretty after that.

"I said sorry, I said sorry so many times, but she never believed me. Never believed me. She used to stare at me with those empty eyes and I couldn't stand it.

"I promised to be good. I promised. She said she'd punish me, like she punished Uncle Bob. But I couldn't be good. I'm bad, so bad. I'm rotten inside."

"Oh my gosh, Annie!" Shila pointed to something on the floor.

It was a large jagged piece of pottery. It had blood all over it.

"She made me do it," Richard cried. "I didn't want to but she made me. She warned me what would happen, but I couldn't behave. I couldn't be good. I'm so bad, so rotten."

He crawled backward and turned himself over. He sat up and looked at us.

Shila screamed. He held out his hands. There was a white

splodge drenched in blood in each of them. That was all that was left of his eyes.

Blood ran down both his cheeks, from where they used to be. He eyelids were red and swollen and twitching.

"I had it coming," he cried. "There's no secret anymore. Now everyone can see that I'm a monster."

OPENING DOORS

I think we met in '78. Actually, it could've been '79. It was at some house party, probably at another squat.

Not sure what Evey saw in me. I know what I saw in her. She had some real assets. Although I didn't look too bad those days myself. Bit less padding round the middle.

She was an activist, a proper campaigner type. She was talking to me about this march for social workers. Winter of Discontent stuff.

"These are the valuable people in our society. The people who care for the sick; who look after the elderly, and the vulnerable. What the government is doing to them is a disgrace."

I wasn't that much into that revolutionary activism business. Sure, I hated Thatcher like every one else. But I was mostly bumming around back then. Didn't really care about anything. Didn't really do anything except smoke fags, sniff glue and get plastered.

But I thought she was sexy, so I made out like I was outraged by union worker pay freezes and wanted to come out in solidarity with the working masses and so on.

The things we did back then... I went on that march. Couldn't have given a toss about nurses or social workers. I just wanted to get off with her. I even made my own little banner, just to show her.

I used to paint houses with my cousin; I was sleeping on his sofa. He had a basement in South London. He used to go out with this wiry bitch. Big teeth and no tits. She wanted me out. I was supposed to be saving the money for it, but I was spending it down the pub or with dealers.

So I promised to paint her house – Evey's I mean; not that other bitch. But it wasn't her house. It was some kind of shelter for... I think it was for either drunks or for the homeless. I think I made out I was some kind of ace builder/worker/craftsman, but I only just about knew how to hold a roller and clean the brushes. Had to steal the paint from my cousin's dad. And the brushes.

I must've done something right, because by the end of the month we were fucking. She was living in a bedsit in Barnes. Used to cycle over there. But she wasn't some street kid like me; she was from a proper family. A Heart of England, Home Counties lot.

But she'd rebelled. She was against her bourgeois upbringing. Down with the toffs! She wanted to fight the class struggle. She wanted to live with the common people. And sleep with the common people – like me.

Of course as soon as I got my hands on her – and all over her – I tried to move myself in. Steve and bitch-face were on at me to move my stuff out, so – and this is what I was always doing – I tried to move myself in to hers.

That didn't go down well with the housemates. They were all lesbians. She said that wasn't on, so I didn't know what I was going to do with myself.

But she had a plan. She wanted to go where the action was. Take the fight against society to the next level.

She said we should move down the Villa Road. That was one of the squatted streets in Brixton – where the real radicals lived.

Now those guys, they were on their own planet, doing their own thing. I liked the idea of a squat because I wouldn't have to pay rent. But this lot thought it was the trigger for bringing down the whole establishment and setting up the socialist state.

It was a fucking nut hutch. Down one end of the street you had Marxists arguing with Trotskyists who were battling with Leninists who were setting up a committee to meet the demands of some other stupid committee they'd set up the week before.

Then down the other end of the street you had primal screamers. The birds who screamed at each other to unlock the hidden instincts of the mind and unlock their emotions and stuff.

That's what the women thought anyway. Us blokes thought they were well dirty. They'd get seduced into going over there. The guys on the opposite side of the road had a telescope on them. Until the screamers found some thicker curtains.

I mean, look, you know, they were good folk, underneath it all. I mean they were mad, but they cared about each other and about other people and they'd help each other out. This is what people don't understand; they were like a family for people who had nowhere else to go. People who had nothing to do, nothing to really live for. No hope for much of a future except the dole or some fucking job picking up litter or sweeping streets. Go somewhere like Villas they'd at least give a shit. Not like the council. Or the fucking police.

But it was a bit much for me back then. Dumb as two short planks back then. And even Evey started to get a bit bogged down by it all. I don't think she'd much time for all this political guff and philosophising.

"It's all very well for them and their talk, but people out there need help now. There are people suffering out there and they don't need talk."

Be honest, I don't think she really understood it. Not that I did either. Still don't. Couldn't tell you the difference between Trotskyists and Leninists or whatever.

She was pretty headstrong. She wanted her own thing going on. They'd been set up there a while, so there was all this stuff that had gone on without her. She was a bit territorial, bit bossy. Probably why she liked me. I'd just go along with anything.

The thing that really made us think whether we wanted to be there or not was that we were supposed to – no, *expected* – to sit in front of a committee to discuss our relationship, our pairing, and what it meant.

They did not approve of the family unit. Ties forced down upon us from the capitalist society. We had to find our own meaning in our 'relationships'. We had to discuss our feelings and how we intended to live and... I don't even know what they thought we were going to say, but I wasn't having any of that shit. That was the one line I drew. I wasn't going to go and talk about what me and Evey got up to in front of a bunch of professors, feminists and perverts. No way.

Evey disappeared for a few days. I think she went to see her parents; maybe it was for money. She'd deny it – but I swear she had more than she was getting off the dole.

She's gone for a while and then suddenly shows back up and says I need to pack my things. She's found a place. Some new place.

I'd been stoned all afternoon, but I get my stuff together and headed after her. She told me she'd bumped into this old mate of hers, Ciaran, and he was about to take over a new squat. He was going to do it with some friends who were about to get booted out of their squat, but they'd managed to fight the council off, so they were staying.

I don't know if Evey talked him into still doing it, or whether he decided just to do it anyway and got her to go along. Either way, there was another bloke about and I wasn't letting him move in on my territory.

He'd managed to pick the locks of this place. That was risky. If you were caught breaking and entering then the police could have you arrested. But if you got in unnoticed, and set yourselves up there, then you could claim squatter's rights. That's how it worked.

The crowbar was the squatter's tool of choice – they were kept like treasure at the Villa Road, some of them hung them like swords on the wall. But the risk was they were noisy. So if the neighbours or some busybody heard you, you could get caught. They also damaged the doors pretty bad. But they were quick – they got you in fast.

What you wanted to do when you got inside was barricade the place. Stop anyone else from coming in. For that, it was better to pick the locks, because the damage wouldn't show and you had a chance of keeping the doors together. You changed the locks eventually, but it was the first few days where you had to be careful. Do anything you had to to keep the place locked down tight.

Evey kept going on about how this place was amazing.

"We can use it to set up a proper centre to help the community. Give people time and let them see how we're just doing good things to help vulnerable people. How could they complain about that?"

When you broke into an abandoned council place, they'd do everything they could to put you off. They'd tear up the floorboards, pour concrete down the toilets – seriously, I'm not making this up. They'd pull out the pipes and wrench out the wires, just to stop you from setting up there. They'd rather these places fell to bits and lay empty rather than let people who needed somewhere to live use them.

This place was spotless. Floorboards, toilets, pipes, plugs – it was all there. Made me think there had to be something suss about the place. When I got there I found there's something she forgot to tell me.

The place was a factory. Four floors. Newly done up. I thought, hang on a sec girl, there's no way this is going to work. This place couldn't be abandoned. The plaster on the walls was new. It just needed decorating. Same with the floors, they just needed carpeting over.

I said to her this was chancing it a bit, wasn't it? This wasn't a derelict; the owners would probably be around in the morning.

That's when this Ciaran shows up. He's short and really pleased with himself. He's a squatting pro. He knows his business. He's a bloody vegan. This place had been boarded up for over a year. It was being refurbished but then refurbishments stopped. He thought the company had gone bankrupt. But when he'd checked the registry, they seemed to still be in business. Maybe they'd just run out of money.

But here it was, this pristine, fixed-up building, lying empty. Everything we could need: bogs, kitchen, even space to park. It was only the upstairs, where the electric hadn't been connected up. Everything else was as good as you could hope for.

This was going to be the community centre Evey always wanted to rule. Her kingdom where she could help the sick, the poor, the needy. And provide a creative space for artists, and poets, and writers. The perfect hippy commune. Not intellectual bullshit – besides the bloody poetry – it was a place just to help people. That was her theory: if you just did good, then people would get it. They would listen. You didn't have to shove Trotsky or McLuhan down their throats.

I wasn't really thinking about any of that though. I wanted to know who this prick Ciaran was and what he wanted. They'd done marches or soup kitchens or something together in the past. He was shorter than me, and a ginger; but he was pretty well built. I figured if I was going to take him I'd have to be faster. I was quite thin; I could throw a punch but didn't have the weight behind me. Bit of a ducker and weaver me. That's how I'd take him.

Not sure what part he wanted to play in Evey's new society, but they were pretty pally. He was fitting bolts to the door. Now we were in, we had to stop anyone else getting in. The windows were already boarded up. It was the other doors we had to be careful of. Anyone with a key could get in.

Ciaran was keeping the lights off in case we were spotted. He said we should get bolts onto the other doors and start nailing them closed in the morning, when we didn't have to be so quiet. Evey kindly hands the bolts over to me and tells me to do it.

I didn't want to leave them alone, but even I was thinking we were on to a good 'un. This was like a mansion compared to most squats. There was no furniture and just concrete floors and lots of dust all over the place. While Evey was thinking of helping the poor I was thinking we could use this for gigs, find an old pool table and do it up. Could have skittles in the hallway...

Ciaran wasn't planning on spending the night, which was a bloody good job. His gear was still at his old squat, so we were there to look after the place while he got his stuff together. This was too big a place for him to look after on his own, which is why he'd got us along.

There was only really the front door, back door and a fire escape. I screwed on the bolts as hard as I could. We'd have to board them up, but couldn't make that kind of noise at night. I don't think we had any boards anyways. Evey went around and checked the windows upstairs with her torch.

It was the end of summer so it wasn't that cold yet, but it was starting to get cold. We set up in the room near the boiler. It was probably meant to be some storage closet. But it was better to sleep in to keep us warm. It was just behind one of the kitchens. We didn't have mattresses; it was fucking uncomfortable.

Nothing happened that first night. If it did, we didn't hear it.

Evey went skipping that first morning. I don't mean jumping – going to skips to find stuff for the factory, alone. It's cos I didn't bloody want to get up. So I was left on guard. After a while I started to wander around. We didn't have any food except cornflakes and half a loaf of bread. No milk.

I wandered upstairs to see what that was like. I hadn't been up before cos it was dark. It was still dark, but some light was getting in around the boards on the windows. There were no fittings up there; no kitchens or bathrooms. Just empty rooms – except for this one that had old paint cans and a few planks of wood and some unused boards. What they'd left after they'd boarded the place up by the looks of it.

I milled about a bit more when I heard a door close. I was supposed to be keeping a look out. If that were the police, we'd have been busted.

I prayed it was Evey – although she would've given us a proper earful. I got downstairs and everything was still airtight, no one about the place. I checked all the other doors and the windows. No one was about. Everything was locked up. I just thought I imagined it.

Evey did make it back soon after. She knocked on and I let her in. She was with Ciaran. They had a whole bunch of stuff tied to a wheelbarrow. She had sofa cushions for us to sleep on. She'd picked them off a sofa left on the pavement – they were clean enough. The sofa had been broken, but these'd be good to sleep on.

Ciaran had his toolbox with him, so it was time to start getting things fortified. They'd found some planks in a building site skip. I said I'd seen some stuff in a room upstairs and straight away Evey starts having a go at me for not bringing them downstairs for the two of them to look at; I've been doing nothing all morning when I could've been helping.

The bit that really got to me was when Ciaran grins at me all knowingly, like as if he's thinking 'typical Kev', like he actually knows me. He decides to go with me to get the stuff, not that I needed his help.

Problem was I thought the stuff was on the second floor, somewhere just right of the stairs. But when we went up there, we couldn't find the stuff. It was pissing it down outside, so we weren't even getting any light either. So we went up another floor to see if we could find the stuff there. Turned out all the paint stuff was on the top floor, and on the left side of the door.

Now I can forget stuff sometimes, but I don't think I even got up that far. Yet suddenly all the paint and junk is up there. I hadn't been drinking – I was dying for one, but I wasn't out my head or anything. It just seemed weird then. Now it really freaks me out.

Later when I was nailing planks over a fire exit, Evey comes over and says, "Did you just hear a door bang shut?" She thought she'd heard someone come in. But I'd not heard anything, or seen anyone walking around except for the three of us.

I got my orders to go on a special job in the afternoon – I got sent to the post office to get a photocopy of the squatter's notice. We had a blank one that Ciaran had lent from one of his mates's copy of the Squatter's Handbook. I made sure I got it quick and got back to the factory in case he was going to try something with Evey. But he was just playing with wires and shit; seeing if he could get the lights on upstairs, but no luck.

We got the notice up outside, round the back. They felt really good about getting that up – but it was just a piece of paper. I couldn't really see how it was going to stop the pigs from turfing us out if they wanted too. But apparently they couldn't.

Ciaran didn't hang around in the evening, which was good. Evey had gone shopping before the shops closed and we had some baked potatoes and beans in the little kitchen. The gas wasn't connected, but we had a couple of little camping stoves.

Evey was feeling too tired for any action, so I went down the local for a couple while she slept it off. Played a few games of pool and almost got in a fight.

When I get back later, Evey's all in a panic. She's heard someone upstairs. Heard footsteps and doors closing. I pick up a plank of wood with a nail in and grab a torch and lead the way up there. We go up all four floors. Go over each one room by room.

We don't find anything. She's a bit spooked. I tell her something must be loose somewhere, like a board or something on the roof maybe. She's not so sure. She's sure she heard footsteps.

She's still not in the mood, so we go to sleep after. But during the night I think I hear something too. Evey stirs but I don't wake her. I get up and walk quietly into the kitchen. I stand there and listen carefully for a few minutes. But I hear nothing.

We had to go sign on the next day. Gave the new squat as our new address. That felt pretty good. I wasn't really spooked out by the noises at that point.

But I had promised Evey I'd go around and check all the boards on all the windows on all the floors, make sure they were all tight and not loose. I hammered in a few nails but everything was pretty secure.

Ciaran moved in his stuff that day. Room next to ours. He was on my turf and he thought he was there to stay. He and Evey were going to go skipping that afternoon, but I stepped in and stopped that happening. I wasn't going to be wandering round in the dark while he and her went off together.

She was annoyed about that and that's when I knew there was something going on. She said I should be spending the time

72

painting, because that was my job, but I could've done that any time.

And anyway, it would've actually made more sense if me and him went out because we could carry more. Not that I wanted to go with him, but you know it would've made more sense that way.

She said she wanted to show him some good sites she knew, but she also knew why I was getting all narky. She knew I knew she wanted to show off in front of him. So she stopped arguing rather than let me make a big show of it.

She was grumpy all afternoon after that. Kept snapping at me. I kept trying to dig at her about him: "Didn't you want to spend your afternoon with me? Rather spend it with the ginger would you?"

"Stop being so childish," she'd say to me. Perhaps I should've let him have her. Let her boss him around the way she used to boss and nag at me.

I wonder if that would've changed anything.

Spent the evening sewing blankets and shit together. That ponce knew how to sew too. I was supposed to go see my mate Byron, but I didn't want to leave the two of them. Especially as she was pissed off at me.

We heard noises that night too. Sounded like doors closing. We got woke up by the sound of a door slamming. Evey had another go at me, saying I hadn't checked all the windows properly.

"Can't rely on you to do anything, can I?"

I told her I sodding had checked them all. All four floors; I'd been and checked them all. Whatever it was, it wasn't because of the windows.

She made me go up and check all the floors again. Didn't see what the point was. If anyone had got in, they wouldn't be hiding would they? They'd be grabbing us by the ankles and dragging us out.

So I went upstairs on my own with a torch. That Ciaran didn't seem to have heard anything; he was busy snoring his head off.

73

I went on upstairs and checked every floor. There was nothing going on. Place was dead. It was weird though, because, by this point, I'd been up there a fair few times. But I never got used to it. I never knew my way around. It was dark, yeah, but it was always different. The stuff you recognised, like certain coloured boards over the windows, or missing floorboards, or dented doors. They never seemed to be in the same place twice. No matter how many times I went up there, I could never tell one floor from the other.

And then when I was checking out the third floor, a door slammed shut behind me. For a moment I was shit scared, because I thought someone must be in that room, behind the closed door.

I went up to it really slowly and opened it. There was no one in there. It was the only way in and out. Windows were boarded shut. They'd not been opened.

I didn't know what to do about it. And I didn't tell Evey when I went downstairs. Told her I'd seen nothing. I didn't know what was causing the doors to slam. I thought maybe it was the neighbours. We had offices on one side and houses on the other. Who knows what was going on in there? But I wasn't thinking it was anything paranormal. Not then.

There were people sniffing around the next day. Evey heard them outside and we managed to get a look at them through a gap in one of the window boards upstairs. They looked like workmen. Maybe they were security. People paid to have these sorts of places looked after, but security guys usually did bugger all. Just looked to see if the place was still standing once a month.

Perhaps they'd spotted the poster. They didn't try any of the locks, so we didn't get worried much.

By this point me and Evey hadn't done it for over a week and I was getting pretty wound up. I didn't like this situation: her, me and him. He was changing her. He was vegetarian, so we were always eating salads. He didn't drink, so suddenly she was cutting back on the red wine and lager. And we couldn't eat this thing because it was from South Africa, and we couldn't eat this because it was from Argentina, and not this because it had too many chemicals in it.

As if I couldn't tell what was going on. He was the high prince of squatters and hippies and activists and she was trying to kiss up to him. She was following him about and asking him how to do everything even though she probably knew all the stuff already.

I was just getting sick of it. We were painting all day so she ought to have been asking me what I thought, not trying to get to know what he thought. I was the bloody painter!

That day I really fancied a curry. I don't know why, but I always loved to have a curry and Evey used to enjoy having them with us too. But when I brought it up, she was all, "no, me and Ciaran are going to go round the supermarkets and take all the expired food out the bin. It's a scandal how much gets thrown away when it's perfectly edible."

Now, I don't mind living in a squat, and lifting furniture from tips, and even living in a house with beggars and drunks and sluts, but I draw the line at lifting food out of bins like a tramp. I mean, for fuck's sake, we weren't paying for rent, we had our dole money. We could afford a fucking curry.

I just flipped out. Jesus, it was doing my head in now. Couldn't I just relax and have a curry without having to wonder whether it was made with South African nuts or chemical coconut milk from Rhodesia or whatever.

I had to go out for a couple of pints, calm down and relax. That place was four floors big, but it was too big for the three of us. I knew what was going on. She'd found the perfect hippy partner and I was on the way out. I knew it, I could see it.

I got back hammered at about one in the morning and Evey was still up.

"Where have you been?"

"I've been out drinking South African wine and eating Argentinian fascist Junta steaks and wiping my arse on pages of Das Capital."

She didn't even roll her eyes. "I can hear noises upstairs again," she shouted at me. "There are footsteps. I definitely heard footsteps."

I wasn't having any of that. "Get your bloody ginger lover on to it, I'm going to bed."

I just dropped straight into bed. But I didn't get two seconds of sleep when I heard her scream.

I stagger out of bed and go out there. She's upstairs and I can hear her running about. I meet her on the stairs running down.

"The doors are slamming shut, on their own."

"What are you on about?"

"I went looking and suddenly the door slams shut behind me, and then when I went to look at it, another door slams shut behind me. Someone's up there, someone's up there!"

"Where's Ciaran?" I ask.

"I don't know, I went to his room and he wasn't there."

"Give me your torch."

I went back downstairs, found myself a piece of wood to use as a bat, picked up a better torch, and went on up there. I kept Evey behind as I went searching again.

I don't know what I was looking for. I was too busy getting annoyed about those two to think about the strange stuff upstairs. But I went about again. I searched each one of the floors, bit by bit, seeing if there was anything there, again. But there was nothing about, again, just as I told her there wouldn't be.

"Someone's hiding here," said Evey. But where were they gonna hide? Place was empty. There's no stuff for them to hide around. I banged my stick on the walls and doors and shouted, "If anyone's up here, you better get the fuck out now."

But we didn't find anyone. Place was just as empty as when we'd moved on in.

"There had to be someone. Doors don't just slam on their own," she said.

"Could be the wind".

"Wind from where?"

"I dunno. It happened to me the other day when I was up here."

"You never said. Why didn't you say anything?"

"It was just a door shutting. It's no big deal."

76

"There's something not right about this place," she says.

"Well you chose it," I says and I go off to bed. I sleep for a couple of hours, but she keeps waking me up.

"There it is again," she keeps saying. I just tell her to give it a rest. It's just some noises. That's all. It doesn't mean anything."

Next day though, Ciaran still isn't about. And Evey's worried because she doesn't reckon he'd just take off like that in the middle of the night without saying anything.

I could barely pretend to care. He's his own guy, he don't have to tell us what he's up to all day and night. I tried to tell this to Evey, but she just kept having a go so I kept my mouth shut after a while.

She's got it into her head that his disappearance has something to do with all the strange shit that's going on in this place. That someone has come in and got to Ciaran. But that makes no sense and I tell her so. No one has been in and out of this building except us. All the doors and windows are banged up tight. No one has come in and kidnapped Ciaran. Makes no sense.

Later she has to go to the phone box and call up some of his other friends and old house mates. She's really worried. I try to be nice and say he'll turn up and that he's a grown up man and he can look after himself. But she takes it bad and says I just don't give a shit.

It's all dead tense after that. We're trying to change the last of the locks, which Ciaran was supposed to do, but neither of us is very good at it and we're getting on each other's nerves.

And the banging upstairs. It keeps happening randomly. Neither of us knows what to make of it or what to do about it. We both think there's got to be some proper reason for it, but neither of us can think of it. It's just there, getting on our nerves and winding us up and making us scared.

She catches me knocking back a beer later on and she suddenly flips out at me.

"How can you drink with everything that's going on? Christ, is that all you know how to do? Get drunk!"

"What do you want me to do?" I shout back at her. "I can't find your fancy friend. I can't stop the noises. You wanted to move into this place. It was your amazing idea, not mine."

She picks up a tin can of nails and throws it at me. I know she has a temper, but Jesus, she suddenly wants to kill me.

"For fuck's sake," I shout at her. I swear she's about to throw a hammer at me, when suddenly there's a huge racket from upstairs.

It's as if all the doors have slammed shut at once. She shrieks and drops the hammer.

They start slamming in rhythm. Like beating drums.

"What the fuck is going on!" I shout.

"I can't take this any more," she screams.

She picks the hammer back up and goes up the stairs. I run after her. This is getting really weird now. This is no random thing. Someone's got to be doing it. It's like tribal. It's really loud; it's really frightening. Someone doesn't like us being here and they want us out.

She goes out onto the first floor and starts shouting, "Come on. Come out. What do you want?"

The sound stops the second we're off the stairs.

"Evey, we should go. I don't want to stay in this place."

She ignores me; if only for once she'd fucking listened. "I don't know who's doing this," she says. "But I'm going to find you. I don't know what you want. But this is our place now. We've got rights!"

It was silent for a moment.

"What's the matter? Show yourself."

It was still silent.

Then a door creaks.

It was just down the hall. On the left. The door just opened up a little.

Evey thunders over there. She kicks the door open and goes inside.

I go after her. I look in and she's there spinning around with the hammer raised up, ready to knock someone's head in. But she can't find anyone. The room's empty. There's not a thing in there. There's just her.

78

"Evey," I said. "There's no one here."

She stopped spinning. She stared at me, angry, breathing heavily. Her mouth dropped open. She was about to say something to me.

Then the door slammed shut.

I shouted her. I tried to push it open; I wrenched the door handle. It was jammed; it was stuck. I couldn't get it open. I banged on the door. I punched the door. It wouldn't open.

I kept shouting her. I couldn't hear her. She wasn't banging on the door on the other side. She wasn't trying to get it open. Why wasn't she trying to get it open?

I slammed it with my shoulder. It didn't budge.

I did it again. It came open easy. I fell down on my knees. She was gone.

The room was empty again. No sign of Evey.

I yelled for her. There was no answer. I didn't get it. How could it happen? There was no way out. I checked. She'd vanished.

I just didn't get it. I didn't understand it. How could this happen?

I ran about, looking for her. Floor by floor. Shouting for her all the time. I didn't know what to do. She'd just vanished. I got all the way up to the top, still no sign of her.

I just didn't know what to do. It was like some magician had pulled a trick on me. Girlfriend vanishes from room – figure that one out! As if I'm Jonathan fucking Creek!

My heart was beating. I was desperate and I was lost. I searched that place, each floor, from top to bottom. And then with nothing else to try, I started searching each floor, one after the other again. Going through every room, floor after floor.

It was like a maze. I couldn't tell one floor from the next. I went up and I went down, and it was never the same. I couldn't even tell you how far I went up. It sounds mental. But I wasn't sure there were four floors anymore. I just kept going up and I went down and I went back up again.

I couldn't get my bearings. She was gone and I was lost.

It went dark outside. I still didn't know what to do. I was

just wandering from one floor to another, through one door after another.

Until I saw I wasn't alone.

I heard someone walking across the floor. I turned around and there was a man there. It wasn't Evey. They were dressed all in black. They were tall.

That's all I saw. They had a torch and shined it right in my eyes.

I panicked. I ran for it. I legged it down the stairs and out into the street. I think I thought they were following me. I'm pretty sure now they weren't, but I wasn't taking any chances.

I got lost. I didn't know that part of town yet. And I just flipped out, you know? I didn't know what was going on. I was pretty sure we'd been rumbled. The owners had twigged we were there, or some security company. Not the cops, they'd have made too much noise.

I didn't know what to do. Evey had vanished. That factory had swallowed her up. And now there were people. Maybe they'd vanish too.

I was too scared to go back. Not right away. I was tired. I was lost. I ended up just sitting and sleeping in this doorway to some old offices. It rained, but I managed to stay dry.

I didn't sleep much. And I got kicked out early by some cleaner. I wandered the streets for a few hours. I didn't have any money. My wallet was back at the factory.

I had to go back. I found my way to somewhere I recognised and I made my way from there, sticking to streets I knew.

I looked the place over from out the front. It looked just the same it did always. Dirty red brick, windows all boarded up, doors barred. Still four floors. Nothing looked like it had changed from the outside.

I went round the back. The door looked like it did before. It opened like it did before. Whoever had found us there hadn't sealed the place back up yet. Squatter's notice was gone though. But that could've just been the rain washing it away.

I went inside. It was quiet. I searched through the place. I checked our room; Evey wasn't there. I checked Ciaran's place; he still wasn't there.

It's just like it was before. Nothing's been moved or kicked about. No one's touched anything.

So the only place to go is back up. I was so scared; I could feel my heart thumping against my chest. And the second I put my foot on that first stair, the noise starts. Doors slamming shut. Opening and closing upstairs now like ticking clock.

I almost turn back; I almost can't hack it. But then I think of Evey and I've got to go on in case I can find her.

I shout her name. There's no answer; the noise just continues. So I go back up to the first floor and the search goes on like it did before. Room by room. Nothing. Nothing over and over and over again.

There are no doors banging there. It sounds like it's the floor above. So I grit my teeth and I go up to the second floor. No doors banging there either. It's coming from the floor above. I look and I find nothing.

I go to the third floor. The doors are all quiet there. It's coming from the fourth floor. That's why it must sound louder, cos I'm getting closer. I go the rounds again; still no Evey.

Then I go to the fourth floor. And now everything is quiet. There's no noise. There's no sound. There are more doors on the fourth floor. At least there was that time. It leads you into a long corridor of them.

I walk down that corridor. All the doors are open. I can see into the rooms and they're all empty.

I start crying. And I say "Evey, where are you?"

All the doors slam shut at once. I jump off my feet; practically shit myself. I run for the stairs. I pelt it down. But then someway down I slip and roll down most of a flight and land on my back on a landing.

I'm hurting. It's all quiet again and there's no noise and I'm just lying there on my back, all banged up.

My heart's beating and I'm out of breath and I'm in pain and I'm scared. But nothing was happening, so I just lay there. I didn't know what to do and my chest hurt and my back hurt.

As I lie there I find myself staring at this beam of light. It's coming in from a crack between the boards over one of the windows. Just a slim ray of light, but just enough for me to see, floating in the air, these little specks. I'm lying on my back and I follow the dust with my eyes.

They're little flecks of paint. They've come from something I've not seen before.

I never got used to those floors but I could see something I'd not seen and that was a crack, a crack in the wall.

I got myself up and I walk over to it. I actually hear it crack and I jump back.

The line is straight, vertical. And it goes up to the top and then across and then back down again – it's a doorway. Another door.

It's hidden beneath the plaster. Someone's painted over a door.

I pick at the plaster with my fingers, but that's too slow and I cut myself. Instead, I made a little hole and went downstairs for one of the crowbars. I rammed it in the hole and worked the panel loose. There's a stiff board there, but it doesn't seem like it's been nailed on too tight to shift. Not many nails anyway.

As the board comes away from the wall and more paint cracks and falls this smell starts to come out. This sticky, horrible smell.

I crow the board far enough away from the doorway that I can get my hands behind. I pull and get loads of splinters and dry paint in my face. I give it another go and I feel it give. I pull it down and let it fall. And as it goes down, arms fall around my neck.

It's Evey. She lands right in my arms and pushes me to the floor.

She's naked. She's been beaten black and blue. She's covered in bruises. Her face is swollen out of shape. Her eyes are open. She's cold. And she's dead.

I shake her. Try to wake her up. But she's gone. I know she's gone, there's no life in her. No breathing, no moving.

And then I feel that smell all over me. I look up, I look into that room. It's full of bodies. Dead people. Propped up, lined up, against the walls. At least a dozen of them there. Dead. Decaying. That smell. That fucking horrible smell.

I couldn't hack it. I just ran again. I just left poor Evey there. What the fuck had they done to her?

I didn't dare go back in. I was too scared. I went and I told the police. Never walked into a police station voluntarily before. But they take one look at me and the state I'm in and they just figure I'm some junkie, some layabout off his head.

I shout at them and have a go at them, tell them about the bodies and eventually they call up the owners and ask nicely if they can have a look around.

They chuck me out and tell me to come back later, so I go back to my cousin's, but bitch-face won't let me in. So I end up back at the Villas, and they take me in for the night. I go back to the police station the next day, wait an hour and get told there was nothing at the factory and get told to piss off.

I flip out and they chuck me out. I went out and back to the factory later, drunk, because I'd never have had the courage otherwise. Locks were changed. Doors sealed again. Proper cover up. It's like it never happened.

Police never did shit. I went to four fucking different stations and none of them did a fucking thing. I went back to the Villas and told them, but they didn't believe me either. They thought I'd taken too much acid and flipped. And when they heard Ciaran had gone too, they thought they'd fucked off together and I'd gone off my head. No one fucking listened to me.

I spent some time living on the street after that. I got chucked out the Villas for drinking and fighting. I did a lot of drinking after that. Didn't stop for about 15 years. I heard Evey's parents tried to find me at one point. But what did I have to tell them? Stupid old junkie like me. She just disappeared and no one cared.

All she wanted to do was help people. What did I ever do that was any fucking good?

DOWN THE BACK OF THE SOFA

Every summer me and my little brother Mickey, we'd have to go stay with our nan up in Wales. It was so our folks could spend some time alone together. So they'd go off somewhere and leave us with Nan.

Our nan, rest her soul, wasn't much fun. She was real uptight, real strict. Me and my brother used to hate it up there. Couldn't stand it. There was nothing to do. It was this little estate of all bungalows, all little grannies and old fogies. I think Nan used to think we should sit around and read books all day. But me and Mickey, we weren't in to that; we were a couple of scallies. We wanted to kick a ball around, climb trees, get into scraps.

So she was always shouting at us, telling us off for running about and making too much noise. She'd say they could hear us stamping on the floorboards next door, which was a laugh – round there they wouldn't have heard a bomb go off. All you heard from the neighbours was them shouting "What!" and 'Still can't hear you."

Even football in the garden was noisy for her. She wanted us to stay inside. She only had three videos – a Looney Tunes one – which was all right – Herbie Goes to Monte-Carlo, and this crap one about these little dogs who look after the land of dreams. We watched them every year until we got bored of them. Eventually we got wise and started bringing some of our own. But we always had to have the volume down.

And if we were good, she'd give us a piece of chocolate before we went to bed. Just a piece; half a bar if we were really lucky. She wanted us to play a game – see who could make it last the longest.

God, she was really tight-fisted. She used to buy everything from this market – never believed in buying anything she couldn't haggle for. And it didn't matter if it were falling to bits or if it had stains or holes. All that mattered was that it were cheap.

Besides haggling, all she did was sit in her conservatory. She'd lie back with a damp rag on her forehead reading or sleeping. She'd go dancing once a week, when she'd send us to the cinema. That was better than hanging around her house, but she never checked the times. She'd drop us off and come get us later. If the film was too short, we'd have to wait for her outside. And if the film was too long she'd have one of the staff come in and get us. Seriously, she did that one time. Gave us a real telling-off after. Everything had to be her own way, all the time.

We'd go to the beach once every visit, which wasn't far away, and the park once, which was even closer. Never twice and maybe not at all if it rained when she was going to take us. The beach was all right, because it had arcades and one of those bingo halls. The park was ok too; it was just a park, like any other.

Mostly it was boring and we didn't like going to hers. We'd moan to our folks about it, but they didn't care because it was cheap to just send us up there and shut Nan up about moaning that no one ever visited her.

But this one year, something really weird happened. And I really mean weird.

Me and my brother, we didn't talk about it for years after. We both thought we'd imagined it. I thought he'd forgot it, but he hadn't. We were just having a few beers and I don't remember how we started talking about it. But when we did, turns out we remembered it exactly the same way.

The football at Nan's had burst the year before, and she'd decided not to get another. She said she was sick of the noise we were making with it. But we both reckoned it was because she didn't want to spend a quid getting a new one.

Good thing was my brother had bought this rubber ball with him, one of those ones that bounces like crazy if you throw it hard. The game was how many times you could throw and bounce the ball before Nan came looking in to see what the sound was. And then you had to hide it before she saw it.

We'd managed to keep this up for more than a day. Every time she came to see what the noise was, we'd pretend we'd been doing nothing. And the ball was real easy to hide, because it was small. We could hide it quick even if she made us show her our hands. She knew something was up, but she couldn't figure out what.

It was the day she always took her trip to the shops. She'd always made out like this was an outing, something we should enjoy. Like it were fun to carry her shopping bags around.

She was in the bathroom caking herself in powder. Me and Mickey were bouncing the ball in the hall. The other thing about the game was that the ball bounced like crazy, it could go anywhere. You just didn't know where it was going to go.

We were bouncing it across the living room to each other. We had to be careful not to knock her stuff over and break it. She had all these dainty little ornaments. Flowery things with women in big dresses and flowers in baskets.

She was taking ages to get ready. So we were bouncing it back and forth. And as we were doing it, we were throwing it harder and doing it faster. It was only a matter of time before it went too far.

I throw the ball too hard to Mick and he goes stumbling backwards to catch it and smacks into the sideboard. The sideboard knocks back against the wall and all the ornaments start to rattle.

We were dead lucky nothing broke. But it made so much noise that Nan comes out shouting "What are you up to?" We both say nothing and she wants to know what the noise was and we both pretend like we don't know.

She sees Mickey is hiding something behind his back. So she wants to see what it is. He says "Nothing", but she wants to see what's in his hands.

What he did was so smooth; it was beautiful. While he shows her what's in one hand, he flicks the ball out of the other. While Nan's still looking at his right hand, the ball lands

86

without making a sound onto the sofa cushions. And when she tells him to show her the other hand, that's empty too.

She knows something's up, but she's not sure what. She tells us both to stand in the hall until she's ready. She goes back into the bathroom and I send Mickey back to the living room to get the ball.

He goes to the sofa while I'm keeping watch. He goes and starts to rummage about down between the cushions.

But he takes his time; I ask him what's the matter, he says it must've slipped right down the back. I look to see what Nan's doing and he makes this sound – like "Uuggghh." I look and see him jump off the sofa.

"There's something down there," he shouts.

I tell him to keep his voice down. What the hell's he talking about? He say's there's something moving down there. I tell him to stop being stupid – he says he felt something sticky, and slimy.

I just want him to get the ball back so we don't get in trouble. I don't care about what he's on about.

I tell him to stop being stupid and get the ball back. I force him to go back in there. He goes back to the sofa and I watch him, telling him to hurry up. He dips his arm down again to get it.

"Hurry up!" I keep shouting.

"I think I've got it," he says. But a moment later he cries out loud and jumps off the sofa. I tell him to shut up, but he's got tears in his eyes. Says 'it' bit him.

Before I can find out what he's on about, Nan comes out the bathroom shouting at us for making a racket. She asks Mickey what's the matter now? He's got his hand pressed up under his armpit. He's about to cry, but he holds it in and doesn't say anything.

Nan says she has half a mind to make us stay at home as punishment. We're not stupid of course; we know she can't leave us there.

All the while in the car, I'm trying to whisper to Mickey to find out what's the matter. He won't say. He won't even look at me. I whisper to him "What's up with your hand?" but he won't bring it out. He's got it stuck under his arm and won't show it.

We get to the supermarket and we get out of the car. While Nan's sorting out a trolley, I snap at him and tell him to tell me what's going on. He still won't tell me, so I pull his hand out from under his arm. I only get a quick look before he tugs it back but I can see that something's had a go at him; there are these scratches on his hand and there's blood on them.

It looks bad, and I was pretty surprised at first. But when I start thinking about it, I reckon he's probably just cut himself on a spring or something. Some metal's just scratched him up, that's all it could've been.

That's what I try to say to him while we're going about Kwik Save. "Don't be such a baby. You got scratched, that's all." But he's not having any of it. Something tried to bite him. There's something slimy living down there. He felt it. He felt it move.

I try to tell him he's stupid and a wimp and he tries to start on me, but Nan's there so he can't.

That night when we get home, he won't even go near the sofa. So while we're being made to watch episodes of Poirot, he sits on this hard dining room chair in the corner. Nan's been having a go at him too now, but he won't say what's the matter to her.

But as the night goes on I watch him and I look at his hand and at those scratches. And as I do, I start to lean back and run my hand along the back of the sofa, trying to see what he could've cut himself on and whether I can find the ball.

I don't put my hand down very far, when I just feel something clammy. I pull my hand back up very quickly, because... did something just move? Am I crazy, but did something kind of... twitch? I don't make any noise. I don't make a sound. But I daren't put my hand back down there. Something weird is going on down there.

We didn't even get a chocolate bar to share that night; we'd been too "difficult" that day. Nan was always in bed by ten o'clock so we had to be ready. So me and Mickey both got ready too. We're both quiet, because we're both freaked out by what's going on with the sofa.

I can't get it out of my head, and I want to know what it's all about, even though I am a bit, scared. I'll admit that. But I also really want the ball back; if Nan gets it, we'll have nothing to do all the time.

So after I've finished cleaning my teeth, I decide to creep out the bathroom and go back into the living room. I walk over there, carefully, not making a sound. I know that house so well I know what floorboards make a noise and which ones don't.

I don't put the light on, but the light in the hall is on, so it's only a bit dark.

I get on the sofa and put my arm between the cushions at the back. Slowly at first, feeling around to see if I can find the ball.

After searching for a moment. I get off and look underneath, see if I can see anything down there. But there's not the ball, nothing.

I get back on the sofa. This time I start to feel my way between the two cushions starting from the front and drag my hand all the way along to the back. There's nothing there at first. But when I get to the end, I suddenly feel something cold. I look down, between the cushions, and at that moment – I swear to God – in the dark, I see an eye open. It's beneath the cushions and it looks up right at me.

I'm scared stiff. Too frightened to make a sound. And then, just as I'm gonna shout, it moves underneath the sofa cushions. Like lighting this thing shoots up from underneath me and wraps itself around my neck. Within like a second, it's got me, this big tentacle. And it's trying to pull me down between the cushions.

I try to grab onto the back of the sofa, but this thing's so strong. It's like a python clamped around my throat. I can't breathe; I can't make a sound. It's choking me and smothering me against the sofa. It picks me up and throws me down into the cushions. Then it starts to throw me from side to side; I'm upside down, my legs are just kicking in the air.

I'm turning blue; it's squeezing the life out of me. I dunno what's going on; everything's spinning.

It smacks me against the sofa and tries to drag me back into the cushions again, and everything's starting to go dark. I'm basically pissing myself; I think it's going to kill me. I was being choked; it was squeezing the life out of me.

I think I'm gonna die. This thing is going to kill me.

Then someone gets on the sofa with me. It's Mickey. He's shouting, screaming. He's on my back, hitting the thing, the snake. Trying to pull it off me. He's jumping on the sofa, trying to get it off me

And it works. The thing lets go. I can breathe again. I go flying off the front of that sofa and go smack against the carpet. The world's a blur, but I'm ok. Mickey comes and starts shaking me to bring me around and see that I'm all right.

If he'd not have turned up, I swear I'd be dead. While he's there checking to see if I'm ok, we both spot something. We see it: the snake, this huge python. It's transparent, see-through, like it's made of jelly. And it slithers along the carpet; just slides right across it. It's like 15 metres long, and it's fast. Like a dart, it slides into the hall and around the corner out of sight.

And me and Mick, we're so shit scared, we just run straight into the corner of the room and hold each other in complete shit-scared terror. After a while, one of us gets up and closes the living room door. But we stay there, like that, terrified, frightened out of our little heads.

We must've been there for over an hour. Where was our Nan? She always used to tell us she never went to sleep until she was sure we'd gone to bed. But you know what? She'd been fast asleep the whole time.

After a while, we got up the nerve to go back to our bedroom. But we searched that place high and low before we went to bed, and even then, I don't think we slept very much that night.

We had a look around the house the next morning. Nan wanted to know why the sofa was in such a mess, but we just pretended we'd done nothing. We couldn't tell her; she'd never believe us. We looked for evidence of the ghost snake but we never found any. We figured it must've got out the old cat flap.

And we thought we hated going up to Nan's already. The next year, we begged, begged our parents not to send us up again. Fat chance. We were up there again, but nothing weird was down the sofa that time. But we were both too afraid to sit on it for the rest of the years we went up there before she died.

I'll tell you what though: we never did find that ball. Think about that, hmm? I mean, what happened to it? Where'd it go?

NOISY NEIGHBOUR

I'd just come out of this bad relationship and now that I was over 30 I was starting to sort of take stock of things. And it had occurred to me that really ever since I'd started dating when I was 15, I'd spent almost no time being single. I'd just moved from one relationship to another.

I hadn't wanted it to be like that; but I'm a people person so I meet a lot of people, socially and in my job. And, I don't mean this to sound kind of arrogant, but I've never had that much trouble getting attention from guys. I look after myself; I take care of myself.

But I was starting to think that maybe I hadn't been very smart with my choices. I would just sort of slip into relationships with guys I found attractive, guys who I found interesting. And then when those relationships didn't go anywhere I'd be disappointed and think 'Oh well; that's just how things go'.

Now, as I've gotten older, I've started to want more, and demand more. And those relationships started to become too casual for me. I wanted something more from the guys I dated. But the way I started those relationships and the way that I chose the guys to go out with didn't change. So I was doing all the same things but expecting different results. Essence of madness, right?

So I thought it was time to actually settle down and think about exactly what it was that I wanted. I'd just broken up with this guy, Dan. We'd been going out for, I guess, eight, nine months, something like that. And I was pressuring him to make a commitment, to settle down with me, and he just wasn't getting it.

Now this was new for me because usually, it was the other way around. It was usually the guys who wanted me to be more serious with them. But Dan didn't want to be tied down or whatever. He's a bit immature, a bit younger than me; you know, whatever – it wasn't meant to be.

So I started to think, ok, what is it that I'm really looking for? What is it that I want? Am I really going to find the guy of my dreams in some bar, some party? Are these the kind of guys I want to spend the rest of my life with? I needed to start taking myself and my future seriously. I'm not getting any younger, right? I look pretty good, but I'm not like a teenager any more.

One of the first things I thought about doing was getting my own place. Stop living in these crummy house shares. Get my own space. It didn't cost so much to rent a room but I wasn't saving any money because I was going out all the time. And I thought it would be nice to have a place where I wasn't always waiting to get in the bathroom or trying to find clean plates and stuff.

My friends never thought I'd do it. They'd say to me, 'Katie, there's no way you can live alone'. As if I can't look after myself. They'd say to me that I talk too much. But, hey, I've still got Facebook, right?

It was bad at first, yeah. I was used to people being around. I like interaction, I like being with people. I'm in event planning; socialising, being with people, is my thing. So as soon as I moved in, I was like, Katie, have you made a mistake? Are you crazy? You can't do this. But I was also like, no, this is what it's about, making choices. Making decisions about what you want, what I really want. Not just going with the flow, going with the crowd. This is about me, and me living for me.

Why did I move into that place though? That neighbourhood... well, I'll tell you why: it was what I could afford. It was cheap-ish, for the city. And I didn't think it was that bad. But you know what? When I saw the place, it was dark, it was winter. It's dark at like five pm. It's not that there was anything wrong with the flat – not at first anyway. It's just that there were like, kids, gangs in the street. Cars racing by at midnight. And then, like, two weeks after I moved in, there was someone stabbed to death just a few streets away – seriously.

And I could see these guys eyeing me up, whistling at me. I'm used to that sort of thing, sure. But I was out here on my own, away from my friends, so I was feeling, you know, kind of vulnerable.

I kept trying to drag my friends over to see me. We had this wicked housewarming party – my God, that got so messy. It was amazing.

But London's London and people stick to their areas, their zones, and I was a bit out in the suburbs. So I was starting to think that maybe I'd made the wrong choice. I mean, that's me, impulsive. New me was still quite a lot like old me – making snap choices and just going with it.

There were good things too. Nobody leaving little notes for me to tell me to wash up or arguing about putting the heating on. And it was good for me not to be out all the time because I did need to start saving money for my future – that's what this was all about, sorting myself out for my future.

It was lonely though, yeah. And sooo quiet. I was starting to use online dating to meet guys and I was meeting with friends, but it was hard – that part when you go home alone to be by yourself, and there's no one there. And if there's these gangs and hoodies around the streets, it's a bit intimidating to be by yourself.

I was talking about this to my friend Susie, and she said to me "What are your neighbours like?" I hadn't thought about it till then but I didn't know who my neighbours were. I'd seen people come and go in the houses either side of me, but I'd never set eyes on my neighbour upstairs, the person I shared the building with. We shared a corridor downstairs but I never saw anyone in there. I was starting to think no one lived upstairs. No one ever seemed to collect the mail, but there was so much junk, piles of old letters. There's probably like hundreds of people still getting mail there.

I was sure I'd heard someone. I'd like heard these footsteps. It could've just been the house; it wasn't new. But I thought I'd maybe heard people moving around upstairs.

So there was this one Saturday night; normally I'd be going out, but I was staying in. And I decided to order pizza, treat myself. So I went into the hall to look through the junk mail, find some pizza leaflets. The hall was dark; there's only a light switch by the front door. And it's on a timer so it goes off after like a minute.

I'm heading to the light, when I hear there's someone on there; I'm surprised. I spin around and I can see there's someone walking up the stairs. I'd never heard anyone come in; but I suppose I never heard anyone come in because I wasn't sure whether anyone lived up there.

There's this guy – I was sure it was a guy – walking up the stairs. He's a big guy; hefty; dressed in black. I shout to him, I'm like, "Hey, hello?" I think he stopped a moment, but then just carried on upstairs. I didn't know if he heard me or not, or if he was just being rude, but I went to the light switch and turned it on. But he was gone.

I thought maybe I'd just been seeing things in the dark, but then I heard the upstairs door slam shut. So there was definitely someone living up there.

I was annoyed. Maybe he didn't hear me, perhaps he had headphones. But the way that door slammed, it sounded like he was some dick who didn't want to talk to me. I only wanted to be neighbourly, be nice.

I was hoping we could be friends. That there'd be at least someone close by I could call on if I needed something, or if I was in trouble. Instead there was just this fat jerk living upstairs.

And there were more reasons to hate him. I started hearing his music. Rock music. Heavy stuff. Shit music – all grrrrr and screaming. Just shouting, not singing. It was loud. I could hear it through the ceiling.

I didn't want to make a big deal about it at first. If it was the weekend and he was letting his hair down, fine. But on weekdays when I was going to work – no, that's not fair.

I tried ignoring it; I didn't want it to become this whole thing. But after a while it was just getting me so angry. I really hoped one of the neighbours might say something, but they didn't. Perhaps it wasn't so loud in the other buildings.

I didn't really want our first conversation to be so... antagonistic. But it started to get to me; bring me down. And I started to think, well, I never heard this guy, not really, not until I saw him on the stairs and he ignored me. Was he doing this now to annoy me? Did he hate me? Had I offended him somehow?

One night it got to me so much. It was like, four in the morning; I can hear it in my bedroom. I got so mad. I went into the kitchen to get a mop and I climbed on my bed and started to bang on the ceiling. Didn't do me any good; it just went on and on and on. I just ended up going to work the next day feeling terrible, like total shit.

So I wrote him a note. Not a bad note, not a mean note. I was just asking him to please turn the music down. I can hear it in my flat, it's keeping me up at night and I have to go to work every morning. Please, please, please keep it down.

I wondered if maybe he was a bit deaf. That would explain why he hadn't said hello to me on the stairs and why his music was turned up so loud.

So I pushed the note under his door and for a few days I can't hear anything and I think, fantastic, success! Peace at last.

But it didn't last, not for long at all. It was a Saturday and I'd had a date cancel on me – not a great start. And it's midnight; I've had some wine, some Haagen Dazs, and then the music starts. It's louder than ever!

God! I thought, what's wrong with this guy? You know, before, it was at least loud but not crazy loud. I could hear, like, the bass through the walls, and it was distracting, it was annoying, but it wasn't making the walls shake.

Now I can hear everything. I can hear the guitars, the vocals. If I knew any of that Slipknot goth crap I could've probably told you who the singer was.

I was so mad; I couldn't take it. I went and I marched upstairs and I banged on that guy's door. It's past midnight for fuck's sake; it was so rude. I banged on the door, and I banged again and I banged louder and louder and nothing happened. He didn't answer; he must've been ignoring me. His music was loud but I was pounding on that door with both my hands, screaming and yelling, "Turn the fucking music down. Turn it down! Turn it down!"

So I thought, right, I've just got to call the police. That's it, it's gone too far. I even shouted to him, telling him what I was gonna do. I went downstairs and I picked up my mobile phone and I called that other number, the one that's not 999. And I say to the operator, police please. And just as those words leave my lips, the music stops. Just like that!

He heard me. He knew I was calling the police, so he chickened-out and stopped. I thought what an asshole. What a complete asshole.

I swear I was mad for days. Just waiting for the music to start again. The whole thing totally had me on edge. I was stressed out!

Then a few days later, I'm heading out and I hear him coming down the stairs. As soon as I hear those footsteps I think, right, I'm giving this guy hell. So I stand at the bottom of the stairs and shout, "You've got some nerve."

But instead of this big, chunky, hefty guy, there's this guy in a suit. And he's young, in his 20s, curly hair, glasses; kind of cute, actually. So for a moment, I'm like, what? Who are you? You're not the same guy.

I don't know what to say. He looks confused and asks me what I'm talking about. I ask him if he's the guy who lives upstairs, and he says no. He's the estate agent. He's looking after the flat upstairs.

"The guy's moving?" I ask him. For a second I'm thinking, yes, this guy's leaving me. I can get some peace. But then the guy tells me that the place has been empty for months. The last tenant moved out six months ago and the owner's been having the place refurbished.

I don't know what to say to the guy. What the fuck is going on? I tell him I've been hearing loud music, late at night. He starts to look worried. Says he's going to contact the landlord. He's not told him about anyone staying there. But I realise, a few moments after, what he's really wondering. What if someone's broken in? What if someone, like an old tenant, has got a key and been letting themselves in.

He doesn't say it, but I know that's what he's thinking. It would explain everything, wouldn't it? Why I was ignored on the stairs; why the music stopped when I threatened to call the police. Probably some junkie. You'd have to be off your head to enjoy that shitty music.

I was pretty shaken up. I was really careful about locking my door and looking out for signs that anyone else had been in and entered the building. Obviously I'm not there all the time, so I don't know really.

But it seemed like whoever it was had decided not to come back because no one was there for like a couple of weeks, at least not when I was in the flat. I took out insurance too, just to be sure.

Then one night, I think about a month after that night when the music was really loud, I get woken up. It's like, three in the morning, and music is blaring out so unbelievably loud.

I literally jump out of bed; it's so loud. I can hear the furniture shaking. The bass in the stereo is distorting. It's horrible. It's louder than any nightclub you've ever been to. I seriously could not hear myself think. I literally couldn't hear anything but this music. This horrible heavy-metal shit, sound of screaming, bass so strong I can feel it pumping in my own body.

I was frightened... and angry! Who the hell was doing this? I wasn't going to put up with this or give them a chance this time. I was just going to call the police. I went searching for my phone, but I couldn't find it. It was so hard to think, seriously, the music was so loud. My ears hurt. I wanted to scream.

I had to go and find my phone. I went to my bedroom door, opened up and more sound hit me. I swear I was almost knocked back a few inches; the sound hit me that hard.

That's when I realised – this wasn't coming from upstairs. It was coming from my flat! It was coming from my stereo!

Someone had broken in. Someone was here, in the flat, with me. I was so terrified; I crept into the living room, not knowing what the hell I'd find. All the lights were off; I was scared to turn them on. Scared at what or who I was going to find.

98

The living room door was open. I walked in slow. The only light was this dim blue light; it was coming from the display on my stereo on at full blast. The living room was empty; I went up to the stereo. The music was so loud; it felt like walking towards an air turbine. I reach for the dial and I turn it off.

The room went dark. All I could hear was my own breath. All I could feel was the beat of my heart pounding. It was all quiet. For a few seconds, nothing happened.

Then the light came on. I turned and right in front of me was this goth. Fat, dressed all in black and leather, spiky Mohican, studded collar, white painted face. And he had a kitchen knife in his hand.

I screamed. He reached out and grabbed me by the hair. He pulled me towards him; I lost my balance. He lifted the knife up – I thought he was going to kill me. He swung it around and put it to his own throat. He cut his throat from right to left.

Blood poured out. He pulled me closer. Dragged my face right up to the wound and held me tight. Hugged me to him. The blood poured over my face. In my eyes, down my throat, down my neck, across my chest. I couldn't scream. I couldn't get away; his grip was too tight.

My face was covered in blood. I started to choke on it; coughed and spluttered it out. He fell down and dragged me down with him. Smothered me on the floor with his fat. I couldn't get away. I couldn't see anything; my eyes were covered in red.

I felt his grip loosen. I kicked and screamed and pushed him off me. I got to my feet. I ran. I slipped in the blood. I fell through my glass coffee table. My hands and arms were all cut. I was bleeding too. I ran out of the flat screaming. I ran down the street only in my nightshirt. It was freezing cold. But I just ran and screamed, ran and screamed.

Some guy saw me running down the street. I was hysterical. He was a cab driver. He took me back to his cab office and called the police. The police wanted to go back to the flat with me, but I wouldn't go back in. I just couldn't go back. I told them what happened; they didn't believe me. Said they'd been inside and there was no one there. They found my shattered coffee table, but nothing else except the knife. There was blood on it but they thought it was my blood. And the blood down my shirt was all my blood from the cuts on my arms. They thought I'd cut myself on purpose.

I went mad. I went crazy. What the hell was wrong with them? He was there! I wouldn't do that to myself. Christ. In the end they sent me to the hospital, I was given sedatives. They then sent me to go stay with my cousin. I couldn't go back to that flat for weeks. I was too scared to. The police, they did nothing. Not a thing to help me. I didn't go back to that flat for months.

I went in and there was all glass on the floor. The knife was gone; I don't know what the police did with it. I didn't stay there again. I got my things and ran out on my contract.

I'm back staying with friends now. But it's not the same. They all think I've gone crazy. They don't believe me. But it did happen. I'm not making it up. It's dark shit; it's so dark and wrong and fucked up, but it happened. It absolutely happened.

STUDIO FLAT

I wasn't naïve. I knew when I moved to London that I wasn't going to be able to afford a mansion. Not on a runner's salary. I should've gone for a house share but I was too anxious about moving in with strangers and my experience of house shares at university wasn't great.

But I'd hoped that by moving out far enough I'd be able at least to get a one-bedroom place. I soon found out that wasn't going to happen. Not if I was gonna make Dad's money last, which I had to. I didn't want to be a runner for long; I wanted to progress. But I didn't know how long that'd take.

In the end I had no choice but to take a studio, and not a very big one. At least it wasn't one of those with a fold down bed. But with the bed it wasn't much bigger than a hotel room. Except that this had a kitchen – three units with an oven, a sink, and a microwave screwed to the wall. Nowhere to dry the dishes. Fridge next to the wardrobe. Ancient television with no digital signal. There was a fold down table next to the fridge, giving me a nice view of the wall if I wanted to sit and eat.

I should never have agreed to it. But I'd seen so many places – many worse – and the estate agent put a lot of pressure on me. It fitted into my budget even though they wouldn't budge on the damn price. I was supposed to send down for my things from home when I settled, but I made no plans because there was nowhere to put anything. There wasn't much space for me, never mind my things.

It's just temporary, I kept telling myself. Stay a year, get another job and then move. Maybe I'd meet some people, move in with them. And it's London; there's so much to do, you just need somewhere to sleep.

I don't know what I was thinking. You can't step foot out in London without haemorrhaging money. It costs a king's ransom to even take the tube. It was buses for me, all the time. And that made the days at work even longer. And it's horrible taking the bus. So many damn people.

It's not a great job being a runner. They expect a lot and give you little. They can be long days once you've started shooting; you're amongst the first there and the last to go. And some of the people... I suppose you get bad types everywhere, but these people... They were just so stressed-out and demanding. And rude. And full of themselves.

There were days when I was treated like shit. You get up at 4:30am to get there for 5:30 and then maybe not leave until 9pm. And you'd spend the whole day buzzing around, fetching coffee, moving cables, going shopping, pushing idiot extras from one place to another and getting an earful if they wanted to go home or were getting tired. I was lucky when I'd get a thank you, and that wasn't very often.

Some of those weeks went by in a haze. I had to be so careful because I kept falling asleep on buses and ending up in the wrong part of London.

The work was so hard. And I was so alone.

I thought I'd make friends. Obviously I knew it'd take time. But I was such a doormat at work, swallowing so much shit from everyone. Nick, he was the popular one. He was the other runner, so much more confident and chatty. People liked popular Nick. I did my work ok, but people preferred Nick. He was more matey with everyone and he was the one who was going out to lunch with producers and editors. I did sometimes, but only if I overheard them making plans or one of them was feeling generous. Not that I could afford to go out anyway.

Nick was so damn together. Breezed through the work. Even when he said he was tired, or hung-over, he didn't sound like it. I knew it would be Nick who'd get the first leg up, either at the studio or offered some good freelancing job. I worked really hard, but that doesn't really count. Not in the real world. It's the talkers who always get ahead.

It was so stressful there. One day just ran into another. And I couldn't get to sleep at night because I was so wound up and thinking about what I had to do the next day. I only dreamt about work; it was horrible.

I wondered whether I'd made a mistake. A real mistake. I was tired all the time. It was so miserable.

I might've felt differently if I had somewhere nice to come home to, but that flat was like a prison cell. Like I'd go on day release, but had to come back to get locked back in at night. That was all I was doing, going to work, coming back, and then staring at the walls. The same walls. I was so exhausted when I'd get home most nights. I barely had time to clean the place. Or take my clothes to the laundrette. I was surrounded by dirty clothes, dirty dishes, take-away packets. I was living in my own filth.

And it was so small. I would get so claustrophobic. I remember once coming home drunk and wondering whether I could piss from one end of the flat to the other. I didn't try it, thankfully, but I bet I could've done in it.

I couldn't even open the fucking windows. There was a kebab shop downstairs, it stunk in the evenings. And the noise on Friday and Saturday nights... I used to take long walks on the weekends, just to get out of the place. At least there are things to do for free in central. Though I didn't mind working weekends – I could always use the overtime. Although that was even more exhausting. I could never win.

I thought about jacking the job in, but then what would I do then? And I was on a year's contract for that flat. I knew I should've gone into a house share, at least I wouldn't have been so on my own. It would've been easier to make friends. I was in an industry that was all about networking. And I was terrible at it.

I didn't want to admit I was a failure. That I'd chosen a job I was bad at and entered into an industry I'd started to detest. I didn't want to admit to my friends or my family that I'd made a mistake. Some of those condescending arseholes had been so snide when I said I was moving. Giving me all kinds of stupid warnings and talking about things they knew nothing about. I wasn't going to give those small-town arseholes the satisfaction, no way. I was going to let them laugh at me.

But I started to lose it. I was burning out and I was miserable. And that's when the shit really hit the fan. When things really started to go bat-shit crazy.

I was sat alone one evening in my room, watching the TV. It was just some junk, a soap or something shit. It was dark outside, I was thinking about getting an early night while I had the chance. That's when I noticed a light come on. There was just a parking yard down below, a few battered cars and some bins for the kebab shop. But across from that was an apartment building. Grey, old, brutal architecture. It thought it was dead, a derelict. I didn't think people lived there.

But there was a light on, parallel, across from my room. I could see right into that room. The curtains were open; there was a woman there. The building wasn't abandoned after all.

I watched her. I couldn't help it. She was a looker. A fox. I had to look.

It was a living room; I could make out some furniture: a lamp and a picture on the wall, not much else. She was a bombshell. Incredible figure. The sort of girl you don't see around very often. And totally dressed to impress, like she'd just been somewhere expensive, somewhere glamorous. Cleavage you could drop coins down.

Then the guy shows up. He's suited and booted. Yuppie, business-type arsehole. Good looking. Stubble. Hair combed up and back. Young-ish.

It looked like they'd just got in. She was rummaging inside her handbag, which was on a table. He was undoing his jacket. He came up behind her, hands on his waist, looking her up and down. She turned to meet him. She took his hands. They looked into each other's eyes and then kissed.

I couldn't help but sneak a peek. But God I wished I hadn't.

They did the passionate embrace thing for a few minutes and then stepped apart. She unbuttoned her shirt quickly. She tossed it on the table next to her handbag. He took a step back and loosened his tie. She stood facing him, bra exposed. He grinned at her from ear to ear.

Then he hit her.

104

I practically leapt off the bed. He hit her, right hook, and she went down, crashed to the floor. It happened so fast – I couldn't believe it.

Still grinning, he leant down and hit her again, and again. He took off his tie; I watched as he put it around her neck. He pulled it hard, crouched down on top of her, and he... he strangled her.

I almost vomited. I almost screamed. He strangled her, like a lunatic, huge smile on his face. He enjoyed it. He was loving it!

I grabbed my phone. I called the police. I didn't know the building's address, but I told them what happened and where I lived. They asked me to count the floors, and it had to be first or second floor. Probably second.

The wait was unbearable. It was well over half hour by the time the police finally came over to my room. I'd just been sat waiting. There was nothing I could do. Twiddling my thumbs while they took their time.

The room was dark now. The light had gone out while I was on the phone. I kept watching the room, hoping the light would come on; that the police would get there; that maybe she was alive. She was probably a prostitute. High-class escort – that would explain the look. He looked as if he could afford one. And it might explain why he thought he could get away with it. Killers looking for women with few ties who won't be so easily missed.

When the police finally knocked, I asked straight away if they'd caught him. They said they were having problems finding the place. I went over what I'd seen with them yet again. These plods – they just couldn't seem to figure it out and were wasting so much time. A woman's life was at stake.

They asked me if I'd definitely seen a light go on. I said "Yes, of course", how else would I have seen what happened? That's when they looked at each other. I asked them what the problem was...

The building was abandoned. Had been for years. There was no power. Even if two people had somehow broken in, there was no power. A light couldn't have come on.

"That's impossible," I said, but they were sure. They'd apparently checked with the security firm who monitored the place. It was abandoned and had been for more than five years. They were waiting for someone to arrive with keys, but they couldn't see how anyone could've got in or how I could've seen the light on. Unless it was a torch, but I'd said it was definitely a room light. It had to be.

They didn't believe me, did they? They started to question me! Rather look for this guy – a murderer – or the girl, who was probably dead.

They thought I'd lost it. They could see the bags under my eyes, my pasty complexion, the state I was living in. They'd probably seen it all before. Guy goes stir-crazy in his 700-a-month rat hole. Probably happened all the time.

I tried convincing them I wasn't making it up. That I hadn't hallucinated the whole thing. What could've put that sort of thing in my head!

But the more they asked questions, the more reasons they gave for why it couldn't have happened the way I said it did. And the more I insisted, the more crazy I sounded. I started to question it myself. If you went mad, you wouldn't know one thing from the other, would you?

They left saying I should get some rest and call a doctor. I kept on at them until they promised that they'd still check out the building, but I'm pretty sure they didn't bother.

I remember the guy saying I should air the place out when they left. Bastard.

I was in a state of a shock. I didn't know whether I'd seen a murder or I'd gone crazy. Both were really fucking serious problems.

I couldn't relax after that. I had to go over and look myself. I'd never been there before. It was right around the corner, but I'd never had reason to.

It was as the cops had said. It was boarded up and fenced off. Big steel wire fence around it. You could get through if you were determined, but why would you? Neither of those people looked like they'd climbed a fence or squeezed between wooden panels.

I didn't know what to think. I felt sick right in my stomach. My head was pounding. There was nothing I could do. I just had to go back to my room and go back to normal. How do you do that? When you've just seen someone get murdered.

I lay awake all night staring at the ceiling. It was as if every time I closed my eyes I could see the whole thing replaying. The look on her face when he smacked her down. The look on his face when he strangled her. The determination, the pleasure; it made me want to throw up.

So much for my early night – I felt like absolute shit the next day. Even worse than normal. I had to get out of that damn flat, but I had nowhere to go – it was a Saturday.

The weather was bleak, spitting down, pissing it down. But I couldn't stay in that room. I just started walking, and kept walking. I made it into Hammersmith and then along the river, then to the museums at South Kensington, where the kids and tourists were too loud. I found a sheltered bench in Hyde Park and rested there. I'd been walking for over four hours, seriously.

What did I do next? I just had to go back again, didn't I? Nothing else to do. I could've gone further into London, but the crowds just made my head hurt.

All I had to eat all day was a bad supermarket sandwich. If I had been smart I'd at least have brought a book with me. It was dark again by the time I got back to the flat, wet, cold and miserable. I waited a long time before I even went through the door. I got back inside and studied my miserable surroundings, the same four walls, and decided I had to do something about this place before I went totally crazy.

I did my best. Tidied up, got rid of some of the rubbish. I had to make the place more liveable. It was what it was. I had to find ways to make it better. I made my dinner, lay on my bed and started to think of what I could do to dress the place up. Make better use of the space. It was a distraction, for a while, but I knew, I really knew, there was nothing I could do about it. It really was what it was. A fucking rat's cage.

I fell asleep in front of the telly. There was nothing worth watching as usual. I was so tired I mustn't have been able to think about the murder any longer. But it didn't last. I woke up a little before daybreak – and that's when I saw it again.

There was a light on in the window across the yard. The same light, the same room. My eyes zoomed in like a camera. It was happening again.

Man and woman, back in the same room with the light on. And it was the same man and woman. It was happening again exactly as it had before.

He watched her; they kissed, they embraced. She started to strip.

He hit her.

I felt like I could hear her scream. It was like a blazing migraine. I clutched my head between my hands.

But I couldn't help myself – I couldn't help but watch it again. I don't know why. It's still so clear in my memory. I can still see his smile in my head, those swift, merciless, vicious moves.

He was so quick, so precise. He knew what he was doing, and he did it with such confidence, such expertise. I knew there and then that this wasn't the first. It couldn't be. He knew what he was doing. He'd done this sort of thing before! This guy was a real killer.

I rolled off the bed and reached again for my phone. But by the time I'd reached it and dialled 999, the light was off again. As the voice on the phone spoke to me, I said nothing. The whole thing had stopped again. Vanished. I hung up the phone and just stared.

There was no one in that building. I'd checked it out myself. And there were no other lights on. It was abandoned. And what I'd seen; it was exactly the same as I'd seen the night before. The same in every detail.

Had I gone mad? I didn't know. I drew the curtains but still found myself facing away from the window. I couldn't work it out. What was I seeing? When did it happen? And why was I seeing it? Why me?

Who was the woman? Who was the man? I didn't know. And I didn't know how to find out. Surely if the police knew something about this, they'd have said something, wouldn't they?

I had the horrible feeling that this was something that had happened a long time ago. That someone had got away with murder. And now I was seeing it replayed. But why me? And how? Jesus, how? Can you tell me? I still don't know how or why.

What I do know is that it really started to drive me over the edge. We were hitting the winter months and the clocks went back. That meant there were days, lots of days, when I barely saw sunlight. It was dark when I got to work and dark again when I got out. There was no sunlight at the offices, and not in the TV studio. Only when I was on an outdoor shoot or I managed to get out for lunch did see any natural light. But the weather was so shit, what I mostly saw was clouds and rain.

And when I got home... I started to get scared to have the curtains open. I got home very late one evening, after doing lots of shopping for a food shoot. I went straight to cooking, and when I turned away from the 'kitchen' I saw it happening again. The action had already started, but I managed just to shut the curtains before the attack.

But my head started pounding anyway. Even though I hadn't seen it, it was still affecting me.

I kept the curtains closed all the time after that. As it was always dark when I was there, that wasn't a hard thing to do. Not that it stopped me seeing it in my sleep. Replaying it in my head. And in my head there were all the sound effects. All the noises I could imagine. The screaming... And I was helpless to stop it.

One night, after a few weeks of the curtains being always closed, I just peeked between them. Just to see if it was still happening. I pulled them apart, just a little... and it had already started. I saw him hit her again.

I turned away, put my back to the windows. But the pain went straight to my head... I slid to the floor. It was horrible. I cried. I cried all night.

After that I couldn't take the risk anymore. The next weekend I got some cardboard boxes, and with tape stolen from

109

the studio I covered the windows. I blocked the whole thing out so I didn't have to see that horrible scene again.

So long daylight.

I started to feel like a vampire, a night creature. I hated that studio flat so much. I hardly spent any time there. I couldn't take the claustrophobia, the stuffy air, the smell. The same four walls. I became like a beggar, travelling from place to place. The studio flat became like the doorstep I returned to each night to sleep. When I finished work, I would go to find somewhere where I could hang out for free and not be bothered. The Royal Festival Hall, the BFI, the Barbican... the best places were the ones where you could hang out for hours without buying anything and no one seemed to mind, or notice, or care.

I would eat food sneaked from the studio, or scour supermarkets for almost out-of-date food. Occasionally I even chanced a bit of shoplifting. Then it was the museums at the weekend. You did have to buy things there, and they were usually busy. But I found my way to some of London's more obscure ones. And I could afford to treat myself a little. Just occasionally.

It's amazing what you get used to. I probably looked a mess – I was a mess. But after a while, it just became my thing. I read books, lots of books. Picked them up for pennies from charity shops.

Nick moved on to another job. I knew he would. I remained; apparently not good enough to progress, but at least not so bad that they could fire me. Those wonderful people.

Nick was replaced by Rhiz; we got on. He was ok. We hung out a few times. I was always trying to find ways to get him to stay out longer, hang out more. I think I put him off by being too keen. Maybe he thought I was gay and trying to chat him up. But he was ok with me. Still hung out sometimes.

I'd stopped really worrying about work. Turns out there are worse things that could happen to you. I'd seen them. When you've seen someone be repeatedly killed, it matters a lot less upsetting some agency queen when you get him a latte instead of an espresso.

My goal every day was to find ways to stay away from the flat as much as possible. To find other places to go and ways to occupy my time. It was hard with me not having much money. But I got used to it. Like I said, it's strange what you can put up with.

After a while I even stopped dreaming about it. Stopped hearing the voices I'd made up for the man and woman. Eventually I was able to sleep without hearing them. But I kept the windows covered and the curtains closed.

It wasn't like I was happy. I was never happy. I was just able to cope. Able to keep a lid on it.

It got to almost Christmas, and while others were at parties enjoying themselves, I was at a loose end still and worried about going home to see the folks. What was I going to say to them and my so-called friends about my time in London? What nice things was I going to say about my shaky career and my lack of friends and my lack of sunlight?

But Christmas came early one night. I had moved on from the V&A and found myself wandering out beyond Chelsea into Fulham when, stroke of luck, I found a £20 note on the pavement. Seriously, it was the best thing that had happened to me in months.

I went to a pub. Treated myself to a pint and a portion of chips. Luxuries. It was freezing outside. I wanted the warmth too. I sat in a corner, near a pool table. It was pretty quiet despite the time of year. Not many people there. I put some money in the pool table and started to play by myself.

I was about halfway through the game. I was doing pretty well but I was also starting to fight back. I was holding the cue about to make a pot when I looked across the bar and saw him in the flesh – the killer! The murderer!

It was him, no doubt about it. He was older, grey in the temples. The vision I had seen of him before must've been a good few years ago, but unmistakeably it was him. I had no doubt. I could never forget that face.

I felt weak at the knees. I dropped the cue and flubbed the shot, but that barely registered. I had found the killer and he was alive.

And he was here, with another woman.

Time had not dulled his looks or his sense of style or his taste in woman. Although I doubted this one was another prostitute, she looked more regular, ordinary. I mean, good-looking still, but not dressed like a high-class hooker. Down-to-earth. More everyday beautiful.

He was smooth as ever. Charming the pants off her. Making her laugh, making her smile. She was playing with her hair – that's a sign they're interested.

I put down the cue. I lost interest in the game – it wasn't important. Here was a killer. And he was with another victim. Jesus, I didn't know what he was going to do with her. I sat myself by a corner table, where I could watch discreetly without much risk of being seen.

They had food brought to their table. He shrugged to her when it arrived, as if to say it wasn't bad, it would do. Obviously not up to his usual standards and tastes.

What was I going to do? I had no evidence. The police thought I was crazy. Anyone would think I was crazy. But I knew this man was a killer. And this woman was in danger.

What would you do? Shrug your shoulders, say "What can I do?' and leave? I couldn't do that. I had no choice but to stay and watch them. This one was a redhead. That surprised me. I thought he would just go for blondes. That'd be his thing, his style. Would that mean this woman was safe? Who knows? She could be another escort for all I knew. I was just guessing.

I sat for over an hour watching them. They were almost sickening, the way they were looking at each other. Giggling and laughing. Playing footsie under the table. And all the while, she had no idea what she was dealing with. What kind of animal he really was.

Suddenly they got up to leave. I downed the last bit of my pint and had to rush to get up and go after them. I had to follow them. What choice did I have?

They didn't take a taxi, thank God, or else I'd never have been able to catch them. Instead they took a long walk. A long walk in the freezing cold. I followed at a distance. Tried to stay far enough behind so they wouldn't see me. But they were so wrapped up in each other that they wouldn't have noticed anyway

They stopped part way through the journey to get off with each other next to a bus stop. It was really difficult to find a way to hang around and wait to see where they were going without drawing attention to myself. I pretended to tie my shoelaces and then waited by a bus stop across the road, worried that they might suddenly jump on a bus themselves. But I guessed correctly, they were stopping for a kiss and a grope before moving on. If only she knew...

I wasn't even sure where we were. We'd walked for over 20 minutes – I didn't know the neighbourhood. And then they suddenly left the road. Just when I wasn't paying attention, they disappeared.

Shocked, I ran forward to where I thought I'd last seen them. They'd gone off the street down some steps. He had a basement flat. Under one of those beautiful London houses you could never dream of being able to afford.

I just caught sight of the door closing behind them. That was it. She'd entered his lair. She was in the killer's home.

What was I going to do now? This could be it. He could be planning it now. Deciding when to take her off guard. He had his tie on. He could be loosening it now right at this very moment.

The living room light went on, but the curtains were closed. I could barely see outlines of people moving in there. Perhaps they weren't moving; perhaps it was just the furniture. Perhaps I was already too late.

I had to do something, and do it now. I thought about calling the police. Yes I would sound mad. I would sound crazy. But if they came out here, spoke to him, spoke to me. Maybe they'd get suspicious. Maybe he'd let something slip. Maybe they'd connect him to the old derelict building, where he must've lived once.

No that was crazy. At best I might talk them into coming down here. I could like, maybe, say I'd seen him strike her? But then I began to panic. How long would that take? It could be happening in there right now. He might already be strangling her. She could even already be dead.

There was nothing for it. I went down the steps to the door and thought about breaking it open. But it looked pretty strong. No, I couldn't do that.

So I banged my fists on it. I banged the knocker. Rang the bell. Then I shouted "Help please, it's an emergency". I thought I saw the curtains twitch through the corner of my eye. I heard movement from behind the door.

I had a sudden idea. I leapt quickly up the stairs back to road level and then climbed up the steps leading to the door of the flats above. When the door to his flat opened, he stepped out to look around for who'd knocked.

In just those seconds I threw myself over the rail and landed right on top of him – feet first! That knocked the wind right out of him. He didn't see that coming!

I've never been much of a physical guy, but I gave the fucker everything I'd got. I was on my feet faster than he was and I was smacking him around the head with my fists.

Then the girl came out, and obviously she doesn't know what's going on. So she grabs me by the back of my coat and tries to pull me off him. That gives him a chance to get back at me.

"I'm calling the police," she screams as he's back on his feet trying to throw me about.

"Call them," I reply. "Stop this murdering bastard."

"You crazy fucker," he says.

We've started to kick up quite bit of a racket so people are coming out of there flats. Obviously the neighbours know this guy – turns out it is his flat. So some of them come to help as we're rolling around, scrapping on this little bit of patio in front of the window.

They grab me and pin me down, but I don't care. I don't care what happens now. I can see it in his eyes and he can see it in mine. He knows that I know. And as I scream to the people around me, as they pin me to the ground, I scream that's he's a killer and that he was going to kill her. I can tell that he's scared. There's a little twitch in his eye, a little delay before he answers back.

"He just fucking attacked me," he pleads, playing innocent. But he knows. He's knows he's rumbled.

The police come along and I tell them how happy I am to see them. And I tell him I'm going to tell them everything. He'll never harm another woman. That he's done for.

I get arrested and taken down the local station. And I tell them everything. To hell with it. What does it matter if they think I'm mad? What does it matter if they think I'm crazy? There are lives at stake. It doesn't matter what happens to me, it really doesn't.

They threw me in a cell overnight to cool off. I didn't sleep; I just waited. I just had to hope that maybe he'd let something slip. Or just maybe some smarter-than-the-average cop thought he'd just check up on some of the things I'd said. Fat chance of them showing that kind of initiative, but who knows.

Eventually they drag me out again in the morning. They put me in a room and tell me, as much to my surprise as theirs, that he's not going to press charges. I couldn't believe it!

They said he was taking pity on me because I obviously had problems. I had to try hard not to laugh my ass off. He didn't want the attention. He didn't want the trouble. It was as big an admission of guilt you could've hoped for, not that the stupid police noticed. I told them so, but they were so fucking oblivious.

I had to do my best not to smile ear to ear while they gave me my warning and my lecture. I needed help; I needed to see a doctor. They were going to check up on me with social services, make sure I sought help. Like heck they were. Once I was out the door I never heard a damn thing.

Of course they told me to stay away from 'Mr Anderton' – that's what he went by. But of course I couldn't do that, knowing what I did about him. I'd saved one girl, perhaps only briefly, but others would get hurt. People like him weren't going to quit.

When I got out I stood vigil outside his flat. I didn't care about being discreet; I wanted him to know I was watching.

Had to still go to work during the week, but afterwards, and on the weekends, I'd wait there for him. He seemed to have vanished – had I really scared him off? Then, just after a week, a For Sale sign appeared outside the place. I really had done it – I'd scared him off.

It felt good for a little while. Just a little. I was conscious that a killer was still free and on the loose.

I tried to track him down. Did everything I could. I even tried to convince the estate agents I was a serious buyer. I toured the house, tried to talk them into giving me his details, but without the finance paperwork, there's nothing I could get.

There's really not much more to tell after that. I went into media buying instead of studio work; that was stable, more boring, but more stable.

And I did my year in that damn flat. After he disappeared, I tore away some of the cardboard to see whether the murder scene would stop. It didn't. It just kept on playing over and over. That's because he's still out there. I wonder if whoever moved into that room sees it now? Whether it drives them crazy too.

Because he's still out there somewhere. And he'll kill again. People like him don't quit. Whenever I walk the streets I look out for him. I've tried to Google him, Facebook him, but I haven't found him. I hope to God someone will one day.

Maybe then I can stop dreaming about it. I may have got away from that flat. But I still get the dreams. And I still hear the screaming. And I still wonder who else he's killed and how long it will be before he kills again.

THE HOARDER

Madness doesn't just happen, not the way people think it does. People think that one day you just snap, but it's not like that.

I was fine. I thought I was. I really did. I was lonely, I suppose. But I didn't go around feeling sorry for myself. I'm not like that. I have my job; I like my job. And I've got friends and I go out. Maybe not as often as I'd like to, the hours at work – I'm a paramedic – that can make it difficult. It's very tiring, and some of the things you see can hit you really hard. You don't always feel much like going out. Especially when kids are involved. That always hits hard, more than anything else, when kids get hurt.

There was the thing with Tony too; he's one of the porters at the hospital. That hit me more than I thought it did.

I put my hopes too high for that. Thought it was like a second chance and let myself get too... attached. Let my heart get broken all over again.

He was – *is* – very attractive. And I don't get to meet many men. Not healthy ones with all their bits still attached.

We went out. We had some fun... and that's all he was looking for, some fun. He wasn't looking for anything serious.

Basically I was there, and he thought "She'll do for now", and then when he was bored he moved on to someone else. I've seen him do it to others; he knows how to work it with women. I shouldn't let it get under my skin. But it does. More than I'd like to admit.

I don't know why I'm talking about this. You want to hear about the spooky stuff, don't you? What really happened to me: mad or not mad? Crazy or not crazy?

We got a call out this one night late October. I was with Rohit and we went out on call to this house out on the _____ estate, which is a rough area.

We drove to this old house on the end of this road and the garden there was piled high with rubbish. Police were there, fire service too. You'd think there'd been a major incident, but it wasn't that.

The house was stuffed with even more junk. It was a hoarder's house. Everything you could imagine was there, and it was in piles, or in bags, or in boxes. And just all over the place.

That's why the fire services were there. They were clearing their way through it all. Social services were hanging around as well. They'd come with environmental health officers to see the man earlier. When they'd got no answer, they checked around the back and smelt the body. Once you know that smell, you don't forget it.

You couldn't really get into the house. The back was totally blocked off with stacks of newspapers. There was a really narrow path through the front door, but hardly wide enough for a person to get through.

The man was stick-thin. Piles of his rubbish had caved in and blocked him in the downstairs bathroom and there was no window. Poor guy couldn't even get any water because that'd been cut off months ago.

They were still shifting things out the way when we got there. We couldn't get the gurney in. So we formed a chain, all of us. Carrying stuff out to clear our way in.

The most random stuff came out. Bags of newspapers, boxes of tin cans, kettles, toasters, bicycle wheels... Things were all gathered together; his rubbish was categorised. He was weirdly organised.

It was hours before we could get the gurney to him. And we barely had half an inch of spare space to move in.

But before we got in, I was passed this box. It was falling to bits. The person who passed it to me practically threw it at me because they could feel it go. So they just passed the problem on to me. Thanks for that...

Stuff was falling out of it. And it was all pottery and china too. I just had to basically guide the thing to the ground so that not everything was smashed. It was all junk but you have to be careful in case somebody complains later that you've broke something valuable. People will try and get money out of you for anything these days.

I saved most of it. I didn't look very closely, but things didn't look broken or cracked. Not by me anyway.

But I did see one thing fall out. It was this little china figure. It was the figurine of a soldier. A redcoat from the Waterloo/Wellington sort of era. His jacket was red, his trousers were dark grey, and his hat was black. There was a little feather in his hat, but that had broken off. He had a little brown moustache and two blue dots for eyes under thin brown eyebrows, and he had his rifle held to his side.

I still don't know why, but the second I saw that figure... I just wanted it. I had a sudden, overpowering urge to just reach out and grab it.

I can't explain it and I still don't understand it. I just wanted it. It was so instinctive. I just had to have it. It was as if I'd dropped my car keys or my phone, my instinct was to just go down and grab it instantly. I wanted this figure so much.

I had my hand on it before I'd even thought about picking it up or questioned why I was doing it – it was like I was magnetised to it. But I didn't get to pick it up because the fireman came and said he thought we should have a try at getting the gurney in and Rohit was having a look to see if we could.

I didn't say anything about the figure because I wanted it so badly that I was terrified that if someone else saw it, they'd want it too. So I nudged it with my foot into the grass, hoping no one saw me and hoping no one would spot it there.

My heart was beating. I was like an addict about to get their next fix. I knew it was there and I had to have it now. I just didn't know why I wanted it.

We struggled with the gurney and I really found it hard to concentrate. The only thing that really mattered to me was getting that figure. I couldn't get it out of my head. Rohit could see I was distracted, so he took control of things. When you do a job like ours, you know when to support each other and help each other out and me and Ro have been doing shifts together for years. He knows me better than almost anyone else.

There was hardly anything left of the poor guy. We had to bag him up before we got him out. There were crowds of people in the street by the time we wheeled him to the ambulance.

That made it more difficult. I had to have that figure and now people might be watching. Worse, they might want it for themselves. I made an excuse to go back and talk to one of the police, because you get to know most of them if you do the job for a few years. And then, just as I was going by, I scooped it up quickly and shoved it in my vest. No one saw me, thank goodness.

I was stealing from someone's house. I've been doing the job for 12 years and I never stole anything. You can get fired for so much less than a bit of pinching. But I had to take it. I just had to. And not knowing why in a way made me want to take it even more because I had to find out why I wanted it. Does that make any sense?

Can't believe I'm asking that. None of it makes sense.

I hid the figure under the seat and while I was driving back with Ro, all I could do was think about it lying there. What if someone found it? Found me out? What if someone took it away from me? I was more worried about losing the statue than I was about being caught stealing.

We had a few hours left to do and Ro could see something was up and he asked and I just pretended I was tired and that nothing was wrong. I just wanted the shift to be over so I could get home and put the figure somewhere safe, where no one else could touch it.

There was a bit of downtime after we took the old man in. While Ro was in the toilet I took out the figure to look at it.

Like I said, it was just some cheap china thing. Not an antique, not even particularly well made. But I was trembling when I had it in my hands. I had stolen it, and I was glad to have stolen it and to have it. It was mine now. No one could take it away from me.

I stashed it away for the rest of the shift and then as soon as it was over, I carefully smuggled it to my locker and into my handbag.

I drove home really fast. I was so happy to get him home. I

was so relieved. I brought him into my kitchen and put him down on the table. My heart was racing. I stood there looking at him and more than ever I wondered what the hell I was doing. Why had I just risked my job to rescue this little man from some hoarder's house?

I felt so ridiculous. I actually thought about chucking him away. He looked even more cheap now under the light. Not even nicely painted.

But I couldn't just throw him away. I put him on the window ledge amongst the flowers. Then I just spent the evening as normal. It was like I'd been a different person all day. I felt so detached about what had happened, like I'd had an out-of-body experience. I was probably in denial about it. Didn't want to think about it. It had all been so strange.

I had some wine in front of the telly that night. And I remember as the evening went on thinking about that little man. And how I'd left him there alone, in the kitchen.

It was just a figure, but I felt like I'd left him on his own. I even went to check on him, later in the evening, before I went to bed. I just stood in the kitchen and stared at him. I'm not sure what I felt then. What was I supposed to do? It was just a figure standing on the window ledge. But I felt strangely better knowing that he was ok.

When I tried to get to sleep that night, I had the strangest feeling I wasn't alone in the house. My house was too big for me really. I didn't really need all that space. I think I thought I might fill it with family, one day.

But that night I felt a presence. And I couldn't get to sleep, because I felt I wasn't alone.

I remember going to work feeling worn down and tired the next day, the worst day I could've done that because there was a motorway pile up. Multiple casualties. And there were families, and children. It was one of the worst things I'd ever seen.

Everyone I know who works at the hospital has something that gets under their skin. For Rohit it's anything to do with eyes. He gets this look on his face; he goes blue and looks like he'll be sick any second. Jimmy, another one of the guys, for him it's severed limbs – fortunately you don't get them so often.

But for me it's children. That's common obviously; everyone gets gutted when kids are involved. But I struggle to keep it together when there's fatalities with children. It was the great getaway before a bank holiday. Two whole families wiped out.

It wasn't even one of the worst things I'd seen but it hit me so hard. These kids crushed to death. You couldn't even see their faces. Yobs and drunks got away scot-free but not the kids, not the families.

I hadn't realised I'd become so vulnerable. I came home from work that night a complete wreck, trembling, lump in my throat. I went into my kitchen and I saw that little man on the window ledge – and I cried. I just completely lost it and before I know it I'm spilling my guts out to him. Telling him everything. Asking him why I put myself through it all when I hate my job and I hate my life. That I'm so lonely and so unhappy and miserable and depressed.

I wanted to help people, you know, that's why I got into it. Why I started the job in the first place. But it's like the same thing day after day after day. And people, for God's sake, people are so messed up. The things they do to each other. You see the worst of everyone and you wonder why they deserve help at all.

It felt really good to tell him. It was good to get it off my chest. He didn't even have to say anything to me. Somehow I felt some of the burden lifted just by saying all this. Just telling him how I felt was good even though he said nothing back to me, I felt better for doing it. It felt like a huge weight lifted off my shoulders.

So that's how it started. I'd go to work, come home, and I'd unburden. I'd sit in my kitchen and go through the day with him. Tell him everything that had happened, everything I felt. Every argument I'd had, every pang of self-doubt and misery. And he just took it all in. Soaked it up like a big sponge. Best listener there ever was. Better than all my friends.

He wanted nothing from me. He didn't interrupt or start

talking about his own problems or go on and on about his kids. He just listened and cared about my problems.

Horrible patient – go tell my soldier. See Tony chatting up a nurse, go tell my friend. I started to store it all up; all the things about they day I hated, or got on my nerves, or made me angry or sad. I'd put them on a list in my head and take them home to my new friend.

It was the best part of my day. It got so I spent most of my time in there talking to him. And you know what? It made me happier. Even when I wasn't talking to him, I felt this warm feeling, that I was more... I don't know, happier in myself. It was like really good therapy. I felt stronger in myself because I had someone else to turn to.

I didn't ask questions about it. I didn't say to myself, why are you doing this? This is crazy. I just thought I was thinking out aloud, and that was why it felt good. I didn't ask questions, because that was to admit that what I was doing was wrong.

And I liked it. That's the truth of it. I liked having someone to talk to. Even if they weren't real. It felt good and I liked it. He didn't judge me, he didn't lie to me, he didn't patronise me. He paid attention to me and listened to me. He was the best friend I needed and that I didn't have.

But there were side effects. Not that I noticed at first. It was a while before I started to feel tired. Really tired. When you get emotional, let it all out, that makes you feel exhausted anyway, so I expected that tiredness when I went to bed. But it started seeping into the mornings too.

I didn't think anything of it at first. I did a lot of hours of work, because, well, I didn't have anything else to do with myself. I did start to feel sluggish, fatigued, a lot. I just assumed I was overdoing it at work. Taking on too many shifts. I just had to cut back, that was the answer.

That's how the house started to get in a state. I don't know how it is with real hoarders but it isn't as if I made a sudden choice that I wasn't going to take the rubbish out and live in filth. It was just that when I came to do things like take the bin out or tidy up the living room or the kitchen, it just seemed like so much effort.

And as the weeks went by, things got worse and worse. I wanted to do something about it. I'd say to myself, you've got to get this sorted out. This place is a state. This weekend, we're going to clear up. But the more I thought about doing it the more it seemed like too much hard work and so much effort. I got tired and drained just thinking about it. I couldn't summon up the strength.

I didn't get hung up on it because all my worries would just drain away, all I had to do was turn to my friend on my window ledge and he would make it all seem fine. He used to whisper to me. I could only feel what he was saying, but I took comfort in it and knew that the mess didn't matter, that it wasn't really important. It wasn't doing me any harm and I could clear it up later.

I liked being with my friend and hearing his whispering words. I was already starting to feel like I hated going to work because we wouldn't be together. The best part of my day was the moment I got home and he would make me feel ok. No anxiety, no stress, no frustration, no anger, no misery – he'd just suck it all in and I'd feel relaxed and calm. It was the only time I would feel relaxed and calm and back to being myself again.

I wanted to be at home more and more, so much so that I pulled a few sickies so we wouldn't have to be apart during the day.

I was becoming more distracted at work, all the time. I was also getting more and more tired. I felt weak, and Ro, he kept having to cover for me. He told me I should see a doctor if I was feeling tired all the time. I just brushed it off, said I wasn't sleeping as much and just needed a bit of time off. My new friend said I didn't need to see a doctor, and that was all right with me. It was just the world outside. It was wearing me down.

Then one day I came in looking exhausted and Ro said to me "Woh, are you ok? You're looking a right state girl."

He didn't mean to hurt my feelings, not Ro. He was just showing that he was concerned. It's just that... I've always been sensitive about my appearance. I'm no pin-up. I'm plain, as you can see, and my weight is always up and down. It's not like I've got much confidence either.

The second he said that I just had to go and have a look at myself in the mirror. And when I saw me, I saw that I had changed. I don't know when the change had happened, but I was so pale now that I looked ill. I was practically going grey. And there was grey in my hair, lots of it. And my cheeks were sunken and the bags under my eyes were heavy. I looked like a junkie who hadn't gotten their fix and was going into withdrawal. My skin was clammy, sweaty. I looked sweaty and I looked it all the time.

The whole day, I kept watching people to see what their reaction was when they saw my face. I kept imagining them thinking, "What a mess", "What's she done to herself", "They let her out the house looking like *that.*"

I spent the whole shift wanting to crawl into a hole and die. If I'd had a paper bag I would've put it over my head. When we were out on call, I tried to stay in the ambulance if I could. When I had to go out I wouldn't look people in the eye. I'd try and almost hide behind my collar, pull it up high so it hid my mouth and at least part of my face. Ro kept asking if I was all right, and I'd avoid answering him. It was the longest day.

I told all this to my soldier and he said to me that it was the job that was doing this to me. That it was all too much for me. And then, I can't remember whether he said it or I said it, but the feeling was, "Wouldn't it be so much easier to never go out at all?"

I don't think I took it that seriously at that moment. I needed my job. That was all there was to it. If I needed another job, I should get another job. Although I didn't have the energy to do that. That was also too much work.

The idea must have stuck because the next day, exhausted as always, I got up and got dressed and stood in front of the doorway and just felt this enormous feeling of dread. Palpable dread. Like something terrifying, petrifying was beyond, and I was so scared of it, *so scared*, that I felt nailed to the spot. That physically, I could not walk the distance. I was frozen to the spot. I didn't want to go outside. I didn't want the world to see me any more.

And his words found their way into my head. It would be better if I just stayed here at home. I didn't need the rest of the world. I could shut them out. I'd be much safer just here, at home, on my own. With him.

I didn't need anyone else.

No one else really cared.

It just made sense at the time. And I would've taken any excuse not to leave the house at that moment.

I called in sick. My hands were trembling as I did it, but I did it.

And that was it. The beginning of my new life. I wouldn't have to worry about work. I wouldn't have to worry about what I looked like. I wouldn't have to worry about anything.

I felt so much better at home anyway. Besides the tiredness and the fatigue, I was so much happier talking to him and being with him than I ever was anywhere else.

I first told work I had the flu. Then I called to say I had tonsillitis. I knew that would buy me a couple of weeks off without being challenged; it's pretty common.

But after a while I stopped calling up. Coming up with a lie, talking it through with them, even that was too much effort, too much hard work. Just the thought of it filled me with dread. So I just stopped calling them. They started to call me of course, but I didn't answer. I couldn't bear it. I couldn't summon up the will or the strength to speak to them.

I went to sit in my chair. And that was how I spent most of my days. Sitting down, snoozing. Half-awake, half asleep.

I was so tired, I hardly ever moved. I'd only move if I needed to drink or eat something. Then I'd shuffle into the kitchen and I'd see and feel him there, and I'd feel fine. That was really good because it made sure if I had any doubts about what was going on, he would take them away. If, for a moment, I had doubts about my miserable, isolated existence, he'd just lift them and I'd feel good again.

He was happy there in the kitchen. He didn't seem to want to move with me. I took him into the living room a few times to talk to, but he always preferred to stay in the kitchen. It became harder and harder to get in there. You'd be amazed at how quickly the rubbish piles up. It started to stink in there. I hated the smell, but I didn't have the will or the energy to do anything about it. And strangely, I knew he preferred it how it was, so I just left it.

The only other times I left my chair in the living room was to go to the toilet and to bed. Although it became more of a struggle to get up the stairs. It was lucky I had a downstairs bathroom. Eventually I stopped going upstairs at all

Almost everything felt like too much effort. As the weeks went on, I hardly washed. Hardly changed my clothes. I didn't like being this way. Feeling so unclean, so dirty. But it was too much work. And if I ever felt wrong or worried about my condition, all I had to do was see my friend and he'd make everything all right in my head. Then I could sleep soundly again for hours.

I had to eat of course, so once in a while I forced myself along to the corner shop. The time between trips going there got longer and longer, so I was always buying tinned food.

And when I walked back home I would sometimes pick things up. Bits of rubbish, cans, bottles, cardboard boxes. He liked those. I knew he would appreciate me adding these things to his collection.

I used to eat food straight from the can – that was easiest. It wasn't as if I could get into the kitchen to use the cooker anyway.

I didn't know it, but I was creating a prison for myself. I had to be able to move around in my home, even if I never moved around much. So the junk, the stuff, would have to go where I didn't go much. So it started to pile around doorways and up against windows, blocking out the light. As the weeks went by, I saw sunlight less and less. Only through the kitchen window, where he stood was there any natural light, and the only exit from the house unblocked was the back door. He was my gatekeeper; I only went out when he said it was safe.

I could hear sounds from the kitchen. I thought it must be rats. It was filthy in there, rubbish piled high. I wasn't so far gone that I didn't know that rats were disease-ridden and dangerous. But he kept saying it was fine, there was nothing to worry about, that I would not ever be harmed while he was here to keep me safe.

But the sounds would get louder. I swear sometimes I would hear things shift and move about – not things moving amongst the rubbish, but actual rubbish being moved around. I wondered to myself, just how big are these rats?

Then eventually, one day I was just lying in my chair when there was a loud knock at the door. I always ignored it when people knocked. I didn't want to see anyone.

But I knew the voice – it was Rohit. I liked Rohit. He did mean something to me. I'd almost forgotten him, but when I heard his voice, it really did wake me up. How long had it been since I had spoken to Ro?

I dropped out of my chair and began to crawl along the floor.

He was banging on the door, as I made it into the hall I could hear him shouting to someone. He was shouting, "What the hell's wrong with this place. What's going on?" and thumping on the door. "Have you seen this? Carina, are you in there?"

He opened the letterbox to look in. I crawled back to the living room; I don't think he saw me. I didn't want him to see me.

I got to hear his wife's voice too, but couldn't make out what she was saying. "Look at the state of the place. Something's wrong here. Seriously wrong," he shouted to her.

I wanted to answer him. Ro and me, we'd been working together for years. We'd been through some bad stuff, seen some bad stuff. I really cared about him. I really liked him. He was one of the best friends I had. And now that he was here, that he'd come to me and was worried about me, I found that I wanted to answer him. I wanted him to know that I was ok. I wanted to talk to him.

But I couldn't. I opened my mouth and I couldn't speak. I didn't have the strength to.

I'd lost my voice. I couldn't speak any more. I couldn't talk.

I lay against the wall, my mouth opening and closing with no sound.

He went away, eventually. I wanted to answer him but I just couldn't. My voice was gone and I was upset. So I did what I always did when I was upset: I went to talk to my friend.

As I was crawling in there I wondered how long it had been since I had actually spoken. When I spoke to him now, did I really speak? No, it was more like he just knew what I was saying, and he knew just how to calm me down or reassure me or tell me to just go back to sleep.

I went in on hands and knees. I couldn't get into the kitchen anymore. There was too much rubbish. I couldn't see him, but I knew he was there. What had happened to me? Where was my voice?

He said it wasn't important. I didn't need to speak to him. He knew me better than I knew myself. What words needed to pass between us?

But what about Ro? I wanted to speak to Ro. He was my friend.

I didn't need friends. I had him. What did I need Ro for? We had each other we needed no one else.

Normally, that would be enough. I would crawl back to the living room and into my chair. But Ro... Ro was more important to me than that. It was as if I'd forgotten him until that moment. He'd been blotted out of my memory. I'd forgotten a lot of people. I had pictures of lots of them, but they were lost now in the rubbish.

I didn't like to think too hard. It hurt my head. But I couldn't let it go. What was wrong with talking to Ro? Why couldn't I talk to Ro?

Ro didn't understand us. I didn't need him. Why did I need him? Why was I letting Ro come between us?

He was angry with me. He wasn't angry with me often. When he was angry with me I didn't dare argue. I just went back to the living room and lay on the carpet.

129

He'd imprisoned me and I didn't even know it. I didn't even know it, but it started to sink in after the thing with Ro. Was it later that night or was it the night after? (The days and hours meant nothing, I didn't know when they passed or how often they passed). I woke up and I found myself crawling to the bathroom. I had been dreaming about Ro. I couldn't let it go. Why couldn't I speak to Ro? I knew Ro cared about me.

I went to the bathroom and put my hands on the sink. It took so much effort but I pulled myself up to look in the mirror.

I had no idea how long it had been since I looked at myself. I never changed my clothes so I never saw my body beneath them. But when I looked into the reflection, I knew...

I was dying.

I was like a skeleton. My hair was falling out. My skin was almost hanging off my bones. I looked like I was dead already.

The shock – it was so bad I fell down on the floor, gasping for air. I was panicking. I passed out; it was too much for me.

I woke up some time later. Trembling. I was dying. I knew it. I could barely roll over. It was like being woken suddenly from a dream. There was almost nothing left of me.

I wondered, if I fell asleep again, whether I'd even wake up. I managed to turn over and pull myself forward along the carpet.

I was facing the kitchen. Piled high with rubbish. I could hear the rats moving again. And then I could see the rubbish moving.

The rats couldn't be that big. There was something else in there. Something growing. Taking shape. Moving.

What it was I don't know, but I was frightened and I tried to move across the floor. I started to wriggle like a worm, pulling myself up slowly on my elbows.

All the time I could hear his voice telling me everything was ok. That I should rest, that I should sleep. There was no need to fuss, no need to struggle.

I fell flat down on the floor again in the hall. That was what he wanted. He wanted me to die so he could live. That thing in the kitchen. That was him. He was coming to life and I needed to die so he could live.

The old man, the hoarder. He hadn't been enough. He had died by accident before my man could suck him dry of all that he had. But now he had fed off me for God knows how long and he was becoming whole. He was becoming real.

I drifted off for just a moment. And in that moment I dreamt about him rising up. Rising from amongst the junk and the rubbish. Stepping forth like some Adonis, smiling at me for giving birth to him. He came up to me. He picked me up off the ground. I was light as a feather; he swung me around like we were in a kind of waltz. My feet never touched the ground. He pulled me close. He stared deep into my eyes. He kissed me. Then he snapped my neck.

I woke again staring at the front door. There were piles of junk in front of it. How could I reach it? How could I get the strength to pull it open and escape? He would never let me. He would never let me go. The door was barely two metres away, but it might as well have been miles.

I was trapped and there was nothing I could do. I lay on my back looking at the ceiling trying my hardest just to stay awake.

I don't know what triggered the idea in me, but instantly I knew that it would work. That it must work. That it was my only chance.

I struggled hard into the living room, grabbing onto the carpet and pulling myself along. It seemed to take forever before I made it to the dresser. Then it took another age before I pulled myself up against it and managed to open one of the drawers. Inside it took not too much searching to find what I had been looking for – matches!

I slumped back to the floor and pulled myself along to the kitchen. The rubbish was now spilling into the living room.

Still lying on the ground, with just a little flick, I lit a match.

He said to me "You wouldn't. Don't be so stupid."

I took no notice. Gently I placed the match against some dry cardboard and ever so slowly the fire caught and started to eat it up.

He was demanding that I put it out. Quietly, patronisingly at first. Like a teacher handing down orders to some stupid child. But I resisted. And the fire it climbed. It grew steadily, but surely.

He got more angry. Started to shout at me, yell at me. But still, I resisted.

I found that suddenly I was standing again. I was on my feet, my body straightening up to stand. He was giving me strength. Letting me have it back. Giving me just what I needed to put out the fire. It was growing.

He knew my plan now. It was like a game of chicken. And he wasn't going to let me get burnt alive.

The smoke was hurting my eyes now. The fire was roaring. But he held back, thinking I must give way first.

But I was only strong enough to go if he let me. And I knew he would let me because otherwise, who would save him?

I knew he would never just let me go but he would let me save him from the fire. He had to. He had no choice. He would burn.

And like some incredible rush, I had all the strength and energy I needed. I leapt into the flames like they were waves in the sea. I kicked and staggered through the rubbish and pushed my way out of the kitchen, through the back door and out into the garden.

Smoke billowed out after me. Almost the whole kitchen was on fire. I was lucky not to be on fire, but my legs were burnt. I could feel it, but I couldn't feel the pain yet.

I landed on the grass and rolled on my back. The fire was in full swing now. Black smoke was rising into the air. I lay there for a moment, just breathing, just breathing.

He was still clutched in my hands. I was dazed, dizzy, exhausted, weak, but I knew I was still his prisoner. After a few seconds passed, I was back trying to stand again. But I felt my strength already slipping away.

I had a rockery. Overgrown now, but I could still see the rocks and I knew then what to do.

I stumbled across the grass. I feel on my knees and then on my face, but I made it to the rockery.

I took a deep breath and brought myself back up on my hands and knees. There was a rock, there was the figure in my hands. All I had to do was bring them both together.

And when I was almost there, two hands landed on my shoulders. Strongly, firmly, they gripped me. My body went still. I froze solid. One hand lifted and began to stroke my cheek. It ran its fingers over my lips and brushed my chin.

The voice said: "We can be together always. We can live for each other. I am yours and you are mine. I will never leave you."

For a moment I felt weak. I felt myself tremble. I felt myself draining away. My back started to sag, my chin started to drop.

"I will never leave you."

But then I drew in a deep breath and inside I felt myself roar. I opened my mouth and from deep inside, I felt it rise up inside me. An almighty scream. I let it out. I was screaming, shrieking, roaring.

I raised the figure up and I brought it down. I smashed it against the rock and broke it into a thousand pieces.

The next thing I remember is that I'm in hospital. I'm hooked up to all kinds of drips and things. My house has burnt down and I'm in hospital only just about alive. But alive. I'm alive and he's dead. He's gone. I never saw him or heard him again.

So that's it. That's my story. You can believe it or not. That's what happened. Make of it what you want.

GLASS EYE

He thought he was so funny. He had this job where he designed shop window displays for places like Selfridges and John Lewis. So he used to work with these shop room dummies. And he'd take their arms and legs and hide them around the flat.

The first time he did it, he put a hand in my knicker draw. I just pulled it open and it was there amongst my pants. He laughed his arse off about that. And that was so incredibly funny he decided he'd do it again. The next time he put an arm in the sleeve of one of my coats so when I pulled it out the wardrobe it fell right out. Absolutely hilarious that was.

I'd enjoyed it the first two times so much, he did it a third time. He put some legs under the bed. So when I go to try and find some shoes I think there's like a dead body down there. I was so frightened I banged my head.

He didn't think it was so funny when I kneed him in his ball sack.

I was seriously not impressed. I was already thinking about chucking him. If someone's really bugging you, you're probably not meant to be together.

You'd think he'd stop after I'd tried to castrate him, but no, he didn't. He waited a bit though. It was a couple of weeks later; I was making tea – for the both of us – and I go and open the cutlery draw. When I look down I see this thing roll down across the knives. It's white and it stops and it looks right up at me – it's an eye!

I screamed so loud the neighbours could hear me. Carlos came in with a big smile on his face. It was a glass eye. He'd found it in the props box at his work. Apparently it was genuine. This had actually been made to go in someone's face. It was someone's real spare eyeball.

I slapped him so hard I almost knocked his eyeballs out. Then I threw his tea over him and told him to fuck off.

I didn't see him for a few days after that and as far as I know he's taken his horrible eyeball with him.

He took me out for a big meal a few nights later, so I kind of forgave him. At least for then.

We went back to mine afterwards. We went to bed and we were, you know, having sex – fucking. He was on top of me doing his thing and I was letting him.

He was part way through when I hear this little sound. I can't tell what it is and then I look over at the floor and I see this thing rolling across it.

It's that disgusting eye. It's rolling on its own across the floor, like a little marble. And then it just stops, middle of the floor. And I swear to you, it rolls around, so that the pupil is facing me. This eye is looking right up at me.

I screamed so hard the people in the next street could hear me. Probably the next town too.

I didn't even know the thing was still in the flat. I was so mad. Carlos said he must've put it in his bag and forgotten about it. But I was convinced it was one of his little tricks.

I thought he must've done it himself. Got it to somehow roll in and made it turn up with string or something. I didn't know how and I didn't care. I chucked him out that night and chucked him out for good. I was going to find myself a boyfriend with a proper job. And a proper sense of humour.

It was a day or two after and I was at home after work in my living room when I start hearing this scraping sound. It's really quiet and I can only just hear it. But I keep hearing it over the next few days. I start to think maybe I've got rats or mice.

It takes a while before I start to think again about the eye. I've had mice and rats before, I know what to expect, what mess they leave. But when I hear this sound I realise it's the sound of something rolling along the floor. When I hear it I keep looking under the furniture, around the bins, behind the fridge. This one time I swear I see it dash across the floor. At first I thought – oh it is mice after all – but later I think, hang on, only magicians have white mice. You don't get white mice scavenging for crumbs in your cupboards.

I try not to think about. It can't possibly be the eye. Carlos isn't that clever. The eye only moved because Carlos made it, and he's not been back since, so he couldn't be moving it now. But maybe he hadn't taken it with him. I did chuck him out straight away. Maybe it was still in my house with me.

It was on the weekend after that; I've just got up and I'm pretty tired. I put on my dressing gown and I walk downstairs to the kitchen to make myself a drink. I go to the sink to rinse out a mug and while I do it, I get this strange feeling that I'm being watched. I turn off the tap and then I hear that little rolling sound.

I stop what I'm doing. Slowly I look down. It's there, on the floor. It's between my legs, looking right up my dressing gown.

I scream and it darts across the kitchen to where the bins are. I pick my colander up off the drying rack and I go over there. I'm going to catch this bastard thing.

I start to kick at the recycling boxes until it rolls out again. I have to be quick – it almost gets past me. I dive across the floor to catch it. It rolls around inside the colander for a moment and then it stops; stops still.

I don't know what to do with it. I definitely don't want to touch it. I slide the colander across the floor and grab a tea towel. I wait a moment, then lift it up, grab it up with the towel and then throw it in the bin.

But that's not enough. I have visions of it somehow rolling its way out the top, even though the bin has a lid. So I take out the bag and I chuck it in the big wheelie outside.

I spent the whole of the day wishing I'd smashed it with a hammer, but I don't want to go rummaging through the bins. The thing might escape.

I couldn't get to sleep that night. The whole thing with the eye was messing with me. I kept looking across the floor to see if I was being watched.

I got up after a while and went downstairs hunting for my handbag to take some paracetamol. While I was down there I heard some rustling from the outside. At first I thought it must just be some foxes, but when I went to my window I could see someone was standing out there, going through my rubbish.

I was pretty tired; I didn't really think about what I was doing. I just went out there in my bare feet and shouted at them 'Excuse me, what do you think you're doing?'

He was this old man. Really tall and dressed in a hat and a big dirty grey flasher's mac. He either wasn't surprised to see me or he didn't care. He didn't like jump or anything. He just turned towards me and blinked his eyes at me. He blinked at me three or four times and then he smiled at me. It was horrible; he had most of his teeth missing. It was a nasty, leery type of grin.

I look at his eyes and I have a really horrible thought. I stepped back slightly and as I did I noticed that I was standing on something. And part of it, a stringy bit of it, was trapped between my toes. I picked it up and it took me a moment to realise what it was.

It was an eye patch.

He winks at me. Tips his hat. And then he goes off down the road, whistling while he walks.

Makes me sick to my stomach even thinking about it.

WEEDS

When Linda died, there seemed to be no point in pretending things could go on as they used to, because things weren't going to be the same. We had been together for almost 40 years; it was rather like losing a limb. You get so used to doing everything together; I really had forgotten what it was like to be by myself.

I was talking to my eldest, Jonathan, and he said something to me after she died that really stuck with me. The life insurance was fairly substantial; our mortgage was paid long ago and this new money meant that I no longer had to work. I could retire early.

So Jonathan said to me, he said I should use the money to do something I'd always wanted to do. Live out some dream that I'd always had.

It was a good idea, but I just couldn't think of anything. And it's not because I didn't have ideas, but without Linda, every idea seemed to have lost most of its appeal. It might have been the grief talking, but I couldn't become excited about anything. Any dreams I'd had were always with her beside me.

There was one thing I'd always wanted but we'd never had, and that was a proper garden. We had this little patch of grass outside the old house, but it had never been much. And around the back we just had this concrete yard. We should've bought a place with a garden; I always regretted the boys never had a proper place to play. We should've moved and we often talked about it, but we never got around to it.

I think what made me want a garden was that it was something to do. Something that needed time and work and care. If I was going to retire I would need some work; now more than ever I wanted something to occupy myself with.

It was silly really. To get a big garden I ended up buying a bigger house; a bigger house just for me. Silly, really. I just had all these empty rooms; these rooms I couldn't fill. I thought that maybe the children could come down during the summer; Jonathan and Gwynn could bring the grandkids. And maybe when the grandkids were going to university they could stay over and... Well, I just wanted an excuse really. But it was a beautiful garden.

It was split onto two levels; a rockery separating the two, with some stone steps in the middle. There's a little pagoda, a bit rotten but salvageable; small pond, patio and a barbecue. The previous owners had just put down poison to keep the plants under control. It was a bit of a mess, past its best but with lots of potential. John thought I might be taking on too much, but that was fine by me. It wasn't like I had so many other things to do.

There's a big oak, completely wrong in some ways for the garden. Just a bit overwhelming but the branches are very strong. I thought I could build a swing for the grandkids; I'll get round to it at some point

It was all rather daunting at first; so much to trim and cut back. I spent most of the first week going to B&Q and back for tools and gadgets and spades. There were quite a few decisions to be made about what to do, what to plant. There was one thing I knew I wanted to deal with straight away and that was this great big boulder. It was dropped right on the rockery; goodness knows how it got there. I had to get these men to come around and take the great big thing away. They couldn't explain it either. Why would you want something like that in your rockery? It made no sense; it was huge – took a small crane to shift it. Cost a fortune; I almost decided to leave it there, it was so expensive.

But the most curious thing happened.

Most of the rockery had been poisoned, so there was only grass and dandelions and a few small weeds growing there now that spring had come back around. I was digging them out, which took me a couple of days. I'm not as quick as I used to be.

139

Where the boulder had been – there was just mud underneath it, as you'd expect. But soon after I'd shifted it these little saplings grew. I was surprised; I didn't know anything could grow so quickly.

Nothing grew like this plant did.

It was baby George's christening, so I was staying over in Bristol. I was only away two nights, but when I came back the things had grown about two feet tall.

They were thin leafy plants, standing upright. And completely black; I'd never seen anything like it. They had jet-black leaves and sort of grubby dark stems. They weren't attractive. I tried to pull one out of the soil; it came out, but it was tough and brought me out in a sweat. It had a sort of dusty finish that left sooty marks on my fingers.

I was completely lost as to what on earth they could be. I had a look on my computer, and when I got stumped I sent a picture to Jonathan to see what he thought. He's obviously better at the internet than I am, but he couldn't find anything either.

Then he asked me, didn't I use to know someone who knew about plants and so on? You know you're getting old when you start to forget about whole people...

Marcus Levy was the father of twin boys who had been in Andrew's class at school. They had been to parties at our house and Marcus's wife had child-minded for them for a couple of years while both me and Lynn were working. I was amazed Jonathan even remembered them; their boys had been Andrew's friends, not his.

So I sent Andrew an email to ask if he knew what had happened to them, because Marcus had been a botanist. As it turns out he was friends with the twins on the Facebook. So through them I got Marcus to be my friend and then I got the chance to ask him about the plant.

He was a teacher now, but he offered to have a look at a photo of the plant that I had uploaded. When he saw it, he couldn't identify it. He was also at a complete loss as to what to say about it.

He offered to come over; he lived not too far away now,

teaching at the University of East Sussex. I had him over to have a look at the plant and for a bit of a catch-up. In the end we didn't talk about much other than the plant; he was absolutely fascinated by it. He'd never seen anything like it.

By this time it had been less than two weeks since I'd shifted the boulder. The plants were now nearly four foot high and there had to be almost forty of them, all crowded up in this small space where the boulder had been. It hadn't rained in all that time and I certainly hadn't watered them, so how they were thriving was a mystery to us both.

Although they hadn't spread beyond the concave left by the rock, they were now sprouting creeping vines at the base that were spreading out to conquer the rest of the rockery.

Marcus dubbed it The Triffid. They'd also sprung these buds at the very top, as if they were about to open out into little black flowers. Marcus was tremendously excited; this was unlike anything he'd seen before, especially in the home counties.

He uprooted one with a trowel, trying to keep as much of the roots intact as possible. He said he would go home and put it in some compost immediately. If it grew so fast in this old soil then he was interested to see how quickly it would grow if he actually fed it. Although I think he was a bit sceptical about my claims as to how fast it had grown.

He told me to let him know as soon as the flowers blossomed. He couldn't be sure the plant he had taken would survive; he asked me to take photographs and email them to him as soon as they opened up.

Well that didn't take long. There was a hot, humid storm, with thunder rumbling and rolling all night and a sudden downpour early in the morning. I didn't emerge outside until the early afternoon when the rain had stopped and the sun had penetrated through the clouds again. I saw that the buds on the black weeds had opened up overnight, revealing these small little flowers. They had five or six petals, each with a little split in the middle at each of the ends. And then in the centre, just this little touch of red, a dark crimson red. The only colour on the whole plant – a blood red.

I went inside and fetched my phone to take the pictures. I took a few close-ups to send Marcus and then, I don't know why, but it occurred to me to smell their aroma. I placed my hand under the petals of one of the flowers. The petals were unusually thick and strangely warm. Not the warmth of the sun shining on them, but as if they actually made their own heat.

I bent towards them to take in their aroma. It hit me like a face-full of powder, like someone blowing flour or pepper into my face. I couldn't see this powder, but I clamped my eyes shut almost straight away.

I felt like I could feel the pollen entering my airwaves, pouring through my sinuses and right up into my frontal lobe. I was desperate to sneeze, but found myself victim to a sudden migraine, a surging, pounding beneath my forehead.

I staggered backwards. The front of my head hurt so badly I could barely open my eyes; it was as if the whole world had turned red. I managed to stumble back to the wall of the house. If I'd have been further away I might have fallen down.

I had bent-double – one hand on the wall, the other over my eyes. I'd dropped my phone. God knows where it was in the grass.

I had to get inside. I didn't know what to do, but I thought the best thing to do might be to wash my face in cold water. I found my way into the kitchen, my head still throbbing. It hurt to open my eyes very much. I had to feel my way there. The water took some of the sting away, but it really did very little. I stood up straight and tried to open my eyes fully. My vision was all blurred. The harder I tried to focus, the more my head hurt. It was as if someone was grabbing what I could see from each side, and was stretching it. My head only pounded harder the more I tried to look.

I struggled my way into the living room and collapsed onto the sofa. I buried my head in the cushions and then I passed out for a little time.

I felt like I was in a fever dream. An endless walk through a shapeless mist of rolling black clouds. I was lost and didn't know where I was. I realised I was lying down, rolling from side to side on the ground. And then this figure came out of the clouds. He was just there, right in front of me, standing over me. He was a shadow; I could see no features, but he leant in close as if to glare right at me.

I woke suddenly, in a terrible fright. I leant up gasping, thinking someone was there with me in the room. But there was no one.

It turns out that I'd been out cold for over an hour. It had just felt like a few minutes. My vision was back, I could see clearly again. But my head still hurt very badly. I went to the kitchen to take some aspirin; that helped a little, but not a lot.

I wondered whether I should call the doctor, but I didn't think they could really help. The sun had come back with a vengeance, that afternoon was swelteringly hot. I didn't dare go back outside, and not because I was afraid of those damn plants but because the bright sunlight hurt my eyes. I'd have to look for my phone again later.

I spent most of the rest of the day lying on the sofa with the telly on quiet and a bag of frozen peas on my head. I felt like I'd gone on one hell of a bender.

I was a little better as the day went on. I took some more pills, but they didn't help much either. By the evening I felt as if I'd lived three days in one, I was so tired. As the sun started to go down, I went back into the garden for my mobile. I found it not so far from those weeds. I drew it towards me by stretching out my leg. I didn't want to go near the things for fear of another attack. I didn't know what on earth they were; all I knew was that I had to get rid of them.

I stood staring at them. Was it just my imagination, or were all the flowers now facing towards me? The black and the little spot of red. They were like little devilish eyes staring at me. Tomorrow the plants would have to go. I didn't care if they were an amazing discovery, they were poisonous and I wasn't going to let them attack me again or anyone else.

My head started to ache under the slightest of strain, so I didn't upload the photos or contact Marcus that day. The screen just hurt too much to look at.

I had a light sandwich for dinner and then settled into bed

quite early. It was still very hot but I kept the window down for fear of the pollen somehow drifting in.

I just zonked out; I felt so exhausted. I fell into a really deep sleep, even in the uncomfortable heat. I was out like a light.

But I didn't sleep for very long. I was awoken by an almighty crash at about two in the morning. I sat bolt upright and suddenly heard sounds coming from downstairs. I thought I was being burgled, that someone had broken in.

There was another crash from the kitchen. If someone was trying to rob me they were making a damn racket about it. I wasn't sure what to do. My mobile was downstairs; I couldn't call the police. The house phone was down there too.

Maybe I could just scare them off. I looked around for something to use as a weapon. There was still noise coming from the kitchen – furniture being knocked about. They were wrecking the place! I had to think of something quick. What I ended up doing was taking the bar out of the wardrobe, the one that all the hangers sit on. Silly really, clothes went everywhere, but it was all I could think of.

I had no idea where I'd left my damn phone. So I had to just try and scare them off. But as I descended the stairs all I could hear were things being knocked around. It was as if they were emptying the cupboards – why on earth would they be after the food? Plates were being smashed, cutlery was hitting the floor...

I stood in the corridor; I was frightened to go anywhere near them. So I just shouted, "Oi – I know you're here. I've called the police."

There was a frantic scurrying through the waste and carnage. I could hear things being kicked and pushed across the floor. And then this hand appeared in the kitchen doorway.

There were no lights on; I couldn't see much. The hand felt along the doorframe and then the body flung itself through. It flew across the hallway, like it had little or no control over itself, and smacked against the wall opposite.

It was a naked man. Heavy, tall, muscular – and caked from head to toe in mud.

It smeared dirt across the wall as it staggered to its feet. It stood facing me, opened its mouth and howled like a beast.

It threw itself at me, clumsily charging down the corridor. I leapt up the stairs as it crashed violently into the front door, slipping on the muck on its own feet.

I had escaped it, but as I dashed halfway up the stairs I slipped and slid down towards the bottom.

The mud man howled and snarled. I started back up the stairs and it grunted and gnashed its teeth, coming after me on all fours. It was faster than me. I reached the top step and attempted to leap into the bedroom – hoping to slam and barricade the door behind me. But it caught me by the back of my heel and I fell.

I felt it grab my legs; it had an iron grip, I could feel the dry mud rubbing against my pyjamas. I tried to pull my legs toward me and I rolled over on my back. I had dropped the rod from the wardrobe in fright – I had no way of defending myself.

It crawled over me like a wolf, a savage animal, drooling at the mouth. I feebly tried to strike at it with my hands but it pushed them too easily aside. It put its hands, fierce and hard, like a clamp, around my neck. The grip was unbelievable; I felt the air spring from my mouth. It threw its head down towards mine; round, bald and horrifying, and it roared in my face, warm drool falling all over me.

I opened up my mouth and screamed. I threw myself up and woke up – it had been a dream. All a dream...

I was drenched from head to toe in sweat; it was as if I'd wet the bed. I was shivering and so out of breath – I felt like I'd run a marathon. It might've been a dream, but I have never, ever, been so terrified in my entire life.

I felt my hands around my neck; the creature's grip had felt so real, so incredibly strong, the feeling lingered even though it had never existed.

I had to go to the bathroom. I splashed cold water over my face and towelled the sweat off my whole body. I was still trembling when I went downstairs to check, just in case, that the mud-covered man had not in fact been here, and that the kitchen and hall were fine and intact, which they were.

Still unsteady, I went back to my room. I've never really had nightmares, but that was the real thing. The most frightening thing I'd ever experienced.

But it wasn't quite over. As I walked back into the bedroom, I saw something strange coming out from beneath the curtains. I thought that at first it might have been a crack in the wall, but when I got close I realised that it was a plant vine, and black...

I threw open the curtains. The vines from the black weeds surrounded and spun around the bottom two panes of the window. They curled around each other in each frame, as if fighting to push their way in.

And they had – the weeds had forced up the window and crept inside. The small vine I saw dangling there was just the start. I threw the duvet off my bed; vines had crept down the side of the bed and made it under the duvet and onto my mattress, two thin sprouts even all the way under my pillow. You could see where my body had been – they had been rubbing up against my side. They had gathered together to make an outline of the left side of my body.

A glass panel on the window cracked, making me jump. The vines were so determined to get in that their pressure was breaking the glass.

I swept them off the bed and forced them back towards the window. Not knowing what to do I went out to my garage and reached for the spare petrol tank out the back of the car. I came into the garden with that, my new spade and my biggest shears. I poured petrol over the patch of black weeds and with matches lit them alight. I then used the spade to sever the vines – I should've really done that first – for fear that they might carry the fire up the side of house and into my bedroom.

The vines had reached and stretched out across the lawn like a snaking tangle of wires and climbed directly towards my bedroom window. I struck and severed the vines and was able to move them across the grass with ease, they didn't have much grip there.

But as the fire burnt, I suddenly started to cough. There were fumes in the air, rancid horrible fumes. I had to go back

146

inside. Coughing, I closed the door and went back to my bedroom. I'd taken the shears with me, and there I went at the vines that had come in through the window, chopping frantically until I could get the window closed.

I watched the fire from downstairs until it burnt down. I was fortunate I did not set the whole garden on fire.

Once the fire was over I set about getting the rest of the weeds off the house. They had climbed so quickly up the wall that they had not gripped it too firmly and I was able to rip them off easily. There were no flowers, fortunately, so no more horrible aroma.

I gathered the whole lot up and threw them in the bin. I thought about setting it alight too, unsure if it could still grow and prosper even out of the soil. I actually got packaging tape and sealed it up, around from top to bottom. And then I wheeled the bin into the garage and locked all the doors.

I collapsed on the sofa after that. It was now almost light. I slept a fair few hours out of exhaustion. When I came to, I washed my face and went back outside to have a look at the garden. There was just soil now, nothing there. The black plants had burnt away. I checked the wheelie bin and saw the vines had indeed made an attempt to make an escape; one small little sapling had pushed up the end of the bin lid. I ripped it out and ground it into the concrete floor with my boot. Without light and food, the things would soon die, I was sure of it.

Still in something of a state of shock, I made some breakfast. I was still trembling. Something had got into my house that night. I don't know what or how. But I had not been alone, not completely alone.

It was an hour or so later that I suddenly remembered Marcus, and that he had taken a sample plant away with him.

I tried his mobile but got no answer. I panicked and emailed him, left him a message on Facebook. But I heard nothing back. Then, the next morning, I got an email from his daughter to say that he was in hospital. I panicked. He had had respiratory failure, a massive asthma attack.

I was horrified. I emailed them straight back but got no

response. I heard nothing for days until I finally learned, from a post on Facebook, that he had died.

I couldn't believe it. Asthma attacks happen, they happen all the time, but I couldn't help but wonder. I emailed the family to offer my condolences and as I did I asked about the plant, in the most polite way possible.

I had to know. If that thing was around it could still be dangerous. I was worrying myself sick thinking about it. Staying awake at night, giving myself migraines.

I got an email back saying they knew nothing about the plant. This email was from one of the twins, who said they had found nothing of that sort in his house. I tried his university too – they knew nothing about the plant. He only taught there, he had no experiments or research.

So what happened to that plant? I don't know. More than likely he threw it away, or someone else did. The vines I threw in the bin eventually starved, withered and died.

When I found out what had happened, I was so upset. So angry. I felt responsible; if I hadn't have called on him, asked him over... I felt responsible.

I don't know why, but I went to the shed and I got my shovel. I went out to the garden and started digging. I went straight to that patch where the black weeds had grown and I dug it up. I dug and I dug. I dug so far down that I caused my body to ache for days and days afterwards. I absolutely wrecked my back. The hole was almost ten feet deep and at least six across. What did I find? I found nothing.

I think I expected to find bones, or a body, or chest, some runes or something. I suppose I had been watching too much television. But I thought that I might find something to explain why.

But there was nothing. Nothing there at all. No clues, no hints, no explanation whatsoever.

I don't know what caused the weeds; I don't know what they were or why they grew there or what they did to me that night. It's as much of a mystery to me today as it was back then.

The garden's in a real state now. Gardening has really lost its appeal.

ANOTHER FACE IN THE CROWD

The NHS reeks of decay. Sickness surrounds you the moment you enter any surgery. And I don't just mean the people, who look sick anyway, but the pock-marked walls, peeling wallpaper, the beige 1970s colours; and then there's the sun-faded posters and chipped, faded floor tiles. No wonder people don't want to come to their doctor. It isn't as if the staff are even polite to you. You're just one more burden on their over-burdened day. Only desperate times would direct you to such desperate places.

The patients I see don't look so desperate, just grey, ghostly and forlorn. I'm surrounded mostly by old folk, rising to the nurse's call either with quiet, faux-dignity, or shuffling and bent-forward, using their partners for support. Besides the olds, there's a young mother who occasionally looks up from a crumpled magazine to shriek at her children. She's probably in her 20s, but looks tired, awful, far older.

Only a perfectly postured Sikh offers any colour. He's putting a brave face on it, looking like he's not one of these people, like he shouldn't really be here. Probably a first visit; maybe just a simple migraine, pain in his back or mild skin rash; something simple.

But that's not me. I'm one of these people; the needy and the helpless. One of society's burdens. It's always been hard to accept that. You go through life presenting one face to the world, trying in some small way to fit in. To be an individual yet also be part of what goes on around you. To be accepted as part of a whole. I've tried, God knows I've tried. Tried to present a me I could live with and present to the world. A me that could be liked and respected and others would want to be with.

But it's all been a façade. A façade that's taken years to create. Those who know me now – and that's not many –

149

probably wouldn't recognise the me of five years ago, definitely not the me of ten years ago. Those were different mes, cast aside, improved, re-written. But the problems, the angst, the neuroses, the doubt, the self-loathing, they still remained. They were just more buried. I played confident, played calm, played rational, played smart; it was just inside that I was falling apart.

It wasn't even a good façade. I could only perform it with the people who I saw every day; it crumbled around new faces, in new situations. You see, that's my problem – *people terrify me.*

It's not rational. I know that, and I've tried to manage it, worked so hard to manage it. I've tried to put aside the fear, talk myself around. But it's never gone away. You can't tell fear to leave you alone and behave. It doesn't work like that.

You see, there's an instinctual fear of persecution. When I meet someone new, whether it's at work, at a bar or behind a counter, I will assume that that person dislikes me, resents my presence; thinks I'm ugly, stupid, fat, dumb, boring, or whatever. I will persecute myself at the slightest provocation; a glance away, a no-laugh at an attempted joke, a scowl or a cold attitude.

There are times when I force my way through, and sometimes things go ok. But that's not enough, and as life has got more complicated it's got harder, not easier. It's a problem that's affected me my whole life. This fear has created a deeply dysfunctional person, a person who instinctively withdraws, who doesn't know how to form relationships.

Where I work... worked... we had quite a small team, but it's got quite large. There are new people and these new people have been there half the time I have been there and already they know more people in the office, have more friends at work, and see those people socially outside of work.

That just doesn't happen with me. I don't know how to do it. I don't think you'll probably understand that – you'll probably take it for granted, the ability to just go up to someone and talk, to start a conversation, to begin a relationship, even a romance. I'm like a ghost in that office, haunting the place, unseen and unnoticed and forgotten about.

And it's not just being shy. It's so much worse than that. The relationships I do have only exist because of forced interaction; they exist because of working closely with certain people and there are certain parameters to those relationships. And because of these parameters, I can interact, have a defined reason to interact. And, after time, these interactions get easier and the people I work closely with don't notice or forget that awkwardness. They get used to me and I get more used to them.

But take me out of that environment and the act disintegrates. If I have to go to another floor, talk to another person less familiar... I put it off, say to myself, I'll go up there in 10 minutes time, 20 minutes, at half-past, at the turn of the hour... When I finally force myself over there, I creep up to them because I feel like I'm being a burden, a nuisance, a problem. Then my heart beats faster, sweat gathers on my forehead, my hands start to shake. I can't control it. Sometimes it's easier than others, but it never goes away. Not really. Sometimes I'll be fine, I'll be doing all right when part of me tells myself that I've overstepped, flown too close to the sun. Then suddenly it hits me, like a panic attack – as if I've gone too far and my body tells me to quit while I'm ahead. I get the shakes, start to sweat and stutter.

Usually people are fine, nice, but it doesn't take much for me to pick up a signal, a glance, a hissed breath, and I'll feel like I'm being an imposition. I can interpret anything as a negative signal. It's instinctual. I just can't help it.

I thought I'd gotten better as the years had gone by. But it's only that I've become better at developing coping mechanisms, better at creating the façade. I always carry a pen when I'm at work; not so I can write things down, but so that I always have something for my hands to do. It's not like I'm stupid; sometimes I know when I'm being ridiculous, when my mind is playing tricks on me. But I don't always know, and being aware doesn't make the feelings go away. Like when you're drunk and you're telling yourself not to be drunk, but you are drunk and you can't hide it.

I do have friends, don't get me wrong; I'm not completely without hope. But I keep them at a distance. Not deliberately, just instinctively. I even feel pressured with them. When I email my friends, I take care with every word. When I text message, I draft and redraft. I feel judged with every syllable and letter. Feeling constantly like you must prove yourself, it's hard work, it wears you down. It makes you feel like you're living a lie.

I've always been at my most comfortable when I'm alone. There's no pressure to be anything, to be anyone, to present any kind of façade. That's why I withdraw.

So how did I find myself a regular of these grim surgeries and these grim surgery people? It's because the façade fell apart. The cracks started to show and I just couldn't carry it off anymore. I started to fall apart and couldn't control it.

I felt trapped – stuck with my life going nowhere. Nothing changing, nothing ever changing. There used to be hope. Hope that I'd meet the right person, become confident, successful, find happiness. That these things would come in time. But they won't, will they? Nothing just happens, nothing ever changes. And I just couldn't go on pretending that they would or could any longer.

These feelings had just been building for... I don't know how long. I kept myself busy, increasingly busy. But in those quiet moments, when I wasn't busy, when I wasn't doing one thing or another, the sadness, the despair, they'd creep up on me. I'd hide from it, find something to do, something to occupy myself, keep up the façade, keep up the pretence of being fine. But the feelings would still be there, lingering away and gathering. And there's only so many distractions you can give yourself.

Just gradually, bit by bit, it was becoming harder. Harder to keep it together. With all my friends moving away and taking their lives in new directions, I was becoming unconsciously more emotionally demanding from the friends who I still saw more often, particularly the people within my work team. They were the only people I saw almost every day and felt safer around.

I was unreasonably demanding of them. I wanted them to love, like and accept me. Not that I let them know that. To them

I was just normal, or a normal as I ever seemed – people do find me a bit eccentric, of course they would.

I was desperate for them to accept me. But we weren't close friends; we were just colleagues. And this made my symptoms of self-persecution more acute. The slightest negative signal, real or imagined, and I'd suddenly find myself spiralling into despair.

I was going on an emotional rollercoaster in and out of every hour. It was ridiculous; I was all over the place for the stupidest of reasons. If I wasn't invited to a meeting, I would feel left out and excluded. If people in my team made social plans and didn't include me, I'd feel slighted, even if none of their plans had anything to do with me. Their busy social lives, family lives, all the things they did without me, made me feel jealous, dejected, outcast, and painfully lonely. I'd become an emotional child, a cripple!

There was this lunchtime when we were all sat in the pub. It was almost the end of the year and people were making plans for Christmas, New Year, and the weekend. And they all had plans – moving plans, wedding plans, holiday plans, family plans. But I had nothing, nothing to do then and nothing to do in the future. So when I was asked what I was up to and I had nothing to say, I made a joke about it. I can't even remember what the joke was, but it was about how I had nothing going on and they all laughed about it.

They laughed too hard. They didn't mean to be cruel; I made the joke after all. But I was hurt – it just wasn't funny. I held on to my feelings until we left the pub and went back to the office. And when we got there I locked myself in the toilet and burst into tears. I knew then that things couldn't go on like this; that there was a crack in my façade and that I couldn't cope any longer.

At least that's what I thought. I forced myself to ring up my local doctor to make an appointment. But they couldn't see me for over a week. What could I do?

I just had to wait. And in the meantime I went back to work. I had to go in every day and pretend like everything was normal. But I was spiralling out of control; I spent every day like I wanted to explode. I was like a bottle with a cork in it; I was fine as long as the cork stayed in, but I would explode if I let it slip out. I could feel the pressure every second of every day. Every moment I was around people it was beating under the surface. Suddenly the question "How are you?" became the hardest question in the world.

The truth was I needed my façade, it was the only thing I had. Without it, I had nothing. Just a sad, worthless, pointless life. But now it was too hard to keep up. What would they think at work if they knew I couldn't cope? There goes my promotion prospects. There goes any chance of me being respected in the office.

I stewed in my juices for nine days. I kept the cork in place until that first time I walked into the surgery and went into Doctor Lund's office. I sat myself down and I just broke down into tears. It was about five minutes before I could get a straight sentence out. I was in pieces. I had fallen apart.

And do you know what happened after that? *I had to go back to work!* Clean myself up, wipe away the tears and pretend everything was normal again. It was torture; I was hanging by a thread.

Doctor Lund was a good listener, better than I expected from a GP. After listening to me get it off my chest, we talked treatments and causes. Anti-depressants came up, but I was resistant because I was worried about the side effects and just being on pills made me uncomfortable.

The problem was that the other treatments involved therapy. I wanted to do that, but this is the NHS; I'd have to go on the waiting list.

Brilliant, isn't it? You've got to put yourself on hold until they can get around to you. You're finding it hard to get up in the morning, you're having these thoughts, these thoughts that tell you you'd be better off killing yourself, that you have no future; that you're done, end-of-the-road done. I was a walking corpse in the making. But you've got to put a lid on it, just casually put those thoughts aside for, oh, just about 3 - 4 months – 90 to 120 days – until they can fit you in.

I went there for help! I went there for hope! And that's the best they could do: "Hold on we'll get around to you when we can".

I was just about lucky. I only had two months to wait. God knows how I made it through; Christmas helped. It was a distraction though it was hardly joyous and I was hardly in a festive spirit. But the family are used to me being gloomy. Another coping mechanism; it's all such a joke that I'm a miserable dick. But it's not funny. What a horrible trap I'd made for myself. It was the same at work – "Oh you're always moaning, always complaining". My misery is a comedy act. All part of the fun.

I had a few weeks of psychotherapy. Besides the depression, my therapist thought I might suffer from social anxiety. Doesn't sound very impressive does it? If it was Asperger's or autism – people can understand that can't they? They know that that's a serious problem. Social anxiety disorder sounds so flimsy, like shyness dressed up and over-exaggerated by wet liberal cry-babies.

Unfortunately, that's as far as I got. After only a couple of sessions my own therapist did himself in; took an overdose at home. Inspires you with confidence doesn't it? When even the psychologists can't look after their own problems. Another life lived and destroyed in secret.

So I go back on the waiting list. I didn't know how to live anymore. I was literally taking it one day at a time. Every day another day on at tightrope. I didn't know myself anymore. I didn't like the things I used to; I couldn't take comfort in the things I used to take comfort in. I felt like a shell, a hollow walking shell.

Work was the worst. They didn't know about my condition – those first few therapy appointments took place out of office hours. I knew I wouldn't be that lucky twice. Then I'd have to tell HR, tell my boss. I don't know how I'm going to do that. I'm holding it together or I'm not, and if I'm talking about it, I'm not holding it together. I'm just a complete mess and I don't want to be like that. Not at work, not with the people I work with.

They don't understand do they? Depression, anxiety, sadness, shyness – it's not real to them. You should just pull yourself together, don't be stupid, get a grip, cheer up, man up… Because being told things like that, it really helps doesn't it? It really, really helps!

So I was back at the doctors, again. In the waiting room again. They were keeping tabs on me, even though not much had changed. I was still waiting for the NHS to fit me in whenever they could get around to me again.

When I finally get my name called, I enter the office and Dr Lund is there waiting. Big man, not fat, but square-faced and big shouldered. He's good at listening, but it's become apparent, as the weeks have gone by, that that's all he really knows how to do.

I waffle and moan for ten minutes, telling him about how hard it is to get out of bed, how the depression has me feeling like a walking corpse – that kind of stuff worries him. We've talked about anti-depressants before, but I've always said I don't want them. The side effects can be quite bad while your body gets accustomed to them. And there's a small chance that they could actually make you more depressed. That you could feel worse.

When you're hanging by a thread, that's a fucking frightening thing to hear.

But it's not just that, there's the social stuff too. Like having a drink – when in England you've got to have a drink haven't you? There's got to be something wrong with you if you're not drinking. It's impossible to enjoy yourself if you're not having a drink! What's wrong with you?

Dr Lund tells me you can drink, you just have to be careful. In all honesty, I don't really put up much of a fight. I've been in a state for months and it's been hard, too hard. And with the therapy it was finally looking like there was some light at the end of the tunnel. But that's gone again. For how long, I don't know. So I thought it was best to just give in and try. I'd say that they can't make things worse, though technically, of course, they could. But the Doctor's good at reassuring me; tells me it doesn't happen to everyone and that if you're prepared for side effects, you can deal with them.

The pills are called Citalopram Hydrobromide, good for depression, anxiety and social phobia. Take one a day for a week and then increase the dosage to two.

I get my prescription, but I put off going to the pharmacy. It was still such a hard mountain to climb. Taking pills means admitting you're sick, and almost like throwing away any chance of you maintaining a normal life. Accepting once and for all that that can never happen. I never wanted to be the kind of person who was dependent on tablets, dependent of drugs.

I used an upcoming work's party as an excuse to wait, as there'd be drinking involved. It was Anya's birthday – she sits a few rows away from me in the office. She's always so damn upbeat. When you're in a foul mood she can be hard to take, because it's like shouting at a little girl or a kitten. She makes me feel bad about being miserable. Everything's so damn easy for her; she's popular and gets on with people easily. Everyone likes Anya.

Especially me – I'm in love with her. Yeah, let's get this part of the story over with...

She's so damn uninhibited; I don't have to work so hard when she's there. Sometimes I used to wait around the office at the end of the day so that I could walk to the station with her. Not that I ever had a chance with her; I don't think she dates men – she was going out with this fitness instructor chick at the time. But just to connect with someone, have a conversation. A proper conversation. Not just small talk, all phony and bland and put on.

But that was earlier on. The team had got much bigger and she made other friends and started spending more time with them. And I found myself getting jealous. I thought we had some kind of special friendship; that's how much I invest in these little moments of closeness. It's ridiculous isn't it? Sometimes I find myself resenting her; I need her but she doesn't need me. I was so easily replaced with others; I meant so little to her. We weren't close at all.

157

But it was her birthday and I went along with the rest of the team. And I had a few drinks and had an ok time; it's not like I'm a complete social wreck. I can make a decent stab at it sometimes, if the situation is right and there are people there who I can connect with. That's mainly people in my team who I know and can work out and understand. Others in the office, they're harder.

Drinking helps in a way. I'm certainly less self-conscious, certainly less reserved. But I sort of blunder in and become over-bearing. I think people probably find me annoying or a bit much. I don't know; I'm really not a very good judge, let's face it. I'm hard on myself about everything. I can make people laugh, that's something I suppose.

I stay quite late, but when members of my own team start filtering away, I see it's time for me to move on. Without my colleagues to lean on, I become a ghost in the room. Flittering from one group to another, and then eventually with few people at all to talk to. Anya has a variety of her own friends there; she's kind of swamped with them. I don't know who they are, or how to talk to them or approach them. I resist the temptation to vanish into the night without saying anything; after a suitable moment or two of preparation I go over and say goodbye. And then I venture out into the cold, walk back to Liverpool Street Station alone.

I always assess and judge these situations, hold a behavioural review in my head afterwards. I do it on the train and on the way home. I try to stop myself, but I can't help it. I obsess over the minutia of the evening. The conversations that went well, the things that didn't. Did they take that comment the way I meant it? Did I buy the right number of drinks? Did they see me start to sweat when I made that joke?

And then it keeps me awake when I try to sleep. All this stupid obsessiveness... I want it to stop but I can't.

I felt terrible the next morning. Absolutely terrible. My head was ringing and I felt low. Really low. When you've got no one to pretend you're happy to, you're just alone with your own misery. I found that pack of pills and I took the plunge. It was a big deal, a big moment, but as so often in life it was anticlimactic. Nothing actually changed; they take a while to build up in your system. You take a low dosage at first to let your body adapt to them.

The weekend went by without much achieved, much done. And I went through the week quietly as normal, haunting the office as usual. Avoiding contact with others outside my usual sphere unless I could help it. Eating my lunch with my team, making the odd joke, pretending all was normal. Walking to the station with Anya on the days she wasn't doing something else, and missing her on the days when she was busy.

It was another pointless week, lived day-by-day, empty and without meaning. Another week survived. Another one lived through.

The following Saturday I upped the dose as recommended. One in the morning and one in the evening. Immediate impact was zero. I felt no different, no less low, no less heavy. Presumably, it needed time to take effect. Besides being a little drowsy, they seemed to be doing nothing.

That next week started like any other, one difficult day after another to face. But it was on the Tuesday, I think, that everything suddenly changed.

I was in Liverpool Street Station, coming up out of the tube and walking into the main area of the station. And as I was walking I saw a shape. I barely saw it at the time, and I don't think I'd have thought much about it if it wasn't for what happened later. But there was a grey shadow; I noticed it just out of the corner of my eye, moving amongst a crowd of people pushing through the ticket barriers. When I looked closer, I saw there was nothing. I thought it must have been a glare, a trick of the light, or just a strange shade cast by my tired eyes at that early hour. I thought little of it at the time.

But it was the same day, that lunchtime, when I was doing one of my long walks, trying to get out of the stuffy office. And as I'm walking through the street, this guy bumps into me, knocks my shoulder. Doesn't apologise or anything – this is The City, after all; the place is diseased with tossers.

I look back at him, as if almost to shout after him – though normally I bottle it. But when I see him: he's just passing around a corner, out of sight, and there's this thing following him. Another grey shadow – just like the one I'd seen at the station. It's hard to describe because it's not like a firm shape, more like fuzz, a mass of moving static, like you'd get from an old TV.

The two events connect in my head. So I turn and go after him. I move quick and turn the corner, and the street is empty – no grey ghost, just this guy. It's like a back street between buildings. This guy, this tall, arrogant-looking asshole; he hears my soles on the pavement. He just turns to glance at me, just for a second, then carries on.

Something's wrong, I know it. I definitely saw something. But I'm not sure what it means. Have I imagined it? Of course I have, and immediately I think of the medication. I check online back at the office; are hallucinations part of the side effects? It just says something about blurred vision. Could that be it? I try not to panic; it's unsettling, but not such a big deal.

I have to quickly click away from the page as Anya comes over asking for me to check her work. She sees I'm looking a bit pale, and I pretend there's nothing wrong. It's hard talking to someone when you'd prefer that they left you alone, not because you don't like them, but because you like them more than they'd want to deal with.

It keeps my mind off the pills and problems at least. There are some compliance issues to sort out, which keeps me occupied. And then the day ends and I go home. I thought a little about the next pill before I took it ahead of dinner; thinking about the grey shapes I'd seen in the morning. Peculiar for sure, but as I'd apparently come to no harm, I took the pill anyway, assuming this effect would pass.

It was another day. I'd almost forgotten about the day before, although I generally don't sleep very well so I'm never at my best early on. That's why it takes me by surprise as I enter Liverpool Street Station and see them – they're everywhere!

Five, six, seven of them. The grey shapes, the living shadows. They follow people; they linger after them as they walk, talk, eat, push and shove. They creep and stalk behind them, like a malicious, malignant shadow. I stand still and I

160

watch them. They're hard to look at; like a bright light, you can't fix your eyes on them. It hurts; you want to look away.

They're everywhere. I stand still, dead still, watching them, scanning the station. There are more – on the upper level, on the platform, queuing in the shops. My heart starts to beat fast. My hands tremble. My anxiety hits overdrive.

I shake my head, they're not real. They're not real! I take a deep breath. I screw up my eyes, close them tight. Drop my head. I count to five. And slowly I reopen them and lift up my head.

Someone knocks right into me, without apology, as usual. I nearly leap out of my skin in fear. They look back at me, but this isn't enough to make them want to apologise, and they carry on. My attention has been briefly distracted; I survey the station again and now everything seems normal. Just the usual sea of people flushing in and out. I relax just a little – it is just a hallucination. Cause to be concerned, but not to panic.

But then I get this hiss in my ear. It's high-pitched, like tinnitus, like when your ears have just popped. I look behind me and there's one there. Looming over me, it's taller than me. I just glance at it – the sight of if swamps my vision. I almost scream. I take off. Rush across the station to the escalators up to the street, shoving and pushing my way out of there.

When I arrive at the office, I'm a shivering, sweating mess, but no one notices. I barely have time to relax when I'm called over by one of the senior members of the team. Some oaf from upstairs has come up with his own creative and is trying to force it on the designers, and rather than tell him his ideas are retarded I get dropped right in it. They want me to tell him it won't wash with legal, the hope being that he'll drop it if it's a legal issue and there'll be no need to go into why his ideas are terrible. That saves the creatives any hassle – how nice for them!

He doesn't quit though; I end up spending all morning raking through his rubbish. In his mind rules are only there to be circumvented. Heaven forbid he should consider that they're there to protect the world from the likes of him.

And I'm struggling to put up a fight because I'm a nervous wreck and stumbling over my words. But that's not a reason for him to consider stopping; that's a sign of weakness he can exploit. These bastards want to ride roughshod over everyone and they'll do anything to do it.

When I get back to my team they think it's so funny. But I don't take it well and snap at a few of them. This isn't the first time they've got me to do their dirty work. This creates a bad atmosphere in the office, for which I, of course, hold myself responsible. It's not my fault; I've every right to be angry. But it doesn't feel that way, and the instinctual persecution starts and takes me back on my emotional rollercoaster. I can feel the pressure; the cork is slipping.

When no one is looking. I creep down under my desk and curl myself up into a ball. No one can see me down there. No one knows I'm there. I don't know why but I just needed to keep the world out, just hide myself away. I need to feel safe, protected. It doesn't really help. I've still got work to do. Deadlines to meet. If only I could just shut it all out.

I must've been down there a whole hour. But no one noticed.

I had to bite the bullet and get back to work. God knows how I got through it. My head was throbbing, my heart was beating hard; I felt like I was in a desperate fever.

I ended up staying late. I knew there'd still be a tomorrow. I had to keep going. Put food on the table. What else was I to do?

I expected to be the only person left in the office, but just as I'm about to go Anya's blonde head pops up in front of me. I thought she'd left hours ago, but apparently she was in a meeting that massively over-ran. She asks if I'm walking to the station...

So we start off and she's prattling on about how her girlfriend's fitness club is doing so well. But I'm only half-listening. My heart is beating fast as we approach the station. I don't know what I'm going to see when I get there and I'm scared. I want to tell her so badly, but I can't just lay it all down on her like that. What's she done to deserve a share of my hell? We're not even close, not really.

Crowds are still pouring into Liverpool Street, even at 8 o'clock. As we approach the entrance, we notice there's some kind of confusion. The road in front is part blocked off. There's an ambulance and there's police; a car has stopped dead in the road, a crowd of people have gathered in front of it.

There's been an accident. It looks like someone's been hit by a car. They're moving the crowd out of the way to get the trolley to the victim. The people part and we can just see him there, lying on the ground, barely covered with a blanket.

My heart stops – it's the man I saw the day before. The one who pushed rudely past me on the street; the one who had the grey shadow following him. I scan the crowd for it. And there it is: the grey shadow is standing a few steps behind him, staring at him. For a moment it's as if the world stops. There are no sounds. No traffic; no herd of feet stamping across the pavement; no policemen trying to move people on. Even the shifting lights of the sirens seem to slow down. I look at the grey shade hovering over him.

That high-pitched sound comes from nowhere and strikes my ears. It lifts its head up and fixes its gaze on me. It looks right at me. The grey shadow has seen me. It knows I can see it and it can see me. Its face is featureless, but I know it's staring right at me, and now moving towards me.

Anya pokes me, asks me what's the matter? Am I all right? I say nothing, then take to my heels and shout "I've got to go," and I run into the station, down the escalator and into the main hall.

But the place is swarming with them! More than before; there must be hundreds of them, walking unseen amongst the crowds. Stalking people without them knowing. I scan the whole station, spin round on the spot. They're everywhere!

The high-pitched sound is getting stronger. It hurts. I cover my ears, close my eyes. I can't block it out. I open my eyes again – they're still all there, but now they've stopped. They've all stopped. They're not following anyone any more. They're all still – and they're all looking at me!

All of them. I'm stood in the middle of the station and they're watching me. The crowds are still moving, the people are oblivious, but the grey shadows have stopped and they're all staring at me.

As if from nowhere, I see one of them drifting through the crowd straight towards me. It moves like the flickering surface of water. It's coming right for me and no one else can see it except me. They know I can see them and now they're coming to get me!

It gets bigger as it gets closer. I panic and scream "No!" People in the station turn and look at me.

I run. I run towards the barriers and leap over them. One of the station staff cries out after me, but I don't care.

There's a train on the platform. It's packed, absolutely jam-packed. I jump on anyway; people sigh and grumble and hiss 'For goodness sake!' as I squash them further into the carriage. But I don't care. For once I just don't care.

The alarm goes and the doors slide closed. I'm squashed against them so close that my breath steams up the window on the door. Turns out I'm on a train going to East London, almost exactly the opposite way from home. But it doesn't matter.

Then I panic – what if they're on the train with me? They're not stuck at Liverpool Street; if they're on the streets, why can't they be on the trains too? What if they're here right now with me? I look around, but can't move much and can't see past the people. For once the crowds are a good thing.

I wait a few stops before getting off. I'm miles out, but glad of the distance. I don't dare go back to Liverpool Street. I hop on a bus that goes to Stratford and take the Jubilee Line back through to Waterloo. It takes me hours and the whole time I have the feeling I'm being watched and that I'm being followed.

I didn't see any of them. I didn't catch a glimpse of one of those grey ghosts for the entire journey back. But I couldn't shake the feeling. It felt like more than paranoia; it felt like instinct. It got worse as I got off the train and started walking home. The weather was terrible now; absolutely pouring it down. I was looking over my shoulder every few moments. I kept walking faster and faster.

I got back home, slammed the door behind me and went upstairs to my flat. I lingered in the hall for a moment. I was home, safe, but I had the urge to go to the window and see if anything had followed me back. I went to the window thinking I must be wrong, telling myself I'd imagined it and nothing had come after me.

But I'd been right all the time – they were standing outside! Four of them, the grey shades were out in front of my house! I had led them home, taken them right to my door.

I dropped to the floor, curled myself up against the wall and put my fist in my mouth. My God, I'd taken them home with me, showed them where I lived! What were they? What did they want with me?

I was in a state of sheer panic for I don't know how long before I was able to ground myself again. It was the pills! I was hallucinating. I had to remember I was hallucinating. This wasn't real. They weren't real. It was my mind playing tricks with me. The fucking pills!

I looked up the number of NHS Direct on my phone, while still crouching and afraid to show myself in the window.

I got put through to this woman, and explained to her that I was taking these pills and was getting side effects. Typically for me I was too afraid to tell her the full extent of the madness, even in this crisis I still had room to feel ashamed and embarrassed.

She asked me what the hallucinations were like. I said it was like shadows moving, that I could see grey shadows walking around of their own accord. She said that didn't sound like a typical side effect of the medication and I asked her what that was supposed to mean to me? I wasn't making this up!

She said to stop taking the pills immediately, which was fine because I'd already forgotten that evening's dose. After less than two weeks on them, I shouldn't experience bad withdrawal. She said she'd leave a message at my surgery for my doctor to contact me in the morning.

I ended the call and sat for a while longer under the window. It must've been almost an hour later before I dared to look again through the glass. I was just on my knees peering over. The street was empty once again. Nothing but the passing traffic.

But no amount of telling myself it was all a fantasy was enough to make me sleep that night. I did not sleep a wink. I phoned in sick to work next day, that's how bad it was; normally I wouldn't have the guts to do anything like that. I just stayed at home all day lying in bed, staring at the ceiling.

Doctor Lund phoned late morning. He said it was extremely unusual for patients to experience hallucinations, especially as intense as I'd described. I didn't want to go onto something else. I agreed to meet in a few days, as soon as I could get off work. In the meantime, it would take a little time for my meds to leave my system and I might feel some mild withdrawal symptoms. As long as I didn't see those things again, I frankly didn't care.

That was Friday. I had the whole weekend to recover, but I didn't dare leave the house. No matter how much I told myself it was all in my head, I didn't dare. There wasn't much food about; I was living on odds and ends from the back of the fridge and freezer. But I didn't feel much like eating anyway. Depression does that to you; takes away your appetite for pretty much anything.

Christ knows what I used to do on those weekends, those empty pointless weekends. The hours just meandered by and I'd sit around watching the TV or playing the PlayStation hoping at some point either might lift my mood, even if only slightly.

But Monday eventually came around again. With a great deal of anxiety I pulled myself out of bed and out of the door. That must've been the longest commute of my life, and on British transport, that's really saying something!

When I reached Liverpool Street I started to tremble uncontrollably. I started to pour with sweat, my heart started to race and my stomach began to churn. But there was no time to stop and worry; the crowds have no patience for anyone who stays still. I was swept along by the masses and ended up back on the escalator, floating up to ground level.

I passed through the barriers and found myself back in the main hall. And as the people busily swept through from one end to the other, I looked among them and could see no sign of the grey shapes, the shadows. I started to get my breath back, relief washed over me. I had nothing to fear, the illusions had gone away.

And the relief of that almost made the day go smoothly. Lessened the pressure behind the cork. I had perhaps the easiest, least uncomfortable day I'd had in a long time. I just kept quiet, hid in my corner of the office and the hours passed relatively smoothly. It was the same the next day too.

Doctor Lund was keen to start me on some other medication. But I still refused. I got quite snappy with him; therapy, proper therapy was what I needed. I wasn't going to put myself through the same nightmare again. I survived this long in my despairing state, I could last longer. But then I started to cry, which made both me and the doctor question whether I really could or not.

I said I'd have to consider it. We had another appointment in a week. Until then things went back to normal, one heavy day after the next. It's hard to spend every morning wondering why you're getting up. Wonder why you're carrying on. To feel like you've got no future. That if not this week then maybe the next you'll find yourself under a train, in the grip of a noose, flat out on the road. To feel like it's just inevitable. That one day the time will come when you'll just resign yourself to it and take a leap off something or other.

Those are the really scary times. Not the hysterical moments, not the times when you want to cry out or crawl under the table; it's the times when it all seems so rational. When you face the possibility of suicide with a sense of calmness and inevitability.

But there was worse to come. The landlord was sending over a cousin to service the boiler, so I had to make sure the place was clean and tidy so he wouldn't give a negative report on me and get me in trouble.

I'm in my room cleaning the window when I hear the floorboards creak on the landing. I'm alone in the house, there's no TV or music on, so I notice it. And when it happens again, I realise someone is in the flat with me.

There are people walking in the hall. The sound starts in my ear – their sound, the hiss. In my house! And I can't see them now. I can only hear them. I can hear their call and I can hear them on the floorboards. The cheap plastic panel floorboards creak under their feet. They're here in the room with me. I see floorboards sink under their weight. The hiss grows louder – they're there, standing right in front of me.

I fall to the floor, crawl up against my wardrobe. The sound is unbearable. I can't see them but I can sense them, feel them lingering over me. Then the hissing sound changes. The high-pitched whistle isn't a whistle at all. It's whispering. Voices; too fast, too indistinct. Hard to understand, like the sounds cartoon characters make when they whisper. An undistinguishable jumble of words. But they are words. They're there, hidden and undecipherable.

I whine and squeal like a frightened animal; I couldn't bear it. Why couldn't they leave me alone? What did they want with me? I just wanted them to stop. I couldn't take the voices any more. My head was full of them. I could feel their presence all over me, like static all over my skin.

"Stop it" I yelled. "Stop it. Leave me alone! Leave me alone!"

I cried. I curled myself up into a ball, screamed into the rug. And slowly, the sound receded. I opened my eyes and looked up. The room was still empty. I thought maybe I was alone. But the floor creaked again. The sound of footsteps. Footsteps walking away. I don't know how many there were, how they had got in or even got out. But there were many; it was a whole group that had come after me.

The ridiculous irony of it all. I spent my life wanting to be noticed by people, to get their attention. Now I was being pursued and haunted by these things. And I didn't know if I was alone or not. No doors were open. They could've still been in the flat with me. I didn't know what to think or who to turn to.

I held on to the idea – and I had nothing else to hold on to – that it must've been a residual side effect of the medication. That the drugs were still exiting my system. Maybe that was why I'd only heard them, not seen them. But that barely rang true – why now? After all those days... and why so intense? And the whispering... the voices... what were they saying? What did they want?

And things were about to get worse. So much worse. I arrived at work the next day to a shit-storm. There'd been a fuck-up on an ad. A compliance issue – something I'd missed. It's hard to explain without getting too technical, but there was a disclaimer I was supposed to have included that I'd forgotten to put on. It was from a week or so before when I was at my worst and I'd just completely forgotten. But the company had been in trouble with the regulator for this sort of lapse before. And our competitors loved to leap upon this kind of mistake and report us for it.

It's so totally unfair. Investors can flush millions down the toilet in dodgy deals, but something like this, total small fry, and I get hung out to dry.

I'm pulled into my boss's office first thing. He's relatively sympathetic, although he is critical that this has happened before. I point out that that was two years ago, when I'd barely started and been thrown in the deep end without enough training or supervision. He understands that, but he knows and I know that isn't going to count for shit – the head of department is on the warpath. It's the knock to company prestige; the butting heads with the regulator that is going to cause issues. Issues that move to the very top of the company ladder. He's going to get heat from above and he's going to want someone to blame, a scalp to be presented. And it's going to be me.

It's so fucking typical. You work hard, put in the hours, put in the days, put in the effort. You do all you can, take pride in your work, do it properly, do it better than so many of those miserable fucks who don't do their jobs right, who half-arse themselves through the day, but have the gift of the gab, friends in high places and other people they can shift the blame to.

I work so bloody hard. But no one ever notices. No one ever cares. No over ever looks up, comes over and says "Good work, nice job, I appreciate what you do". I was bloody invisible until I fucked up – only then did they see me. And all they saw was failure. Some little nobody they didn't have to give half a shit about.

After meeting with my boss, I had to run to the toilet. I locked myself in and started to cry uncontrollably. Coming to work, miserable as it was, was the only stable thing in my life.

I sat on the toilet but slid down onto the wet floor – I didn't care. I just had this despair, throbbing inside me, pounding inside me, and I had to let it out.

I was in the disabled loo, which offered some privacy. But someone heard me. I got a knock on the door; someone asking "Are you all right? Hello?" I covered my mouth, moved away from the door and edged quietly into the corner. They knocked again... tried the door; I trembled, trying to breathe as slowly as possible. They said they were going to get someone. I crawled quickly to the door to listen to their footsteps as they headed away. I was frightened to go out and be seen. When I was sure no one was in the corridor, I chanced it.

I was lucky – no one saw me leave. I headed for the stairs, where there'd be some privacy. I sat on the steps between floors, trying to get my breath back. But that's when the whispers started. The grey shades were near me. I could hear their incessant whispers. I couldn't take it. I just couldn't take it. I couldn't breathe.

I ran down the stairs. I tried to get away from their sound. They must have been following me; I could hear them all the way down. Only when I got down into the lobby and was surrounded by people did the sound stop. I looked such a manic mess; the security people even lifted an eyebrow. I went outside, hid around the side of the building where there was less people traffic.

What was I going to do? They were all against me now; they really were. There was nowhere to go, nowhere to hide.

The sound of the shadows had lifted, but they could be anywhere, waiting for me in any place.

I tried to think. I was in a mess. I was in trouble. But I was dealing with two separate problems. Side effects and a work mistake. They wouldn't last forever. I could pull myself together. I could get through this. Jesus, what other choice did I have? I had to get through this. I had to get a grip. Get a grip.

I got a call on my mobile. My boss was calling. How long had I been away from my desk? I didn't bother to answer; I had to get back up there. But what would be waiting for me when I got there?

I was on a knife's edge. I can't even describe it; I thought I was falling to pieces, like my body might just collapse under me. I had to walk close to the walls so I could keep myself steady.

I don't know how I made it, but I got back to my floor and my boss was there with one of the senior designers – he jokes that they'd thought I'd jumped off the top of the building. If only he knew.

I apologise; say that I went outside for some air, that I was feeling pretty ill when I got in and now I felt a lot worse. My boss says it's good that I made myself scarce. The head of department had walked through the office and might've thrown me out the window.

He's going to be out all afternoon, so there'll be no stringing me up today. I get to wait until tomorrow. There's going to be a meeting with HR present to discuss my performance.

It was just one mistake I plead. An easy mistake. He sympathises with me again, but it's my job not to make those mistakes. Ultimately I'm responsible. He says I can take the afternoon off as I'm not well. But I'll need to think of my response. To consider my defence. It's not an official disciplinary, not in name anyway. It just might as well be.

I found myself riding the tube around London for a few hours. I was supposed to be thinking of my defence, but all I could think of was how many pills would it take? Where at home could I hang myself? Where would I get the rope? Could I really do it here? On the underground? Just step off the platform? I would need to time it right, so the train didn't have time to stop. Or would jumping on the live track be enough. Which one was it?

In the end I did nothing. I'd like to say I'd changed my mind, but I just thought I'd fuck it up and make things worse. I went home and sat in front of my computer trying to think of what to say in the meeting. It was my responsibility not to make those mistakes. I could complain and moan about conditions, a lack of appreciation and so on, but I had fucked up. That's all there was to it.

As it got dark I got a supportive message from Anya, asking if I was ok. I was lifted briefly by the fact that she cared, but then I got distracted by what I should say back to her. I ended up not replying because I couldn't decide.

I started to think the easiest thing to do was just to surrender. The head of department wanted blood, so why fight? Make him look the one in the wrong by admitting I'd made a simple mistake. Point out that these things happen rarely. Make his response seem totally over-blown.

Maybe that would work. It was the best I could think of. I slept so little that night. Kept imagining myself being frog-marched out of the building: "You'll never work in this business again!" It's not like they could fire me for one mistake. I'd been there for years. But they'd find a way to ease me out. Once they want you gone, they can find a way. I wouldn't be the first. Those miserable fucks know how to get you. Maybe I'd be lucky and get a pay off.

I looked an absolute wreck that morning. I was so groggy I'd almost forgotten about the shadows. Hadn't even bothered to look for them in the station that morning. I actually thought maybe I'd finally seen the last of them.

The meeting was set for 11am, making it hard to avoid Anya and explain to her why I hadn't answered her text. I even kept my emails off in case anyone in the team asked me about the meeting. I think they all felt too awkward to come and talk to me; they could see that I was a mess.

I kept my head down in my cubicle so no one could see me until the time came. My boss appeared by my side and asked me to come with him.

They were waiting for me in a sterile meeting room with the sun shining too brightly through the windows. The fat head of department looked like a pig about to stick its snout in its dinner. To his right was a sour-faced woman from HR. I didn't know her name, but her and the head of department were thick as thieves.

My boss sat next to me and it started. The HR woman talked for a bit about the process and why we were here. She talked about the complaint a little and then handed things over to the head of department who started to lay into things. He complained at great aggressive length as I'd expected. My boss interjected a few times, but I wasn't listening.

I don't know what was said; I nodded and said yes a few times. But as soon as I'd walked through the doors all I could hear were the whispers. They were there with me, in the room, the shadows. Their voices invaded my head and after that I was lost. Those people could've offered me their apologies and given me a 10k pay rise and I wouldn't have noticed.

I felt paralysed. These whispers washed over me, filled my head. Was that them there? Could I see silhouettes standing behind the judge and jury? Shapes just visible in the sunlight?

There was only one thought in my head as the whispers overwhelmed my conscious: how hard would I have to jump at those windows to break through? We were nine floors up, high enough to ensure a sudden, violent end. Make a nice scene of it all. Very dramatic. Very messy. And they'd know they did it. They'd know they'd pushed me too far. A small bit of comfort before the end.

And it would be the end. The end to the misery. The suffering. It could all be over. I just had to break-through. Could it be done? I'm not un-strong when it comes down to it. But that glass is made not to break. Would I have a chance? Could I do this one thing? Is this a challenge I can rise to? To not have to face any of this any more? To not live this life any more?

It was the only thing I truly wanted to do.

They'd stopped talking. They'd stopped a few moments ago and noticed me looking through them. They were confused.

My boss put his hand on my shoulder. I looked at the judge and jury. I rose from my chair and walked to the door and left. I marched straight down the stairs. No one rushed to follow me.

I went to get my bag – it was under my desk. Some of the team noticed me and turned their heads like meerkats as I made for the door. I still had some in my bag – the pills. I'd forgotten that. I'd put some in my bag to take at work and forgotten to throw them away.

As I entered the fire exit and descended the stairs I dug my fingers into the blister pack and took out each one, a total of 14 pills, and swallowed them one after another. A week's dose in one.

I walked all the way down to the reception. I didn't have my entrance card and leapt the barriers, disregarding the complaints of the security men. I wondered how long it would take the pills to get into my system. I walked around the building three or four times. My mobile went off in my pocket; I dropped it down a drain.

I clenched my fists and started a firm, resolute march to the station. I was breathing heavily as I reached the escalator and journeyed down. I walked into Liverpool Street and wandered through the main hall looking all around. They were here. They had to be here. They hadn't left their nest. I knew it, my instincts told me.

"Where are you?" I screamed. It seemed as if the whole station turned to look at me. And then tried not to look at me. That's Londoners for you.

"Where – are – you!" I shouted again. "I know you're here. Show yourselves."

Less people were looking now. They were giving me more space.

I breathed in and breathed out. They might be hiding, but they were here.

"Don't be shy," I shouted. "Come out." I was turning around and around, making myself dizzy.

And then the whispers came. I laughed. The familiar whispers – I was calling them out and they were answering my call. If they wanted me, now was their chance. They could come and take me away. Do whatever it was they did to people. It didn't matter. They didn't need to be coy. I was offering myself to them.

"Come on," I shouted as gradually they started to appear, shifting ethereally through the station. Circling round me like a pack of dogs, like a storm around its eye.

"Come and get me!"

The circle got smaller and smaller and as I watched them surround me. One must've slipped from the pack and come straight at me. I turned right into it. It came over me like hot sweaty air and I almost screamed. Everything went dark.

Everything was silent. Everything stopped.

I stopped. When I found myself breathing again, I felt like I hadn't done it in an age. I felt the ground under me; I was lying on the floor.

My eyes opened and I gasped for air. I must've collapsed. I was on cold, hard ground. But not where I fell. I'd been dragged across the station. I was near the second entrance, the one on ground level near the suit and card shops.

It was night now. The station was closed. Shutters sealed the entrance and covered all the shop windows. I was closed in.

All sound was absent. There were no trains moving. No footsteps. No sounds from outside. No sound of cars or night buses. No late night revellers. Nothing.

But it wasn't the lost time that got to me, or the silence, or being trapped inside the station. What got to me was all the bodies.

The station floor was covered in bodies. Scattered from end to end, bodies of all ages, young, old, black, white, tall, short, fat, slim – it was a very diverse massacre.

There were hundreds, maybe thousands of corpses. A vast panorama of the dead. I had to step over them to move anywhere. Some seemed like they could just be asleep; others wore more obvious battle scars: legs were snapped, necks were

175

bent and broken. There were holes in heads, clothes caked in blood, bodies burnt to a crisp.

Where was I really? I couldn't still be at Liverpool Street. I was there, but I wasn't. Where had all the people come from? Why were we shut inside? Why were the lights still on? Was I dreaming? I didn't feel like I was dreaming.

It was as if hundreds had just dropped dead during rush hour, and they'd just sealed them up in the station. Like victims of a sudden plague quarantined.

But then why did they all look so different? It wasn't just their injuries that singled them out; it was the clothing, the fashions. Even this close to trendy Shoreditch some looked preserved from a different age. Fresh bodies from the not-so-fresh 70s and 80s and even decades before. Perfectly preserved as if they'd died only yesterday.

I had to walk carefully, trying not to tread on anybody or anything coming out of them. And then, surreally, I spotted a cleaner.

He was by the underground ticket office. He had his cleaning cart with him and he was sweeping up around the bodies as if them being there was just normal.

I looked around again. He seemed to be the only one here with me. The caretaker of corpses.

I walked hesitantly over to him. I didn't want to shout; it seemed disrespectful amongst so many dead people.

He was wearing a reflective jacket, but the tatty blazer he wore beneath was a relic of another time. A time when to work on the railways was something you were proud of and that pride was expressed in a fine uniform. In contrast, his trousers were grey and stained and he had odd shoes on. He had a deep smoker's tan and knotted, grey, greasy hair.

He saw me coming and quite deliberately paid me no attention.

"Hello," I whispered.

He frowned, and with a slight twist of the neck said, "Yes?"

"Where am I?"

He looked at me like I was an idiot. "Liverpool Street Station." He continued to sweep the floor.

I kept on. "Who are these people?"

"No good asking me. I'm just the cleaner."

"Where did they come from?"

He shrugged. "They just show up. We get new ones quite regular. We're gonna run out of places to put them".

He lifted and emptied his dustpan into the cart. "You're a live one?" he asked, only half-interested.

That startled me. I realised I didn't know. I wasn't sure. "Yes, I'm alive, a live one," I said in a panic.

"Don't often get live ones. Usually they're gone by the time they get here."

"But you're alive."

He smiled wryly. He pulled down the collar on his jacket. Even on his darkened skin, a ring of thick, deep bruises were visible around his neck.

He went back to sweeping. I didn't know how to deal with this.

"How do I get out of here?" I pleaded.

"Out? Mostly it's folk who want in. I don't know if there's even is a way out."

"But you said it was Liverpool Street. There are exits – surely."

"We find that people don't want to leave," said a new voice.

I turned around slowly – all my hairs were suddenly standing on end. Just behind me was a man not just smartly dressed, but dressed to the nines. Tailored within an inch of his life.

He wore bright blue. But it was the gleaming shine of his smile that hit you first. His teeth were perfect. As was his hair. As was his everything.

It was a moment before I recognised him; he was the man who'd died. The man killed in the road that day; the man I'd seen followed by the shadows. He was standing in front of me, not just alive again, but practically shining like a light

His voice sent shivers up my spine. Something about the sight off him seemed to send all my senses haywire. I felt euphoria, I felt fear; I felt like I needed to run for my life.

"You're suffering, I can hear it like a drumbeat." He tapped the side of his head with two fingers.

I tried to look away, to back away, but I couldn't move without tripping over a body.

"Who are you?" There was something horrible about his eyes. They were too bright, too blazing; I couldn't look directly at them, it made my head hurt.

"It doesn't matter," he said. "I'm like you. They called out to me and I heard them. And now I'm here among friends, good friends." He opened his arms wide "In this special place."

I was tensing up. When I tried to speak, it was suddenly so difficult. "I don't like it here," I could barely get the words out. Something was happening to my body.

"Do you know who these people are? They're people like me, like you."

I was becoming rigid. I was panicking. My heart was pounding; I felt like my jaw was stiffening shut.

"They're dead." I stuttered.

"This is a peaceful place where we can all live together. You're afraid; I can see that you're afraid. I can feel your heart, it beats with pain. It is so hard to let go and face the truth.

"You're here because you belong with us. We called out to you and you came."

I was paralysed.

"This is our sanctuary. A place where no one need be afraid. No one here feels despair in their soul. This is a place where no one is judged. We are who we are, and we find comfort and peace together, here."

He put his hands on my shoulders. His touch made my senses go wild. I wanted to leap out of my own skin. But I couldn't move.

"I feel the pain in you. I feel your hurt. I feel it all. You've suffered so much. Don't hold back, show me. How are you feeling inside? Don't be afraid. Just show me."

No – he couldn't do that to me. He couldn't talk to me and ask me how I was. I couldn't take that. Christ, I couldn't hold it in. I could barely ever hold it in.

I found myself weeping again. I felt tears fall down my cheeks. They felt alien, like they'd come from somewhere else.

"I was like you once. We all were. But then we let go. And it was hard and it was frightening. But we all finally found peace."

I tried to speak. All I managed was a whisper, a sob.

"You can't go on like this. You know you can't. This has to end. Let us help you. Let us show you the way. And then we can all be at peace together."

"All it takes is a step" – a woman spoke into my ear.

"We can help you find peace" – said another.

The bodies were rising. They were standing up as if they'd only been asleep. I was surrounded by people. Were they dead or alive? I didn't know.

"Let us help you."

"We can carry your burden."

"You don't have to suffer."

"It's better to let go."

The crowd parted. The man in blue led the way. Two of the corpses took me arm and arm and guided me along after him. The crowd cheered and chanted me on my way.

"Come on."

"You can do it."

"All it takes is a second."

"We can help you".

They walked me through the station barriers, the crowd pushing through after me.

The man in blue walked halfway along a platform, and my guides, a woman and a man, put me in front of him, my body now an alien thing I could no longer control.

There was a rumbling in the distance. All else was quiet again. The crowd was there with me but they were silent.

The man in blue put his arm around my shoulders.

"Are you ready?"

I can't even remember if I answered or not, or what I even would have answered. A train was coming into the platform. It brought light with it, a great overpowering light.

"The time is now. It takes just a moment."

He took my head and twisted it around. I was looking down at the rail tracks.

The roar of the train grew louder. The light grew brighter. The sound drowned everything out. I felt myself trembling again. My legs were jelly. I was barely holding myself up. Was I in control again? I was standing. I was not falling.

"It's now or never," shouted the man. "It's time. Just let go."

I wanted to go, to fall on the tracks. I wanted to do what he said. I wanted to please him. But I couldn't move. I was locked to the spot. My stomach was twisting in knots. My body was shaking. Uncontrollably shaking.

The sound of the train was deafening. It was coming into the platform fast. It wasn't slowing down.

The man grabbed me. He grabbed me hard, as if to throw me. "What are you waiting for?"

My head turned towards him.

His face! In the beaming light it was changed. Deformed. Wrecked. Destroyed. This was his real face. The broken face of a man dragged under the wheels and scraped across the tarmac.

I felt him put his weight against me. I looked back to the tracks. He was going to throw me off the platform. The knots in my stomach tightened. My back spasmed. My chin rose. My head went back.

I was blinded by the light.

I felt my body hit the ground hard. I could taste acid in my mouth.

I landed on flat ground. I could feel my body again. It felt terrible.

I could hear voices. Distant voices. I was aware that people were close to me. But I could only sense them. I could not see.

There was movement all around me. The light was gone. It was dark, gloomy again. A shape moved over my eyes. They wanted to know if I was awake. I heard them, but I did not want to answer. I wasn't strong enough.

The activity continued. I spasmed again. I was being sick. One of the voices – Anya. She was there. I felt hands under my shoulders. I was being lifted off the ground. Voices asked the crowd to clear. I was placed on a trolley, and taken slowly to an ambulance. Alive. Unwell. But alive.

At the hospital my stomach was pumped. I felt like someone had taken out my insides, run them across some sandpiper and thrown them back upside down. Apparently I didn't talk for days. It's so hard to remember. The whole thing was like an out of body experience.

I didn't say much. One of the few things I remember is Anya coming to see me. She came to see me and to see if I was ok. She did care about me. And I turned away from her. I told her to leave me alone. Because it was just too painful to be near her.

I was committed. They took the whole pill-swallowing thing as a suicide attempt. There were no other explanations and I never really told them the full story, of all the shadows and all the bodies.

It was weeks before I was able to talk at all about it. I had these nightmares. I had to be sedated when I went to sleep because they would come for me in my sleep. I would see that man's mutilated face and he would just stare at me and wouldn't say a word. He'd glare at me with his horrific eyes for what seemed liked endless hours without saying a word.

I was a wreck. A mental and physical wreck. I was broken, totally broken. You don't really ever get over something like this. Not the horror anyway. The behavioural stuff, the psychosis, yes, you can treat that and it's hard, and it takes years and some things you can get better at. But the horror, those faces, that station, that place. Did I try to kill myself or did something else try to kill me?

It did finally get me the attention and help I needed. It was a pretty risky cry for help, but finally I became a priority for treatment. But it was a long, long road to recovery. I am still recovering.

It was heavy therapy for me. Cognitive behavioural therapy. An attempt to repair my damaged patterns of thinking. The constant negative reinforcement.

You get your thoughts stuck in a loop and it starts to destroy you. To break the cycle, you have to learn to think differently, and that's not easy. It's not like being taught a new lesson at school, it's trying to re-write the very way you instinctively behave so that when someone doesn't smile at you when you order a pint, you don't take it personally. And that you really believe it's not personal; you don't just try to tell yourself it's not personal, you actually firmly believe it. It's sounds silly, ridiculous, but that's madness for you. You can't deal with the small everyday stuff other people can deal with.

There's no hell like the one you make for yourself in your own mind. And I'm still not free of that hell. You can't just learn to be a whole new person. You can't rewire your own mind overnight. It takes time, years, to unlearn what you learnt in a lifetime.

I've still got so much of that anxiety. It's like a rubber band. For all the times I feel confident in my interactions with other people, they'll be a time when suddenly it all comes back and I snap back and it hits me hard. Maybe one day I'll finally get over it and be able to lead a more normal life. A life when I can just be with people and not fear that they despise me and are going to say so.

Really, I'm one of the lucky ones. It doesn't feel much like it sometimes. But I'm not dead. I'm alive. And I'm not... in that place. Wherever that place was.

I mean, I might have actually gone to hell. All those times I hear people say, "It was hell at the train station this morning" – they really don't know what they're talking about. I guess NHS waiting rooms aren't so bad either, in the wider scheme of things.

I still get the nightmares and when I'm in crowds sometimes, out of the corner of my eye – maybe I see something, maybe I don't. But I get that same sensation of wanting to leap out of my own skin and I just have to go and get as far away from that place – wherever it is – as possible.

After the hospital, I went to live with my mother for a while. Arseholes that they might all be, the company still paid me through my illness. Even they thought it was distasteful to cut off someone who'd gone off the deep end.

I had to go back of course. I'm saying that, but maybe I didn't. Perhaps we could've parted company over the phone. But I felt like I had to go back. I had to see that place one more time so I could move on.

And it was all the same of course. The office, the people – nothing physically was different. But yet, when I was there, it was as if everything was behind a sheet of glass. Everything seemed to be a different colour. And I felt like if that glass was shattered, the world beyond would just come through. That somehow the world was at its weakest here. There was just a thin layer between this world, and a dark place somewhere else.

Whenever I get that feeling. When I think I've seen the shadows or the man in blue, I wonder to myself whether I've found another one of those places where the world we see and believe in is so thin. Thinner than it is anywhere else. And that there's some other place beyond. Somewhere frightening just beneath, where evil, real evil, lives and exists and can tear us apart.

I saw my colleagues there – back in the office – and I spoke with some of them. It was even nice to see them. And there was Anya of course, and I shared a quick drink at the café with her and tried to pretend I was all mended and fine. She was caring. She was kind. But we've not stayed in touch.

I took the bus there. I couldn't face the station. Not at least, from the underground. I had to approach it slowly. Work myself up to it. Even as I approached the escalator entrance, I felt that physical revulsion. I almost turned back. But I didn't and I went down there and it was normal. It was how people see it every day.

I couldn't see any grey shadows. And I couldn't hear any whining static sound in my ears. But they were there, those creatures, whatever they are. They were there somewhere.

That's the thing about despair. You can't see it. You can't hear it. But it's there. And it's always closer than you think.

THE WIFE

I've known Greg my whole life. We lost touch after college, when I went to work in Manchester, but when I was back visiting Mum and Dad I'd see him around, bump into him down the pub and so on.

I don't want to speak ill, but he was always a wuss. He was a wimp when he was a kid and he was wimp when he grew up. He was a nice guy, don't get me wrong. I liked Greg. But we weren't close at school, because you just wouldn't hang around with a square like him. Always had a note from his mum to get out of games. You know the type of kid.

Later, when you're grown up, it's different and even though he was still kind of the same, we became mates. He was easy to get on with. When I moved back he'd started hanging around with some of my old friends and I got to know him too.

But Greg had a problem, and that was his missus. I'd heard he was with someone and when I bumped into him just before I moved back he said he was engaged. Then a few months later I bumped into him again and she was there. I thought she was pregnant. Later when I was talking to my mate Ed, who we both went to school with, he said she was just a big girl. Each to their own; she was sort of pretty in her way.

Didn't get invited to the wedding, no surprise there, we weren't mates then. But next time I saw her, she was big. And I do mean big.

Ed had mentioned it, but I didn't believe him. I thought he was talking it up, for a laugh. But she'd piled on the pounds. The kind of girl they'd put on a scooter these days. Or a forklift.

Joking aside, she wasn't a well woman, and not nice either.

First time I met her she barely said a word. As shy a thing as you could imagine. You wouldn't have thought she'd be any

185

trouble. But it quickly became obvious that he was completely under her fat thumb. He was taking her orders.

She didn't go to work. She stayed at home. Now that'd be ok if she was looking after kids but they didn't have any. Can't remember what job she used to have, but she didn't work any more. She was ill but we never found out what from. There was always things wrong with her: her back, her legs; she was depressed, she was stressed; it was one thing after another.

She didn't go out much. And it was Greg's job to look after her, to provide for her, to be at her beck and call all day long.

If he was out, she'd call him and summon him home. He could be out with us having a drink and she'd call him up and he'd have to run off home to her. Otherwise, he'd have to be back before 10. He had a home time. 37 years old and he had a home time.

It was just something you got used to. We never really talked about it, not while Greg was there anyway. When he went off home you knew why and you said goodbye like it was normal. We knew why he was going, and he knew that we knew, and was probably glad we didn't bring it up.

Wasn't really our business to say anything. We all felt sorry for him. It was pathetic, but that's how it was. His choices. He never really had a backbone.

The only time I ever saw him stand up for himself was, ironically, when someone had a go at her.

We, sometimes, would make... occasional... fat jokes... about her.

One time Ed said one, drunk, and forgot Greg was there. He said she was so big she had her own postcode. Greg was livid and started going on about how she was unwell and needed looking after and how the council wouldn't help and how the NHS were useless.

He was defending her. She was running his life and making him miserable and he was defending her. It was ridiculous. It made no sense.

She hated us. She never had us over. We had Greg over, but she never came. Not to a barbecue or for dinner or anything. If we saw them together in the street, she'd basically ignore us. She'd check her phone or do something else, like carry on shopping. She was just rude.

He used to cancel on us a lot because of her. Sometimes, if we were expecting him at the pub, or we'd invited him out somewhere, he might cancel last minute. There'd be no excuse, just a "Sorry guys, can't make it tonight" text. We knew why, but he wouldn't admit it.

The one time I lost it with him was when we were going to see The Levellers. He said he was definitely up for it. So I said I'd get him a ticket. I joked – but not really joking – about whether he'd pull out. I knew it wouldn't finish before 10pm.

I text him during the week and he said he was looking forward to it. But on the night, nothing. He was a no-show. I didn't actually think he'd drop out. Not when he's spent £25 on a ticket.

It was just sad. A man who couldn't leave the house because his wife said so. He didn't show his face for a few weeks after. Still made him pay for the ticket though.

Then, one day, she died. Totally out of the blue, no warning signs. She dropped dead. And dropped is the word – she fell down the stairs and broke her neck.

Her funeral... That was something. Didn't know they made coffins that big. Those were some hefty pallbearers. It's amazing we got through that one. We had a few drinks and none of us made a joke all day. Wasn't easy.

He was really upset. And we did our best. We could see he was broken up. But we were thinking, he's finally free! He can move on and meet someone nice. He didn't have to put up with her any more.

It seemed like it was a new beginning for him. We had to still pretend we were sorry she was gone. But we were also trying to be positive. Sneak in the odd silver lining. Like the fact he could stay out late, if he wanted to.

But he didn't ever want to. He still kept going at 10. And we didn't say anything about it, just as we didn't before. Force of habit we thought. But as the weeks went on, the old habit didn't go away.

So one night Alf says to him, "Greg, you don't have to go early. Stay, live a little."

This was a Friday. He didn't have to get up for work. So we twisted his arm, said we'd get a curry. Why not come along?

He didn't really want to. We seemed to talk him into it, but he was checking his phone as it got close to 10. He waits until we're on the quiz machine then slips out and heads off. It was weird. You'd think he'd be trying to make the best of it.

We were trying to keep an eye out for him. We wanted to make sure he didn't, I dunno, top himself, or do something stupid. We used to call on him a lot and invite him around to our places. But sometimes, he might still cancel on you last minute, and with no real excuse. He'd have a headache or stomach ache or something that obviously wasn't true.

We were talking, me and Ed, and Ed said he'd called on Greg and found out he still had all her things there. He hadn't got rid of any of her stuff.

We talked to him about it later and we offered to help him sort the stuff out. He says he should, but he hasn't got around to it. We push him a little, force him to name a date. It's not good to be stuck in the past. He needs to move on.

We go to his the next Saturday. When we show up he's uncomfortable and fidgety, and then, when he's making us a cuppa, he just breaks down. Says he's not ready yet. He can't do it today. It's too much for him.

So we take him out and give him a few drinks, play some snooker; we try to take his mind off it. And he's ok, for a while. But we say to him, it can't wait forever. We're gonna come by next Saturday. He needs to be ready for it.

He just nods. Doesn't say much, but agrees to it.

By next Saturday, Ed has a cold and leaves it to me. Cheers mate.

I go over and Greg's nervous and fidgety again. But this time, rather than try to put it off, he says he'd rather do it himself. She wouldn't like it if other people were touching her things.

I know what he's doing. So I tell him he can't put it off.

I've got better things to do with my Saturdays. We're doing this today.

To show him I'm serious. I get out of my chair and head for the stairs. He grabs me and shouts: "No you can't. You can't go up there!"

He's frantic. He's desperate. He's trying to block my way and I'm just about to say something to him. But then I hear the floor creak above us.

"You've got someone up there?" I say to him. And he looks away from me, embarrassed.

"That's great Greg. You don't need to be shy about that. It's great you've found someone."

"No. You don't understand," he shouts. He's sweating. He's trembling. Then he whispers, "She's not dead."

The second he says it, he puts both hands over his mouth and backs off. Like not even he can believe what he's just said.

I think he's cracked. "What are you talking about?"

"You need to leave," he says. "I'll be fine. But you need to go."

"Greg. I'm not going."

"Please. Just leave. I don't know what I'm saying. I'll be fine. I just need you to go."

I look upstairs. I did hear the floor creak. But that could just be the house. Hell, it must be.

"Greg, your wife's dead. You know that, right? We had the funeral, remember?"

"I remember," he says. Tears fall down his face. "She died. But..." He looks up the stairs, like he's looking up at her, looking for her advice.

"She's not there Greg." I decide I'm going up there. "I'll show you."

"No, wait!" he shouts.

They only have a small terraced house. There's just two bedrooms upstairs. One just stores old boxes and junk. Then there's the bedroom. I go inside and it's empty.

"Greg, there's no one here."

He stands in the doorway, tears in his eyes.

I open the wardrobes and look under the bed. "Nothing in here... nothing down here... There's no one here, is there?"

He doesn't say anything. I say it right to his face "There's no one here. I want you say it."

"No", he whispers.

"No. That's right."

And that's when I hear the toilet flush.

Suddenly all my hairs are standing on end.

"Greg... who's that?"

He doesn't say anything.

"Greg, tell me. Who is that?"

"You should go. She won't want to find you in here."

I hear the lock on the bathroom door snap back. I feel a kind of shot go up my spine. The bathroom door creaks open. There's the sound of footsteps on the carpet.

Greg and me, we start backing into the corner of the room. We can hear her cross the landing. We're practically holding each other, waiting for the horror to come through the door.

It's half closed. It starts to open.

Greg screams: "I'm sorry – I told him not to come up here. He..."

The door opens all the way. But there's no one there. The sound stops.

I feel my heart beating like the clappers. I'm trembling, but Greg is shaking so hard he looks like he's going to fall to bits.

He grabs me. "Why'd you have to come up here?" He's shaking me. "Why'd you come up here?"

I try to push him off. I shove him so hard he falls down against the bed. He's crying.

I go to pick him up. "I'm getting you out of here."

"I can't leave" he whines. But I'm not having any of it and he doesn't put up much of a fight.

I drive him back to mine. He spends the afternoon sitting in my living room, staring straight ahead like a man in shock. I don't say much to him. I don't know what to say. I don't know what to do. I think about calling Ed or someone else. Maybe a doctor. Maybe Greg's parents.

I can't add it up. Greg might be losing it, but me? I heard that noise too. And you can't catch madness. There had to be some proper explanation. But I couldn't think of one.

So I put the telly on, make him a drink, and say, "You can stay here as long as you want. You don't have to go back to that house."

He says sharply, "But she needs me!"

"No she doesn't. She's dead. She doesn't need you anymore. You've got to move on son."

He twitches. And, in a tiny, quiet voice, he says: "It's not that..." He's struggling to say something. He looks around, as if she might be listening, hiding just out of sight.

"I want to move on. But she... she won't let me." He starts to cry again. "She's angry. I let her down."

"No offence Greg. But if it was me, I don't think I could've put up with everything you put up with from that woman."

"I pushed her."

You should have seen his face.

You should've seen my face.

"She was struggling up the stairs and I pushed her. I just knew that I could. I watched her fall. I didn't know if she'd get back up again. But I hoped she wouldn't."

He breaks down, weeping, struggling to speak.

"I was supposed to be taking care of her."

What do you say to someone who says all that?

I hid in the kitchen for a few minutes.

Jesus. Greg was a murderer. Greg, of all people. He'd really done it.

He could go to prison for this. But I couldn't give him up. Not Greg. If there was anyone who didn't deserve it, it was him. He might've done it, but he was pushed. Pushed into pushing her. I wasn't going to grass him up. Not for this.

"Greg listen to me," I said. "It doesn't matter what's happened. Everything's gonna be ok. You can stay with me. You don't have to go back to that house. I don't know what's going on, or what you think is happening there. But it's time to let it go."

"I can't leave her," he cried.

191

"She's dead Greg. She's not there. How could she be?"

He didn't look very convinced.

"She's dead, isn't she? Say it with me Greg. Melinda is dead."

He couldn't. He burst into tears again. I put my hand on his shoulder. What was I supposed to do? I didn't know how to deal with this.

That was the longest day. I let him cry it out and then made us some dinner and we watched more TV. He didn't say much. He barely moved from his spot on the sofa. I kept having to tell him to eat or drink something.

I put the football on and that kept us going. Then, late in the evening, we're watching the highlights and he gets up to go to the loo. He's gone a while. A really long while.

I start to wonder how long it's been. I check my watch. It's 9:50pm. Almost 10 o'clock.

His home time.

I rush to the hall and see his coat and shoes are gone.

I should've known. I should've guessed he'd make a run for it.

I get in my car. How much of a head start does he have? I reckon he's been gone about 20 minutes, give or take. If he's walked it or run, he's probably not there yet. Unless he's taken a taxi.

I drive up and the lights are on – he's beaten me. I knock on the door, really knock hard. "Greg! You've got to let me in."

There's no answer. Maybe I should call the police. If he's as crazy as I think, he could hurt himself. And just when I'm thinking that, I hear screaming. Greg is screaming.

I decide I'm gonna force the door. I force it with my shoulder. And it fucking hurts like hell.

He's in the kitchen. He's burning his hand in a George Foreman grill. He's pressing the lid down with his right hand and burning the left one inside. There was smoke coming off his hand. His own hand!

I grab him and pull him away. We fly from one side of the kitchen to the other. Pans and plates fall down on us as we crash into the cupboards.

"What the fuck is wrong with you?"

He's screaming in agony. His hand is red and pink and black. The grill is on the floor, lying open, burnt skin still sizzling on it.

He's hysterical, screaming, howling. I don't know what to do. He's scaring me now. I'm shit scared. I don't want to touch his hand. I don't want to do anything that might make it worse.

I get out my phone to call an ambulance. I start to dial.

I turned my back on him for like two seconds. Just when my phone starts to ring, I hear him walking on broken plates.

He brains me with a frying pan. I drop my phone. I fall forwards. My phone slides into the hallway. I try to crawl after it but don't get far. He cries out. I brace myself.

The second hit knocks me out.

Some time later I wake up and I'm in the hall. I'm dizzy. My head is ringing. Just lifting my head is so painful. The room's spinning. And the smell... It smelt horrible.

I feel like I'm going to be sick. I can barely make it onto my hands and knees. It smells like rotten eggs.

It was gas! The place stunk of gas!

I got onto my feet, but I couldn't walk straight. I had no balance. I was falling from one side of the hall to the other. I had to get to the kitchen.

The door was stuck. There was something jammed underneath – old towels. I managed to shove it open. All the gas rushed out. It made me choke.

Greg was lying flat. The cooker's open and all the hobs were turned on. I turned them off and got the windows open.

I didn't know how long I'd been out. But I could tell by the look of Greg that I'd been out too long. All the colour was gone from his face. He'd been sick on the floor. He was already cold.

I managed to call 999 before I passed out again. I don't remember what happened when they arrived. I had to be taken to hospital. It was all too much, you know.

I got treated for concussion. But it was too late for Greg.

Poor bloke. It's not easy to poison yourself with gas these days. Natural gas isn't poisonous. It took him ages to suffocate and die in there. Fucking hours.

I tried, you know. I really tried to help him.

He left a note. He had it scrunched up in his hand, the one he hadn't almost burnt off.

All it said was 'Sorry'.

I don't know whether he was saying sorry to me, or to someone else.

And that's the worst part of it. I don't know, when he decided to kill himself, whether it was because he wanted to get away from her, or because, in his twisted head, he thought he had to be with her. That he needed to kill himself so he could go wherever he thought she was. Because he thought he had to. So they could be together.

I hope not. I really hope not. I want to believe he's found peace. I really want to believe that.

MASTER OF SPIDERS

My sister hates spiders. She's terrified of them. So it was obviously absolutely essential for me to love them. And they really are fascinating creatures. A spider's silk web; that's *the* strongest material in the world. Even with all today's technology, we've never been able to find a way to replicate it, to manufacture a material that can recreate its tensile strength. We're not even close.

But I needed these weapons against my sister. She's four years older than me, and when you're a child, that's a big difference. A big difference. I don't think she ever really got over me being born. Obviously she was the only child and then I came along and then I turned out to be gifted and that's always been a big deal because since then the focus has always been more on me than on her.

That's not my fault. That's just the way it is. It isn't as if my parents disowned her, but they saw I was very intelligent, highly intelligent, much more so than the average and that naturally took their focus. Quite frankly, what did she expect? She certainly didn't have to take it out on me. What did I know? I was just a kid, even if I was a gifted one.

So naturally I would seek weapons to redress the balance should she try to bully me and push me around, which, by the way, my parents were always far too light on her for. She would get away with things I could never get away with. If her test results were down at school, they weren't getting on her back. Not the way they were on mine.

At first it was just little spiders – I might just capture them outside and put them in her room, or drop them in a glass of water she was drinking when she didn't notice. And that got me a few jumps and screams and few punches in the arm, all of which were worth it, totally worth it. At first my parents didn't think I was behind it – as if I could be the master of spiders. But eventually they started to get wise to it, probably because I was enjoying it so much. I had to come up with another approach and that's when I unveiled my master plan.

I was collecting this part-work magazine, Bugs. Fascinating facts for kids about insects. I was always reading stuff like this, well above my age group. And with this magazine every week you would get a piece of a model tarantula. Not one of my favourite arachnid families, but they're what most kids would've heard about. They've got the reputation – quite undeserved – of being scary, deadly spiders.

It was a big model; the legs stretched out to about the size of an A3 sheet of paper. But the best thing about this model spider, by far the best thing, was that it glowed in the dark. It was going to scare the absolute pants off my sister. And I was definitely not disappointed.

I snuck into her bedroom while she was in the bath and placed it under her duvet. I then – and this was the clever part, the really clever part; to make sure she really got the full affect I replaced her light bulb with a broken one. She wouldn't be able to turn the light on. She'd just use her desk lamp, keeping it pretty dark, and change the bulb in the morning. That I predicted correctly.

It sucked totally that I couldn't see her uncover the spider. I weighed the consequences of hiding away in her room somewhere, but I couldn't find a spot where I wouldn't be seen and where'd I still get full view.

I could still obviously hear the scream. I can still hear it now, in my head. She was hysterical. It was incredible, just incredible. I'll admit my plan was a little short-sighted. I knew my parents would come down on me like a ton of bricks – I was prepared for that. What I hadn't quite planned for was the immediate wrath of my sister. As I said, she's bigger than me. That's actually still the case; Wendy has always been unusually well built.

I only just managed to get to the door in my room to barricade myself in. My parents had to restrain her. It was complete chaos. But I couldn't have been more pleased with the result. Even if it did mean being grounded for a month. It was shock and awe, and that was how I dealt with my older sister, shock and awe.

But my fascination with spiders was not just about sibling warfare. I absolutely, sincerely loved these creatures. I sort of still do.

They are just astounding. Arachnophobia is just the most ridiculous of fears. Hardly any spiders are in any way harmful to humans. And those that are, you know, actually, they're not the big hairy ones they'd have you believe were deadly on TV. People have that misconception; the most dangerous to humans are actually very small, like the general size of most household spiders.

My fascination was entirely genuine. And I wanted to know more and obviously I wanted to go and visit London Zoo. Because, let's face it, London Zoo is cool. I knew that, I'd seen it on the television, on The Really Wild Show, and I wanted to go, why wouldn't I?

Not an easy sell to my parents. Trips to London are expensive, there's the four of us to pay for, transport, food, yadda yadda yadda. Oh and now suddenly Wendy is against zoos. They're boring or wrong or whatever. Essentially she's getting back at me. So transparent and so typically petty of her.

Mum and Dad tried to get me over it with other zoos, but just like a kid who's being made to eat Tesco cornflakes instead of Kellogg's Cornflakes – no, they're not the same and I knew that and I wasn't going to accept any cheap old second best.

It took lots of nagging but I wore them down. When Wendy went on a Brownies' camping weekend away at the beginning of the Easter holiday, I argued, successfully, that if they were going to pay for her to go on such an outing, I deserved something as they were effectively spending money on her that they were not spending on me. And that wasn't fair. Not fair at all.

Besides, they knew they would so obviously enjoy a trip to London Zoo. Who wouldn't? And without Wendy it would also cost less and we wouldn't have to put up with all her sulking and moaning all day.

In actuality, however, it was not her that I should've worried about. It was Mum and Dad, because... well... really, they've never been the best-matched parents in the world. My father, he's kind of extrovert and impulsive and funny, and always, kind of, ready for action. A real fun type of guy. And my mother, she's more of your buttoned-down, planning, well-organised, thoughtful kind of person. In some ways, they complemented each other, but more often they just clashed and drove each other nuts. And to go on a day out down to London... nothing could've spread the wild fires of discontent between them.

Mum went into major planning mode, as she does. While my dad... let's be honest, I think he'd admit that he sometimes deliberately provoked her by being difficult. Being slower than he should be or not picking up things he should have. He dragged his heels; we were late leaving the house, we almost missed the train – things got off to a tense start.

When we arrived, I obviously wanted to go straight to the bugs and insect exhibits, but my parents were like "What's the rush?" Though as soon as Mum started planning our route, Dad had to go off schedule and do his own thing almost immediately.

But London Zoo is great. There's the whole penguin thing, which is fun, and the meerkats and the... You know, sometimes it's the animals you don't expect to be interesting that you find to be interesting. Anteaters, for example – they're huge. I was expecting these little dog-sized things like in the cartoons, but they were these huge shaggy animals, over a meter long. I just wasn't expecting that. And what I wasn't also expecting was how dull the lions were. Lazy, lazy animals, just lying around getting the lionesses to do the work for them and just waiting to be fed.

Finally we got to go where I was dying to go to – the bug house. At first I was kind of disappointed because it obviously wasn't all spiders. I don't know why I thought it would be. But I was a kid, I had strange ideas.

But the spiders they did have... I was acting like a guide to my parents, taking them through tank to tank, talking them through the species, most of which I recognised; I had amazing recall even then.

They had such exotic species. I knew they had the golden orb spiders (nephila clavipes) but I wasn't expecting deinopis subrufa – the ogre-faced spider, which has these amazing big marble-like eyes. And there was bagheera kiplingi, a jumping spider that's – guess what? – the only vegetarian spider in the world. Well, at least known to science at this point. There's still, you know, a remarkable amount of species we probably haven't even discovered. You'd think after all these centuries of exploration we'd have seen it all. But new species are found all the time. It's just incredible.

I might as well have been conducting my own tour of the spider section, because I was talking my parents through the spiders – telling them about paraplectana, a spider that mimics a ladybird's spots, not to ensnare prey, but to put-off prey, because ladybirds are so disgusting to eat. Imagine the evolutionary path that led to that? It's just extraordinary.

So I was telling my parents about this and I was being so fascinating myself, sharing all this knowledge, that other people started to notice and they started to gather around and listen to me. And before you know it one of the curators was there listening and saying how much I knew and how impressed he was with all the knowledge I had.

His name was Christian Bachmann.

A name I will never forget.

He was so impressed with how much I knew about spiders that he decided to show me something special. Just me. He allowed me to hold and touch one of the spiders. But not just any spider. He took me to the far end of the spider house to one large tank and there, in all its glory, was theraphosa blondi, the goliath birdeater. And if its name makes it sound big, there's a good reason. It is *the* largest spider in the world. They can grow up to 28cm long. Think about that – that's almost as long as a classroom ruler.

He let me hold it. Well, part of it – it was too big to just hold in both my hands. And this one was still bit shorter, more like 22 – 24cms long. People all around me were scared and frightened. But I wasn't it. This was a beautiful, amazing creature. I was only scared that I might hurt it or drop it. I could've watched that spider move for hours, such grace, such precision, such a perfect specimen.

I begged Christian Bachmann to show me more. He was very kind. I was just some kid, going on and on about spiders, and he was a guy who had his job to do. But he still let me help feed the birdeater. That freaked my parents out, the dried flies he had to feed them. I could not have been more excited. Just watching him move, this beautiful creature. I never in my wildest dreams thought I'd get to be that close.

My parents did literally have to drag me out of there and told me to leave the man alone. I wanted his job. I wanted to do it all myself.

I totally spoilt the afternoon. I threw such a tantrum about being dragged away from the bug house that I saw Christian Bachmann look at me like I was a nightmare. And he walked away from me. And when I saw this and realised he was revolted by my behaviour, I thought I'd lost my new best friend. And I blamed that on my parents too.

We went around a few more exhibits but I was basically refusing to look at anything. I had my arms folded and kept my head looking straight at the ground. Mum, ever the disciplinarian, wasn't taking this behaviour lightly. When it became clear I was not going to give up my tantrum, she threatened to take me home. My dad was less embarrassed by my behaviour. He said she was taking it too seriously. If he – by that I mean me – was going to sulk, let him sulk, we can still enjoy the place. Besides which, the park was only going to be open for an hour or so longer, so it didn't make any sense for us to leave.

Representing his opposite view of parenting, my father suggested a bribe. He would get me ice cream, if I behaved for the rest of the day. I consented, basically, and we saw the aquatic mammals and the ancient sea turtles and a variety of creatures and ended up at this café where my father went to get ice cream and I was still in a sulk, but basically improving, and at least looking up and around at things.

Mum, however, is still kind of tense. And then the worst thing possible happens. She sees my dad chatting to the woman behind the counter and sharing a joke together. And when my mum sees that...

I should give some context here. At the time even I didn't know about this, but my father had had an affair, or at least had slept with someone else. Mum now thinks that he had all kind of affairs, but she never has really forgiven him for leaving her. They were mismatched, but my mum didn't want to let go. Anything but be on her own.

So him chatting to this woman, this pretty younger woman triggers an argument and they start to go at each other.

"Can't I just talk to a woman?"

"This is how it starts isn't it?"

"You're paranoid."

"You can't help yourself."

Obviously, I'm hating this. I can't take this. I don't know how to handle this because I'm young. Even a smart kid like me can't hack it. And I was angry at them both for the way they were behaving. And I was the one supposed to be behaving like a child. Were they any better? I don't think so.

So I ran off. I didn't want to be listening to them and I think some part of me was thinking, this'll show you. I'm going to disappear – this will upset you and you'll deserve it. And they were so wrapped up in their stupid row they didn't even notice.

I didn't really think I'd get very far. It took a few moments to realise they hadn't seen me. They weren't coming after me. And with me actually free to do what I wanted, I decided to go back to the bug house. Why not?

Imagine my horror though when I got there and found it was locked up already. I was pretty devastated. Until I saw a staff door not closed properly. It was hanging just a little open.

Well I just couldn't help myself. I pulled it open and peered inside. There was no one there. One door led back into the bug house. But now I was here, I wanted to explore the private and forbidden. To get a look behind the scenes...

201

It was so quiet. Heading in the opposite direction I walked into a changing room with lockers and a shower, which then lead into a storeroom with metal shelves stacked with tools, replacement tanks and other assorted things. There was also a huge metal container, which I guessed, rightly, was a chiller where they kept the insect and animal food.

It was all very dark, most of the lights were off and there were no windows. And the place was deserted; there was no one about.

I ended up in a dark corridor with a few doors – the first to an office and the next to a break room. There was no light except from the last door at the end of the corridor. There was a dim glow coming from there. And this strange sound. A scraping sound mixed with a tapping sound.

I was kind of scared, but still curious. I went to the door slowly. It was open far enough for me to look inside without making a sound.

It was the security room. The light was coming from stacks of television screens showing scenes from around the park; from the pavements outside, to the enclosures and viewing areas, even the door outside the bug house were I had entered – without anyone noticing me.

How? Because the man in the security room was not watching the cameras. He was stretched over a chair. His head was dangling over the back. His arms were hanging from his sides.

He was shaking. He was trembling. The chair legs were scraping across the floor and his shoe heels knocking against the tiles.

He was covered head to toe in spiders. Hundreds. Thousands. All kinds of species. The small. The large. The rare. The exotic.

They walked and crawled over him. Moved in and out of his clothes. Up his sleeves and trouser legs. In between the buttons on his shirt.

They walked over his face. A huge, hairy tarantula rested over one of his eyes. Webs were being made on his chest. Between his fingers. Over his shoelaces.

He was breathing fast, short, sharp breaths. Like a man having a fit. As an adult, I look back on his face. His breathing. His trembling. It was… orgasmic. This was a man in a state of ecstasy. Sick ecstasy. Twisted pleasure.

He turned to look at me. Christian Bachmann. Spiders fell from his face, from his lips.

"Get out," he screamed. "Get out!"

I ran. Of course I ran. I got the heck out of that building. I was running about outside in a panic and somehow found my way into my mother's arms. She was searching for me, in a foul mood, and was puzzled by the automatic hug I gave her.

She yelled that we were leaving. With or without my father. Although he managed to catch up.

I could hardly speak. I was so terrified. I wanted to tell my parents. But I didn't think they would believe me. Why would they believe me? They might've noticed I was behaving strangely, but they were too busy being angry with each other and working really hard not to speak to each other. So I was just sat there. Paralysed with fear. I could not speak. I felt like being sick.

What the fuck was that? To this day, I could not tell you. To this day. And I'm an intelligent man. A scientist. And I cannot begin to describe or understand what the fuck was going in that room, right then, with that man.

When we got home, my parents got the privacy they needed to have their full blazing row. I just went to my room, crawled beneath my sheets and stayed there. No dinner. No food. I just went to sleep eventually.

They'd pretend to make it up in due course. But not before ruining the rest of the holidays. When Wendy got home, they still weren't talking. When she found out it had all started at the zoo that was her excuse to start blaming things on me. She's always blaming me for things that have nothing to do with me.

I had nightmares for days after. When I saw a spider, I was scared. Suddenly I was worried they were after me. That Christian Bachmann really was the master of spiders. That he could control them. And through them he could spy on me.

I would check my room every night for spiders for the rest of the holiday. Every night. I would move around the furniture. Check under the bed. In the back of my wardrobe. I would check everywhere. For over a week I looked. But then things started to calm down at home. And my parents had a truce.

Soon I was going back to school and things started to return to 'normal'. I still didn't share what had happened with anyone. I just didn't want to think about it. I wanted to think it was from some other reality. That temporarily I'd just stepped into another world and that it was some strange isolated incident, unexplained and unrepeatable.

Life just went on. For just a little while.

I was going to bed on a Friday evening. I had cleaned my teeth. I'd changed into my pyjamas. I was looking forward to going to sleep quickly so I could wake up soon to watch Saturday morning cartoons. Things were well and truly back to normal.

Only, just as I was about to turn out the light, I spot, on my desk, a spider moving. Just a small, common house spider – tegenaria duellica – crawling behind a pot of pens.

I'm scared. I creep over and tip out the pens and drop the pot on top of the spider, trapping it.

I'm relieved, until I hear a voice.

"I see you."

My floor is covered in spiders. They weren't there a second before. Now there's millions. Crawling across my floor. Crawling on my naked feet.

I jump on the bed, but they're already climbing up there. They're climbing the walls. They're climbing the curtains. Falling from the ceiling.

"Help me," he whispers.

I look up. He's there's. Christian Bachmann. In a giant spider's web. He's wrapped up like a mummy in spider's silk. The spiders are spread all over. He looks at me dead-eyed and screams, "Help me!"

He spits spiders from his mouth and they hit me in the face.

They're on the bed. Raining from above. I get beneath my sheets and start screaming. Screaming. Screaming.

My sheets are ripped off. I scream so hard I wet myself.

But it's Dad. "What's wrong? What's going on?"

I'm basically having a fit. I don't believe him when he says there are no spiders and that I've been having a nightmare.

I wasn't asleep. I swear to you. Look at me. Look at me in the eye. I was not asleep. I was not having a nightmare. Maybe I was in some kind of nightmare. Some kind of projection. But I was not asleep. For that moment everything I saw was real.

Don't ask me to explain it. There's no explanation. And believe me, as a scientist I find the lack of a real, rational explanation a real fucking problem. A harder pill to swallow than anything else.

The next day, my parents come over to me. They're all serious and they take me into the kitchen and they tell me that that nice man who we met at the zoo, Christian Bachman, has died. And they wanted to tell me in case I saw it on the news, which I probably would do.

They tried to explain it to me, but I just took the newspaper off them and read about it for myself. It's reported as a strange mysterious death. He was found dead at his home, where he was found to have a private zoo of arachnids, which he could've not have legally owned. He must've bred and stolen them from the zoo, or even smuggled them in.

In any case he was supposed to have died because he was experimenting with spiders venoms and poisons and had injected himself with them. You know, before meeting with you, I went back and I did my research and I looked up these old stories. Some of the papers, they had ridiculous theories about him trying to synthesise narcotics out of spider venom, that it was some kind of drug binge.

It just makes no sense. The amount of venom you could extract from a spider... It's tiny, the number of spiders he'd have to have. And if he injected himself with venom, he must've known what was going to happen. He was an entomologist, even if he was just working at London Zoo. He was qualified. It doesn't make sense.

205

He could've been bitten by accident. But none of the papers say that. I mean, I expect the tabloids to be making stuff up, but it's in the serious papers too. He was injected with venom, with a syringe.

Maybe he was trying to build up an immunity. But then there's the other things. What I saw that day. I just don't...

... I don't get it. I stand before you a scientist. And I have seen things and experienced things I cannot in anyway explain. That scares me. That really scares me.

I don't think I've got anything else to say. When I look at a spider now, I think, what do you know? What do you know that I don't?

PRINCE OF FOXES

When I was little I used to watch the foxes playing at night. They weren't playing, not really. They were scavenging or hunting or whatever. But to me it looked like they were playing games. I used to give them names, but I couldn't really tell them apart. They could do whatever they wanted, and, in my head, they were all friends, having good times together.

I'd watch them from my bedroom window, after Nan put me to bed. On the other side of the fence at the end of her garden was this unused land where there was a disused railway line. You could still hear trains; there was a line running a bit further away. But this part was dead and overgrown with grass and weeds. It probably really upset people in the neighbourhood, but no one did anything about it.

I'd sit up late and watch the foxes appear and disappear; crawl under or climb Nan's fence and disappear into this world under the grass that was theirs. A secret world. I used to think about it and dream about it a lot when I was growing up. Because there was nothing I wanted to do more than just disappear.

I loved my Nan. She was the best thing in my life. My parents would drop me off at hers when it suited them and she would look after me and everything would suddenly be normal. There'd be breakfast in the morning, my lunch would be ready to take to school; my shirt and my skirt would be clean and ironed. I'd be at school by nine and I'd be picked up at 3:30. It was all predictable and stable. She cared for me; looked after me properly.

When I was with Mum and Dad I never knew what was going on. Sometimes Mum might get me from school, sometimes I might have to wait ages. Sometimes Dad would get me. Sometimes I might get picked up by someone that worked for him, who'd I'd never met before. My teachers would have to call him to check I wasn't being handed over to some paedo who'd come in off the street.

When I got handed over to my Nan, I knew what was going on – Mum and Dad were getting rid of me. So I'd scream and cry and whinge, but that never made a difference. My parents, who were supposed to love me, wanted to pass me over to someone else; an old lady who was strict and wasn't much fun.

But then I'd get used to it. I'd suddenly know what it was like to have a real parent. Someone who looked after you. Someone who cared about you and paid attention to you. Helped you with your homework.

That can't have been easy, getting me to do homework. Mum and Dad didn't really care, so I didn't care either. But then my Nan started making me do it and started to get on my case if I didn't. And I got to like the attention. I never got much of that at home.

Dad was a criminal. He owned a garage, which was his 'legitimate' business. And I guess you could probably get your car fixed there. But the parts were probably stolen. And he might steal bits of your car without you noticing. Like your air bags.

Dad never did any of the work. I never saw him get his hands dirty. All the work was done by teenagers and a few other hangers-on, creepy old guys with names like Mick and Dave and Keith. They'd check out the cars and then go to the office and tell Dad a bunch of stuff. Dad would come out and spout a load of bull to the owner. Make out it was worse than it was, but you were lucky because he just happened to have the parts you needed. So it was going to be expensive. But not as expensive as it could've been, and at least you'd get it done today.

You went in to get your spark plugs changed and left with a new gearbox, windscreen, wheel rims and exhaust. And new spark plugs that didn't work properly.

That was just his regular work. He did other stuff too. He never told me exactly how he was making his money, but he wasn't that bothered about keeping it secret. He'd boast if he thought he was onto a winner, especially if he really got one over someone. I know he was into stolen goods, stolen cars obviously. And he did drugs too, both sold and took them.

I picked up on all sorts of things, not that I really understood them. You don't know what's normal when you're little. Not until you see it. And then you know you're the one who's different.

Nan was careful not to say bad things about Mum and Dad. She was good like that. But I knew. And there'd be these little comments here and there.

She was afraid to upset them. Mum was vindictive; if they rowed she'd threaten not to bring me over. But that wouldn't last because it was too easy for them to dump me there. They didn't always tell her that they were bringing me over. They might just show up. But Nan was always happy to have me.

Can't have been easy for her to bite her tongue. She was a tough woman my Nan, a real battle-axe. She would not take shit from anyone. She definitely didn't take shit from me. There was no pudding if I didn't eat all my dinner. No staying up late on school nights. No staying up late ever if I didn't do my homework first. I would get angry and say that Mum and Dad let me do I wanted. But she wouldn't have that. She'd stand her ground until I did what she wanted.

I might throw a tantrum and say I hated her. But that wasn't true. It dawned on me slowly that she wasn't the problem. It was confusing to be told to do stuff and be made to follow rules and actually find out good things would come out of it. Like having clean clothes and nice food.

When I actually did my homework, my teachers were pleased with me and encouraged me. When I stopped, because my Dad was like "What are you doing that for?" my teachers were disappointed in me. And I realised that made me unhappy.

Because I wasn't really free to do what I wanted at home. I was free to keep my head down and stay quiet and not get in the way.

I wanted to be like the foxes. They moved about in secret and they didn't have to depend on anyone. They really were free to do what they wanted. I wasn't.

Dad thought he was really clever. He thought that because he never did a day's work, he was a genius. Easy money was the best money. But we never had any money. It went out as soon as it came in. He'd splash it out on clothes and new TVs and all kinds of things we didn't need.

If he'd been smart he'd have done smart things with it. But he didn't. He just kept robbing and cheating and stealing.

I don't really hate him though. He spent money like an idiot, but he could be fun. He was a big kid. I'd come home and find he'd splashed out on a new football table or bought a games console or that we were going out to a Wacky Warehouse or something. He was kind of spontaneous. He'd just go off and do stuff and that was pretty fun.

He was dumb as fuck. But he loved me, mostly. And if that doesn't sound like much, it's a lot more than I got from my Mum.

I'll never understand her. That bitch. I don't know how she could come from my Nan and be so different.

You had to love her, that's all she cared about. You had to love her and give her all your love and affection. She'd suck all she could out of you and it'd never be enough. She was like a vampire.

I remember being very little. She'd be playing with me and looking after me and would just suddenly change. She'd go cold on me. And then nothing I could do would make her like me again. I could scream and shout and she'd look at me like I was nothing.

It's like she couldn't trust it. A child had no choice but to love her, so that wasn't enough. It wasn't real. What could a stupid kid give her?

She always wanted attention. Her and Dad would have these big rows about her flirting with other guys. But she loved that. She loved the attention, and if Dad got angry and got in some fight that was better, because that meant that he loved her.

He used to come home in a state sometimes. Blood on his shirt, cuts and bruises, black eyes. But it was all part of their 'thing', they'd row and fuck and row and fuck, and get pissed up all over again.

Dad wasn't allowed to spend more time with me than her. I had to compete with her. And she always won of course.

I remember the time he bought me a huge Scalextric set. I was so happy. Me and him; we started to build it in the living room. I was never much into girly stuff. I'm still more of a tomboy.

But straight away, Mum was pissed off. Said we were making a mess. She'd hoovered or swept up or whatever – you know, the bare-minimum. That house was a shithole.

We were building the track and she was being ignored. So she tried to get in on it and started trying to build and was getting it wrong and didn't know how to do it and got bored with it. And I kept getting annoyed with her because she wasn't doing it right, and she had a strop. She was spoiling our fun because she couldn't be part of it.

I went off to the toilet and when I came back she was on top of Dad. One hand down his trousers. I just went back to my room. The Scalextrix went in a box and never came out again.

Mum had me young. And Dad married her, to his credit I suppose. They tied the knot straight away; she didn't want me showing on her big day.

That must have stung Nan bad. I don't think she was at the wedding. I don't think they spoke for a while. She didn't like Dad. Nan's a suburban snob. I could tell she was better off than Mum and Dad; she lived in a much nicer house. If cheating and scheming was so good, why did we live in this shitty council terrace and why were we hiding behind the sofas when people came to knock at the door?

Nan had two daughters. The wrong one died. Horse-riding accident I think. And then her husband, my granddad, died. I think that's when she started talking to Mum again. Because I'd been born then and Nan wanted to know her granddaughter.

She wanted to make sure I was ok and looked after. Because she knew they couldn't be trusted to do it. She was probably lonely too. Old woman, on her own; not many friends.

211

I remember seeing her cry one time. Mum and Dad had come to pick me up and I saw her watching from the window as I got in the car. She went away from the window when she saw me looking at her and didn't wave goodbye.

I asked Mum. "Why is Nan crying?" And she said, "Because she's a silly old woman."

Nan was ok to them, but they didn't bother. They called her a cow, said she was stuck up, a bitch, tight-fisted. She wouldn't lend them money. She refused too. She would buy things for me if they asked, but would never give them money. She was too smart for that.

I knew Nan wasn't a bitch. When I talked to kids at school, life with Nan sounded a lot more like what was going on with them and their parents than what happened with mine. I wasn't even supposed to tell anyone what my Dad did for a living. Mum told me not too. And that was weird because he was supposed to work at a garage. Why was that secret?

I was pretty quiet as a kid. It was the safest way, just be quiet and stay out of the way. Another thing I thought I had in common with the foxes.

But I could be pretty temperamental too. I would just boil over and get angry. Get so frustrated I just couldn't keep it in. Like if I really wanted to do something, like get some help with my homework, and Mum just decided she couldn't be bothered, after she said she would – I might just suddenly explode. That was a bad idea. Mum was much better at tantrums than me.

She hit me sometimes. Not all the time. Just a few times. I remember one time she just picked a belt up and smacked me across the face. I don't even remember what I did to deserve it. Even she looked shocked she'd done it. But when I started to make a lot of noise, all the sympathy went. She shoved me in my room and told me to shut up. She'd do anything to make sure she got the last word in any fight. I just started to bottle everything up.

I don't know what the teachers at school must've thought. They were probably afraid of Mum too. The stupidest thing of all about my Mum was that she had so much fucking pride. If

212

someone accused her of being a bad parent, all hell would break loose. She could not possibly be a bad parent.

I didn't tell my Nan when she hit me. I was afraid if I did, Mum would get angry and wouldn't take me to see her any more. It was always best just to go along with what Mum said. It hurt less.

Nan didn't like the foxes. They'd shit in her garden and make a mess of the bins. And then there was the noise they'd make at night. Nan was always complaining about it, but I thought that was them singing. I thought they were cute, she thought they were nasty and dirty.

One summer, when I was eleven, Dad had some business abroad, and Mum went with him. They dropped me off at Nan's, and said they'd be back in about a week. But they didn't come back. Not for ages.

Me and Nan were together for months. It was honestly the happiest time of my life growing up. The longer it went on, the better it was.

She was strict, but she could be fun too. She bought a paddling pool for the garden. I loved that. She liked games and she liked playing with me. She'd sit with me and build Lego and do jigsaws. She'd watch TV with me and let me watch what I wanted.

Nan became my normal, everyday parent. We had no idea where they were, and as the weeks went by the new school term got closer. Nan didn't have the keys to my parents' to get all my school stuff. She had to buy new stuff, call up school and find out what books and things I needed for the new term. And when I realised Nan was putting money on the table, I asked to be part of the tennis club and the school band and other stuff. She didn't think they were stupid or a waste of money.

A few weeks before school started, Nan came into the kitchen and was complaining about the foxes again. She said she could hear them at the bottom of the garden at night and she'd found they had a nest down there. There must be baby foxes, she thought. She could hear them behind the shed.

She said she wanted to call in an exterminator, but she couldn't be that cruel. So she just complained all the time instead. She wished she hadn't told me, because straight away I wanted to go out and see the foxes, and feed them and pet them because I didn't really understand that they were wild animals.

Nan couldn't convince me. I loved the foxes – they were cute. I'd seen Animals of Farthing Wood on TV. I just knew they were friendly and I wanted one to stroke and love and cuddle.

I wanted to see the little fox cubs. She told me I couldn't. I wasn't allowed to. And that was supposed to be that. But I could be stubborn too.

I snuck downstairs one night. I was used to doing what I wanted in secret. And I knew Nan's bark was worse than her bite.

I poured the foxes a bowl of milk and I let myself out the back door.

In my bare feet, I walked across the grass to the shed, which was in the far corner of the garden. I was pretty quiet. I didn't want to scare them.

There was a gap between the back of the shed and the old fence. When I got there, I couldn't really see anything. But when I looked carefully, I saw a little light reflect off the eyes of a fox looking back at me. It looked like the den was just beneath the neighbour's fence.

I kneeled to put the bowl down. But there was a noise above me, from the roof of the shed. A boy appeared from nowhere and dropped down in front of me.

I dropped the bowl and fell on my back. I was really surprised and really scared. The boy was a bit older. His face was dirty and his hair was long and a mess. He was skinny, very scrawny. And naked; I could see his willy.

He let out a screech, just like the foxes did. I got up and ran back to the house. I locked the door behind me and stared out the window.

Nothing happened for a moment. Then a fox crept out from behind the shed. It stood at the end of the garden and watched me.

I watched him back. After a little bit of staring, he went back behind the shed.

I was scared and confused, but a little excited too. I'd just seen something weird and wonderful – a boy who lived with the foxes. I watched from my room for hours to see if I could see him again. But I didn't and I got sleepy and went back to bed.

The next day, while Nan was busy with breakfast, I went back to the garden. I went around the shed to see if I could see the foxes or the boy. I couldn't see anything behind the shed. It was a tight space.

When I walked to the patio, I noticed something really weird. The bowl I'd taken out last night, and left in the garden, was there by the back door, waiting for me.

Nan wouldn't have done that. She'd just have taken it inside. And I was sure she hadn't been out. I hadn't spilt all the milk when I'd been surprised by the boy. The foxes must've drank it and brought it back for me. I couldn't explain it any other way.

If I'd been a bit older, I'd have thought it was a joke. But as a kid I thought I'd really been right about the foxes all along. That they really did have their own special world. They weren't just animals. They were special. And one of them could transform into a full-size boy.

I was so excited. I'd discovered some kind of magical secret. I thought about telling Nan. But I didn't think she'd believe me. And she hated the foxes. This was going to be my secret. I liked it that way.

I started to put bread out for them at night, in secret. I'd stay up late and watch them, waiting for them to take it. But I'd get bored and fall asleep. In the morning the bread was gone.

Then one time, I saw a cat try to take the bread. And from nowhere the foxes showed up and scared it off.

They knew I was watching every night. They'd just been waiting for me to go to sleep. They were clever. Really smart.

I became obsessed with foxes. I started to draw them at school, read about them in books. But I was careful not to let Nan know about them. Others would scare them off and I might never find out about their secrets.

I had to be even more careful when school started, because Nan was putting me to bed earlier and making sure I

215

was doing my homework in the evenings. Even if I didn't have any, she'd make me tell her what I'd been doing at school to check I was learning things and paying attention.

Besides the foxes, things really were about as normal as possible. I had a new uniform, a new kit for sports, new shoes, nice new stationary. I felt like I was going into school a whole new person.

I joined the netball team. Tried to convince my Nan to buy me a trumpet to play in the school band. She wouldn't budge on that one because they were expensive. So it was the recorder, but as most kids had been practicing for years, I gave that up because I didn't want to be in a beginner class with little kids. I kept that secret from Nan and pretended to practice in my room for a few weeks.

We even started to plan for my birthday in November; it's the day before fireworks night.

I didn't really think that I'd get anyone to come to a party. I never really had friends growing up. It was always the same story – I would make a friend and then want to spend every living hour with them. And then when they didn't want to spend every living hour with me, they'd start avoiding me and I would get angry and have a tantrum at them and then they wouldn't be my friend any more. I got the reputation for being a psycho. At least that meant they left me alone rather than just bully me.

But Nan was always positive: "Of course your school friends will want to come". She even had me starting to believe it. I was in the netball club and although they'd been mean and nasty at first, some of them noticed that I wasn't bad at it and started being nicer. I thought maybe we could have a party. I wasn't ashamed to take anyone around to my Nan's.

We shouldn't have let ourselves get carried away. We both knew deep down that they'd come back eventually. There'd been no letters, no postcards, no phone calls. But they had to come back some time.

I was wishing that they wouldn't. The way I felt about them wasn't so confused anymore. I just hated them, and I didn't want to live with them anymore.

We drove past the garage one time; it was still open. This tall thin guy was there, talking to the customers. I had no idea who he was, but I'd find out soon enough.

They showed up just before Halloween. Me and Nan were talking about what costume I could wear to the school party when their knock hit the door. Me and Nan knew, instantly. It was Dad's knock. We felt like the rug had been pulled out from under us.

Mum came in with fake hellos and happiness. She came over and hugged me while I stood like a statue. They were both tanned. Dad had a gift for Nan: a cheap bottle of wine he'd bought duty free.

Nan was shaking. I'll always remember the sound of her voice when she said, "Where the hell have you been?" It was thin and croaky; her old voice just couldn't handle how angry she was.

The row began. As they shouted at each other I walked off and went outside. I stood in the garden and looked out into the night and I cried. If I could've vaulted over the fence I would've. I hoped the foxes might come out from their hiding places and lead me away. That the boy, who I now wasn't sure if I'd imagined or not, would come and take my hand and show me a way to another world where none of this was happening to me.

My Dad shouted at me from inside the house. I barely heard him. He came out and grabbed me by the arm and said we were leaving.

He went with me to my room where we threw all my stuff in bags. "We're getting you out of this place" he said, as if I'd been living in some hellhole, rather than the best home I'd ever had.

Mum and Nan were still rowing. I heard Nan say, "You don't want her, you never wanted her. You don't even care about her."

"I'm her fucking mother," Mum screamed back. "She stays with me."

"Let her stay for Christ's sake."

"Oh she's going," says Dad. "And she ain't coming back either."

217

Nan tried to grab me, to hug me. But Mum got in the way and Dad dragged me outside to the car.

Mum slammed the door and sat on the back seat with me for some reason. Probably wanted me to feel sorry for her. You always had to feel sorry for her, what she had put up with. She started saying bad things about Nan, saying I'd be much happier away from her.

"I hate you," I whispered.

She heard me and said "What?" So I said it again "I hate you". I said it louder, and louder and louder. I jumped on her and hit her, over and over shouting "I hate you, I hate you, I hate you."

Dad pulled the car over, dragged me out, put me over his knee on the curb and smacked me in the street. I lay with my face down on the back seat for the rest of the journey, screaming and crying until they carried me back into that house and locked me in my bedroom.

God I hated them. I hated them from my gut. I just wanted to escape. Go anywhere. Be anywhere else but in that house with them.

But what could I do? I was still in primary school. They were still my parents. Whatever fantasies I had in my head, I knew I couldn't ditch them. They'd just drag me back. There was nothing I could do.

Things went back to normal. All the things I'd started to like, the regular stuff like being picked up from school, nice food, help with the homework – all that stopped. A few quid for the netball club, what was the point of that? "I used to play in the park when I was kid, and didn't have to pay for it," Dad said. "You've got a football, go play in the park."

Nan was a forbidden subject. I wasn't allowed to talk to her or about her or visit her. That was that.

For weeks I barely said a word. Mum started getting angry at me for being quiet, which was weird because she used to like that before. After a few weeks she stopped cooking for me. I was old enough to do it myself and she wasn't going to do it if all I did was sulk.

I hid out in my room where I spent my time drawing and making up stories. Ever since I'd seen the fox boy I'd been trying to imagine who he might be, what he might do, where he might go. Even though I'd seen him only once, I knew that he was in charge of the foxes. I'd read that they were solitary animals. But they were working together at my Nan's; I'd seen them. This was some kind of fox gang.

Was he a fox or was he a boy? I came up with an Alice in Wonderland kind of story where, in the grass and weeds of the scrubland behind my Nan's house, there was a portal to another upside-down world. There the foxes were human. When they went through the fox hole, this giant hidden fox hole, they came to our world where they turned into foxes. Like the foxes we see every day. And when I – because I was the star of my own story – went to their world, the opposite happened and I turned into an animal. I was a squirrel. They came to our world to experience what it was like to be an animal, and I went to their world to do the same. Animals were free and they weren't cruel or selfish or nasty. Not in my world anyway, because these animals were also people.

The fox boy, he was the foxes' dog in their world. He was their loyal guard dog, and when they came over to our world, he became a real boy. But he still behaved like a guard dog and protected them. He was my best friend in both worlds, because he always looked after me.

It was a silly story. It didn't make much sense. But I needed the escape.

I spent my birthday at the fireworks night at the local cricket club. My parents got drunk while I stayed in the playground looking after five and six year olds. It was the same every year. We didn't go because I wanted to. It just happened to be my birthday. I got a new bike at least.

It was around this time Terry appeared on the scene. They called him Uncle Terry to me, although there was no way he was my Uncle. And I don't just say that because I hated him from the moment I saw him. I say it because he was tall and thin; my Dad was pot-bellied like a pig. It was him I'd seen working at the garage.

He had big teeth and stunk of cigarettes, even more than Mum. He'd call you babe, or sweetheart, or gorgeous; even though I was 11 years old at the time. He was friends with Dad and they seemed to know each other from years back, but I'd never set eyes on him before. Suddenly he was over a lot. Him and Dad had something going on, and it wasn't just a few drinks down the pub or selling stolen cars.

Terry was more careful about talking about his business. He didn't just say stuff or boast. If he saw me around, he was all 'charm'. Pervy, weird charm.

He was a bigger drinker than both Mum and Dad. And even more unpredictable. He might show up in the middle of the night, bringing the party with him. Dad was suddenly away a lot doing stuff with Terry.

If anyone else had got him up in the morning, my Dad would've been up in arms. But when it was Terry, it was all fine. He was in awe of Terry. He seemed to want to impress him. He was always kissing up to him.

Something was going on. I didn't know what. Even Mum didn't seem to mind Terry being around. She didn't seem to mind him spending so much time with Dad or them being woken up in the middle of the night. Whatever was going on, she was in on it too.

Christmas was horrible. I got told off for not being excited about my presents. I was too old for dolls and I didn't really want to play video games. But I got a telly for my room, which was something. Even more excuse never to go downstairs.

We had Christmas dinner at a pub. Terry's mob showed up. I sat around until my Dad sent me home. Spent the evening on my own.

New Year's Eve was even worse. Dad had a house party with the music turned up really stupidly loud. Terry's gang came over and they ended up rowing with the neighbours, yelling at them over the fence. Terry tried to climb over and start a fight. It wasn't even 10 o'clock.

The police showed up before midnight and there was another big row. Terry and some other guy I never saw before got arrested. The party moved to a pub down the road. I got left alone again.

I remember going to my room and spotting Mum's handbag on the bed in their bedroom. It normally never left her side – her cigs were in there.

I took it and found what I was looking for – her address book. I didn't know how to get in touch with Nan. I didn't have her number and I didn't really know where she lived, not how to get there anyway.

I wanted to speak to her so much. I wanted to hear her voice so badly. I thought she might still be up. Mum and Dad normally sent me over and we'd watch the telly. But with me not being there, would she still be awake?

I rang her at about 11:30. It rang for a long time.

When she picked up, when I heard her voice, I started to cry.

"Katy is that you?"

"Nan. I want to live with you. I hate this place. I hate living here. I hate my life," I said.

Nan started to cry as well, she sounded tired. After I told her all that had happened over the past few months, she said it had to stop. She was going to make it stop. Mum and Dad didn't take care of me properly and she could have me taken off them. She'd always thought about it but now she was going to do it. Speak to a solicitor and social services and finally have me taken off them.

It was music to my ears. I was so happy, I thought she was going to storm through the door the next day and take me away with her and I'd never have to see them again.

I went to sleep happy. It was all going to be over and I was going to live somewhere else.

But nothing happened. Weeks and months went by and nothing happened. School started again and things were just back to normal. I was too stupid to write Nan's number down, I just put the address book back in Mum's bag and then when I wanted to call her again and find out how she was going to save me, I couldn't.

I waited ages. The call finally came in March, but it wasn't the call I wanted.

Nan had had a stroke and she was in hospital. As her next of kin, Mum got the call to go and see her.

I remember her telling Dad. Even she seemed to feel bad about it. Her mum almost dying triggered something even in her dead heart. Not enough to take me along though. When I overheard them talking, I demanded I go with her. But no. I was still off limits to Nan. She still hated her that much that she wouldn't let me see her.

When she came back from the hospital, I overheard them talking about her. Mum said Nan didn't even know what day of the week it was. Or what was going on around her.

Nan was in hospital for a few weeks. I begged to see her, but Mum and Dad said that was a bad idea. I would get upset by seeing her.

When it was time to bring her home from the hospital, Me and Mum went over to hers to tidy up. Her house was a mess. That wasn't like her. She'd been unwell a while before she ended up in hospital. She'd had several small strokes that had knocked the life out of her bit by bit. We found out that one of the neighbours had spotted her on the floor in the living room and called an ambulance.

I remember when Dad brought her over that day. She was so frail.

She was always old, but she never really acted old. She was active and determined and alive. And now she could barely stand up on her own. She looked like a skeleton.

She didn't even remember who I was. Mum had to remind her. Then she said, "But Katy's just a baby." She didn't know where she was and what was going on.

She had to be looked after like she was a child. She had to be fed and helped into the shower. She had to be helped to dress and helped down the stairs.

Mum was caring at first. She looked shell-shocked when she looked at Nan. Nan was this strong, powerful person and now she was like a cripple. Mum stayed with her and helped her like a daughter should, for a while at least. The effect started to

222

wear off quite quickly. It didn't take her long to start complaining about what she was having to go through, what she was having to do for Nan and how disgusting it was to watch her shower or watch her use the toilet.

It was always the same with her. Do some work, stick with it a little bit, start moaning about it, then moan about it all the time, then give it to me to do instead. I knew by the third day of Nan coming home that it'd be me who'd end up looking after her. So I started helping early and being helpful and trying to make things easier for Mum. I might've been a child, but I knew I was going to have to be the grown up and help Nan get better.

And she did get better. Bit by bit. But it was slow. After the first few weeks, she needed less help. She was still easily confused by things. She kept calling me Becky – that was the name of her other daughter. She kept saying she wished Mum was more like Becky. That really didn't help things.

When Mum realised the Easter holiday was coming up, she knew that was the time she could pass Nan on to me to look after. Dad, in a rare showing of backbone, told her it was a bad idea, but I knew he'd cave in. Once Mum started going on about how hard things were on her and started using her tears, he'd just fold. I was angry and asked him if he'd be helping out. He looked at me like I was an idiot and said he'd be busy at the garage. This was obviously women's work.

So every day, all Easter, I looked after Nan by myself. I had to help her up in the morning, help her on to the toilet, help her into the shower and shower with her. Then I'd bring her downstairs and make her breakfast. We'd eat it at the kitchen table, because there was no eating off your laps in the living room in her house. I still followed all her rules.

We'd sit and watch telly together. Maybe we'd talk, maybe we'd play a game, although she was always forgetting what she was doing or where she was.

It was so hard. I had to sit and talk to her about the same things over and over again. She'd been so sharp before. She would forget who I was or confuse me with Becky, and I'd try not to get upset about it. She'd get better. I knew she would.

223

She got a little better every day. And just maybe I could stay and keep living with her.

I started to tell her my stories about the foxes. She didn't seem to mind. She seemed to enjoy it. She didn't seem to hate the foxes now, but maybe that's because they didn't come around any more. The neighbours had bought a huge guard dog who barked all the time and who scared them off. To top everything else off, it looked like I'd never find out their secrets after all, or whether I'd really seen the boy or not.

One night I was walking her up the stairs, and she thought I was Becky again. She started to talk about me "That poor girl Katy," she said. "Adele and that ape she married. They don't look after her and they don't love her. God knows what's going to become of her. She's going to grow up dumb and stupid like he is. I know it. I feel so terribly ashamed about what's happened to her."

She was still talking about it when I put her to bed "I should've done more for her. I'm going to regret my whole life that I didn't do more for that poor girl. You'll look after her won't you?"

She brushed her hand across my cheek. "You're such a good girl, not like your sister. I can always rely you."

I could barely hold in the tears and went down stairs to cry in the kitchen. Listening to the neighbours dog bark made me think how alone I was. Even my fantasy fox friends had deserted me.

I was sure she would get better. She could still help me. I could still have a home here. But Easter wasn't going to last forever. Once I went back to school, she was at the mercy of Mum again. I could come over in the evenings and on the weekends but that was all.

I tried to convince them, Mum and Dad, to let me stay at Nan's all the time, but that made them suspicious, like I was trying to run away and stay with Nan, like Nan had wanted. I don't know why they couldn't let me go, they didn't really want me. But they thought I was their property. I belonged to them, so why give me away? In their own heads they thought they were good parents; I was just a moaning, miserable brat.

I tried to tell Mum how much Nan still needed me. She snapped at me and said she didn't need me to tell her what to do. I couldn't be sure she'd do anything right to help her. She only cared about herself.

I cycled to school in the morning and over to Nan's in the evening. Nan had managed to get used to a routine, she just needed help doing certain things because she wasn't very strong. She struggled to get in and out of bed and down the stairs. Mum should've always been there to help her with that. But she'd come over when it suited her and Nan would just have to wait in bed till she got there.

In a sick way that probably helped her get better quicker. She started to remember what Mum was like, so that made her get more self-sufficient. So she dragged a chair to her bed so she could grip something when she needed to get up. She started to go up and down the stairs on her bottom.

You couldn't keep her down my Nan. But it wasn't enough. Not in the end.

She caught a cold. Just a stupid little cold. But she was too weak. About a month after Easter things were getting better with her, and even she was telling me not to go over so often. She hated me worrying about her. I was looking forward to half term so I could be there all day, but she was telling me she could cope with more. Mum was only doing her shopping for her now.

So I was only going over a couple of nights a week. And when she started blowing her nose and saying she had a cold, I didn't take it seriously. She said she was fine. But she always said that. That's what people always say.

I let myself in one day and I knew the house didn't smell right. When I shouted for her I got no answer. I got worried and ran upstairs. She'd fallen out of bed. She was staring up at the ceiling, but she wasn't moving.

I pulled the duvet over her, ran downstairs and called 999. I waited for them in silence, not really believing what had happened. I remember that I was shivering. I felt cold, even though it was summer. When they got there, the ambulance people, I barely said a word. I just showed them upstairs. And when they started to ask lots of questions, that's when I started to cry. I just cried and cried.

Mum was sad when she came over, but it was a performance. She needed the people who were there to see that she was upset. But she didn't really care.

Her and Dad talked to the police and the ambulance people for hours. I talked to them too. Telling them the same story over and over. When they finally stopped asking me the same stupid questions I walked outside into the garden. I was tired from talking and crying and I wanted to be alone.

I was feeling like the loneliest person in the world. That all my hope for a better life was gone. My one and only friend was gone and there was no one left. I was stuck with my parents forever.

As I walked around, I hit something with my foot. There was a plate on the patio. A plate with a slice of bread on it.

The plate was cracked and chipped and dirty. The bread felt fresh. I looked at it closely and saw teeth marks on the one corner.

The foxes had brought me bread. They'd given me a piece of bread just the same way that I used to bring them bread before. And they'd been brave enough to come, even with the neighbour's dog barking.

I could not believe it. I didn't know what to make of it. This was proof. Absolute proof that the foxes were not normal foxes. Even though I'd written all the stories, there'd still been a bit of doubt in my mind that maybe I'd imagined it all. I hadn't seen them at Nan's for months. There'd still been this doubt, but now there was none.

Nan wouldn't have fed the foxes. She didn't keep broken plates and she wouldn't have given them fresh bread. The foxes had left bread for me because they felt sorry for me.

It was hard to really know what I was feeling at the time, but it was like knowing that someone, something out there, cared about me still. That maybe I wasn't alone after all. I can't tell you how much that meant to me at the time. How it made it feel like all hope was not gone. That it stopped me from falling into total despair.

In the weeks after, I found out that Nan still had one last trick up her sleeve. Even though she was dead, she was going to do one last thing to help me.

She can't have been cold by the time Mum and Dad started talking about what they'd inherit. That night I crept out on to the landing and I could hear them trying to work out how much everything was worth – the house, the car, her pension. Who knew what money she had tucked away. They could certainly move out of this dump. No council house for them anymore.

They couldn't wait to go to the solicitors to talk about the will. But they changed their tune pretty quick. Nan left everything to me.

They should have known something was up when they were told that they had to bring me with them. They barely spoke to me on the way home.

The house and all Nan's money was to be put in a trust for me until I was 18. How much she had, they wouldn't tell us. I bet Nan wanted it that way, to keep it secret from Mum and Dad.

Mum and Dad could live in Nan's house, but – and this was the bit that almost made me laugh out loud – they would have to pay me rent. It was a really small amount; basically to cover the costs of managing the trust.

I had to stop myself laughing that whole journey home. Nan had totally fucked them over. She'd given me everything I needed so that one day I could have my own home, my own money, and I could turf them out as soon as I hit 18. I had over six years to wait, but it would be worth it, just waiting for that day that I could show them the door...

When we got back, I was sent up to my room and they both had a blazing row in the kitchen. It was the first time hearing them fight made me happy. They'd tried to argue it with the solicitor, but he'd told them it was all perfectly legal. They could contest of course, but they couldn't prove she wasn't of sound mind; she'd done the will ages before.

227

They couldn't have afforded a solicitor anyway. They had even less money than before because they'd been throwing it around because they were expecting Nan's money. And they had to pay for the funeral too.

But things were worse than I knew. They were actually desperate for money. Or at least Dad was.

I was on the toilet when I heard him and Terry talking outside. Something was up, Dad was panicking and Terry was giving him a talking to. He was saying, "I warned you, you should've walked away."

And Dad was like "I almost had it. I was so close all I needed was one more win."

"But you're in the shit now, aren't you? Jesus!"

Dad was begging him for help, but Terry wasn't having any of it.

"Sorry old son, if I had it, I would. You know I would. But I've got it all tied up in this business, where you should've put your money, like I told you."

"Then I'm fucked", Dad said. "He's not going to let me work it off is he?"

"He doesn't know you. He ain't going to give you any work. He just wants his money."

"Then I'm fucked. Totally fucked."

Terry told him to keep his voice down. I didn't hear what Terry said next, but Dad didn't like it. He didn't like it one bit.

A few days later Dad revealed he was selling the garage. It was sold fast, and the price he got for it caused more rowing with Mum. I don't know if Dad told her why he needed the money. He'd been gambling, that's my guess. But he tried to spin it another way – he needed money so he and Terry could set up their business thing.

I'm guessing there was enough left after he'd paid off his debts for him to hand some over Terry. I wouldn't be surprised if Terry had set the whole thing up. Got him into debt so he'd sell up the garage and give half over to him. Now that Nan's money was all going to me, it kind of made sense that he needed to find another way to fleece my Dad out of cash. Terry wasn't his friend any more than he was my Uncle.

Terry was setting up a security company. That's as much as I could work out at the time. I didn't know why it was such a big deal, but I'd find out.

After Nan's funeral – which was just another excuse for a piss-up – we moved into her place. While I owned the house and all the money, the furniture and all the stuff inside the house did go to them. Presumably it was just less complicated to do it that way. They sold anything they thought might be valuable, including Nan's car, but that wasn't worth much.

Dad just pretended like it was his house and just seemed to deny that he was living under my roof. Mum had to make a bit more of an issue out of it.

"Don't you get any ideas," she'd say. "This is our house. The family's house, and you'll do what you're told. Do you understand me?"

I'd just sit in silence, so she'd repeat herself: "Do you understand me?"

Our arguments always went like this now. I'd refuse to answer and when she'd get angry and start yelling I'd get up and go away. If she was in a particularly bad mood she might grab me by the hair, pull me back and shake me. Then I'd have to answer her.

It was war between us now. Nan wouldn't have died if she'd looked after her. I hated that bitch and I was at the point where I wasn't shy about showing it.

It helped that I had a bit of a growth spurt. Mum wasn't very tall; by the end of summer I was almost her height. But just because I was getting cockier, doesn't mean she was less vindictive. When I ate one of her yogurts this one time, and told her I didn't care, she went outside and slashed the tires on my bike. You couldn't win; she'd go to any length to get one over on you.

There was no telling when she might go off. I learnt never to joke about owning the house. When she got angry with me for not taking my shoes off, I said I didn't care because it was my house. So she said, "Watch this," and took a kitchen knife and scraped it across the wall, taking off the paint and plaster.

229

"If you want there to be anything left of this house when you get to 18, you'd better change your attitude and show me some respect."

That one sunk in. Her and Dad could wreck this place and make it a dump like they did the last house. But later when I saw Dad have a go at her for ruining the paintwork, it made her look pretty stupid.

It was a rough summer. I couldn't wait for high school to start. It was a chance to meet new kids and start fresh. It was more fashionable to be stroppy and sulky and introverted there. My fashion sense was somewhere between goth and grunge. I was the girl who the other girls bought cigarettes from, because I was always stealing them from Mum and Dad. They always had a big supply, either stolen or bought duty-free in bulk. And I'd steal them from Mum's handbag too, just for the hell of it. She suspected me sometimes, but never caught me. The whole house stunk of fags anyway. It wasn't like she could smell them on me.

I used to smoke in the garden. They were happy to let me do the gardening. I made them think I was doing them a favour. But really it was so I could get to know my fox friends better. The neighbour's dog had gone – I reckon they got sick of its noise too. The foxes had started to show up again. I'd seen them out of my window.

I cut off the bottom corner of the shed door so they could squeeze in. I put some dog beds and some blankets and things in there for them to keep warm and sleep on. I filled bowls and buckets with water, and sometimes milk if I could sneak it out of the house. I left bread and other leftovers for them too.

I wanted them to know it was a safe place for them and they didn't need to be afraid of me. Because they still wouldn't come close to me. I was still a person after all and it was only natural they should be scared. But I wanted them to know for sure that I was a good person who wanted to be their friend.

They'd come in and eat the food, and maybe sleep – I saw their fur on the blankets and so on. But they were always gone in the morning. I stayed up some nights waiting for them and when they saw me in the shed, they would run scared. So I used to sit outside the shed instead. When they'd see me, they still weren't sure. So I'd throw them some bread, but that didn't really help. The next night, I threw them chocolate instead. That made them think I wasn't a threat, because no one nasty would throw them chocolate.

They started to go into the shed with me watching. One or two of the larger foxes would stand outside and watch me, to protect the others just in case. So I'd save the chocolates and biscuits for those guard foxes and they liked that. It got to the point where they stopped going into the shed and just waited outside for the treats.

I didn't see the fox boy. But when the weather changed and the ground got softer and dirtier, I could see muddy human footprints in the shed. They were very small. Too small for the fox boy. These were the footprints of little children. There was more going on than I knew about.

It felt good to have this little secret world to myself, away from everyone else. To have this magical thing going on. I was coming up to 12, but I wasn't old and cynical enough yet to believe that magic was impossible. When you live with the kind of parents I did, you wished every day that something magical would happen and take you away from everything. I didn't know how the foxes were going to do that, but just knowing magic existed meant that maybe something good would happen.

I was already going to inherit a house and maybe a fortune. Good things definitely could happen. Even with Mum and me being at war all summer, I was kind of positive that I had a future.

But there was a big bombshell coming. On Halloween, days before my birthday, there was some totally unexpected news.

Mum was wearing a sexy witch costume. She was getting older, but she didn't dress like it. She wanted me to help her with her corset.

"Thought I'd wear it while I still can. In a couple of months your Mum's figure will be gone."

She was trying to get my attention, but I wasn't interested.

"D'you hear me? Things are going to change around here."

"Why," I said, not really caring.

"You're going to have a little brother. Or sister maybe. Hopefully they'll be less of misery-guts than you are."

That came out of nowhere. I thought a little brother or sister was off the table. Dad didn't look like he was up to it. With the drinking and smoking and eating, he wasn't looking very good. He was gone all hours of the day now, working late and early shifts. His and Terry's business was about building security, looking after industrial estates and derelict buildings. If this whole thing was supposed to be making us rich, it wasn't happening very quickly.

I didn't even know if my little brother was going to survive the pregnancy, not with Mum's habits. She got wasted that Halloween; I was surprised she didn't miscarry. But the pregnancy carried on. She stopped smoking, heavily at least. I caught her having one or two in secret, but that was pretty good, for her. She only drank sometimes too.

Dad seemed pretty thrilled. He wanted a son. Not some sulky girl. I couldn't carry on his legacy. Whatever that was.

I wasn't sure what it was all supposed to mean to me. I wasn't worried about the baby having all the attention, because I never got any anyway. If anything, having them look after the baby would take the attention away from me. Make my life easier.

That was a stupid thought, because pregnancy made Mum a bigger martyr than ever before. Her mood swings were worse and her tantrums more extreme. Although as she got bigger she got slower; I was less worried about her hitting me.

I pretty much was already looking after myself: making my own meals and washing my own clothes. As the months went on I started doing these things for her too. They were both on my case if I didn't.

While this was going on, I was making better friends with the foxes. My growth spurt meant I was tall and strong enough to climb the fence at the back of the garden. That made it much easier to do my experiments in secret.

I flattened some grass and started to sit there with my treats ready for them. And when it was dark, one by one, they'd come for the chocolate and milk and bread, and sometimes biscuits; whatever I could steal or buy with my cigarette money.

And just slowly, over the weeks and months, they started to let me touch them. They were getting more comfortable with me. Some were scared. But some were more confident. Some I started to recognise, night after night. There was one with a patch on his forehead, another with a damaged ear. There was one with a little limp.

Patch – as I called him – seemed the most confident. Most of them jumped back if you put your hand near them, but noticing Patch was one of the first to always arrive, I started to give him more than the others. And then one night, when he was drinking milk, I just reached out and stroked his forehead. He seemed not to care about it. I stroked him across his head and behind the ears and he didn't seem to mind. He didn't seem to care.

I couldn't stay out long because it was winter and it was freezing. But when it got warmer, I could spend more time outside. And I'd talk to them and tell them about what was going on, about all the stuff with Mum and the baby and creepy Uncle Terry and whatever was going on with school.

I don't know when I first realised I was being watched. Not by the neighbours, or my parents – I was always careful about sneaking out and I always spoke quietly. And I never went out when the neighbours were in their gardens.

But at night, when the trains went by in the distance, light would shine through the grass and weeds and I could see him. He'd be a few dozen feet away, watching me silently: the fox boy. He was checking up on me, making sure I wasn't being cruel to his foxes. He was their protector. I'd been right all along.

When I spoke to the foxes, I wasn't really speaking to them. I was really speaking to the boy. I wanted him to hear me. I wanted him to know who I was and I wanted him to know that I was in love with him. And as time went on, he seemed to get closer, just a little bit closer every day.

By the time Mum was ready to give birth, the foxes were like kittens. I could hold them in my lap and stroke them. They were starting to fight for my attention. They would only come out when it was dark, so it was hard to see them by the time it got around to summer again. I had other stuff going on, like exams.

School was ok. Out of all the years I spent with my parents, this was a pretty stable time. Mum was distracted with the baby stuff and was enjoying the attention. I just had to help her out here and there and keep myself quiet and she wasn't much of a problem.

I had some friends at school, but I still kept to myself mostly. I didn't really think people wanted me around. My parents didn't; why would anyone else?

I hung around with the smokers mostly, where they hid around the back of the gym. Where they thought the teachers wouldn't see us.

I also started to get noticed by boys. I think because I was tall I looked a bit older. I sort of experimented a bit, but I wasn't really interested in them. They weren't really interested in me either. They were just using me. I knew it and it was fine. There was only one boy I was really interested in. I wasn't sure how old he was, or if he was even real. But he was my hero. The others were just distractions.

Mum gave birth in June. I got home one day and there was a note on the fridge to say she'd gone to the hospital. I didn't like rush or anything. I was totally not excited about it. I just figured the kid – we knew it was a boy – was going to be a noisy pain and I'd end up cleaning up after it.

I phoned up the hospital, found out where she was and took my bike over there. I didn't even ask if she was ok. I just thought everything would be fine.

Dad was thrilled with his baby boy; she looked like she was over it already. Dad showed me him, little baby Connor.

I fell for that little bugger straight away. All the teenage 'not bothered' stuff just went. It was as if all the maternal instincts skipped a generation. In like, seconds, literally, I went from not caring to going "Aww look at his little face. His little eyes. His little nose."

He was pretty cute. When he was quiet. He was difficult at first. Even more difficult than I was, apparently.

I think of those days, when Connor was born, and they make me feel really happy now, even though at the time it was really hard. I still had school and mock exams to do and I had to look after this screaming child – and the baby she'd just had.

Mum loved Connor when he was quiet or giggling and smiling, but the second he was trouble, she'd bitch and complain. Until she realised that I was much better at getting him to quieten down. Then she got jealous, but she still wasn't any better at it.

I didn't complain. I got to love it; changing him, holding him, feeding him. I just didn't mind. I just took to it. I did get annoyed at having to get up in the night to feed or change him, but when I'd look at those little blue eyes and that quiff of blonde hair, I couldn't stay mad, even if I had an exam in the morning.

I could let Mum get up and take care of him – and sometimes I did – but I was too worried about her doing it wrong. I was watching her all the time and trying to get her to hold his head up properly and heat his bottle up right. I had to try and do it subtly, but sometimes I just had to shout at her. That'd cause a row, but I'd stand my ground when it came to Connor. Anyway, the more I went on at her the more she got annoyed and let me do it. For once that was fine with me.

Whenever I got home from school, it was straight to Connor to see how well she'd looked after him. Give him a full inspection. See if he'd been changed. See whether she was watching him or listening to the baby monitor. If he wasn't changed or he was crying and she was nowhere, I'd go ape shit.

Connor bought out Dad's generous side. He was all over him. There was nothing he wouldn't buy that baby. He spent so much money on gear, stuff we didn't even need, not for months at least. He even pitched in to help sometimes.

Maybe he was feeling guilty for not being around enough. He was working weird hours, lots of them. He wouldn't tell me why, but he said it'd pay off in the end. Terry knew what he was doing...

I couldn't spend much time with my foxes while all this was going on. I still left food for them most nights. I'd spend time with them while Connor was asleep and I was sure Mum was watching him. I'd tell them all about him, what he was learning, what sounds he was starting to make. And the boy would watch, and I'd pretend not to stare at him back.

One night, after I'd been to feed the foxes, I saw Dad talking to someone by the front door. It was the police.

I asked him what was going on. He was worried, but pretended not to be. He said he'd be back later. "Don't tell Mum, she'll only get worried."

Dad didn't get back for hours. It was very late. But not late enough for Terry. He banged on the door after midnight and woke us all up. They had a long, not very quiet chat, the three of them. I knew something big was up, but I didn't want to know. And they weren't going to tell me anything anyway.

Things were tense for days. I'd walk into the room and Mum and Dad would suddenly stop talking. I asked and Mum said it was none of my business. I tried Dad when he was alone and he said, "It's nothing you need to worry about love. It's gonna work itself out."

He wasn't very convincing. I don't think I'd ever seen him afraid before. He was actually scared. I could see it behind his eyes.

The night before he died, I walked in on him in the bathroom. He was sat on the toilet – with all his clothes on. He was smoking a fag and just sitting there.

I told him he should just tell me what's going on. "It's just all bullshit," he said. "They've got nothing on me. The pigs would have to get up pretty early to catch me out."

He said it was all just some problems with work, but he was going to sort it out.

"Me, you and your Mum, we're going to go on to bigger and better things. I promise. Things are gonna be a whole lot better soon sweetheart."

He was just lying, so I walked off and used the downstairs

toilet and went to bed. Mum woke me up in the morning and told me to get dressed. When I got downstairs Terry was there waiting in the kitchen. That's when they told me Dad had been out drinking and died in a car accident.

He'd got hammered at this out-of-town pub, got in his car and gone too fast down a country road. He'd lost control, landed in a ditch, gone through the windscreen and died of head injuries.

When they'd finished talking, I just got up and left. Mum shouted at me "Aren't you gonna say something? That was your father. Where's your respect?" I didn't see her crying. I didn't see her shed one single tear.

I didn't really know what to feel. It confuses you having bad parents, because you hate them, but they're still part of you. And part of you will always want them to love you and care about you.

He was a prick and he was a thief and a criminal, but he was still my Dad. And he wasn't all bad, not when it came down to it. There were times when he could be normal and he could pretend that he loved me. It wasn't all bad. Not with him. He was an idiot, not a monster.

I still hated crying about it, because part of me did hate him, and then I hated myself more for crying over him when he didn't deserve it. He'd brought this on himself. He'd done this to himself.

I had nothing I could do with my anger or my pain. It was the summer holidays; I had nowhere to go to and no one to talk to, not that I had friends I could rely on anyway. At night I went out to see my foxes, but talking to them, just made remember how lonely I was. They were just animals, and they were my only real friends.

When the foxes saw I had no food for them, they started to mope off. When I saw him watching me from the distance I shouted at him "What are you looking at? What do you want? Why won't you say something?"

We'd had this thing going on for months. And all he did was stand there and say nothing. What was wrong with him? Why didn't he want to come near me? I could stroke the foxes in my lap but he'd stand there like a statue. Always close but too far away. It was like he didn't want me either.

Things went from bad to worse. At Dad's funeral, Terry was sat with us on the front row, acting like he was one of the family. I still couldn't see what was staring me in the face.

He and Mum were sat together drinking at the meal afterwards. By the evening the whole thing was out in the open. I'd gone home with Connor early. I'd put him to bed, but he'd woken up and I'd just spent almost an hour trying to get him back to sleep again when Mum and Terry got back home. I was going to yell at them for the noise but I saw them in the kitchen all over each other.

That's when it all fell into place. It never did make sense that Dad was getting hammered miles away from home in a pub he'd never been to before. But it did if it was a set up. I knew Terry was there that night. He told us he'd left hours earlier, but that's not what happened. He got Dad tanked up, stuck him in a car and let him drive back knowing he'd go off the road and get himself killed. He could get Dad to do anything Terry. I bet it was easy.

The police had something on Dad, and Dad was going to grass. He was going to tell them about Terry and all the shit they were doing together. So Terry took care of him.

And Mum had to be in on it. The speed in which Terry moved in after Dad died... they must have been at it for months. They didn't even wait to make it look decent. I didn't pay attention to what Mum's comings and goings were, not unless she was looking after Connor. She could've been fucking him while I was at school, while Dad was at work. She went out a lot. She had plenty of chance.

No wonder Mum didn't care that Dad was working all hours. She was getting plenty of attention from someone else. Terry had Dad wrapped around his little finger. Why not give him late shifts so he and Mum could screw behind his back?

It was like having the rug pulled from under you. It took time to really put it all together. If Mum and Terry had been having an affair, how far back did it go? How long had it been?

Because I had a new baby brother. A little brother almost 13 years younger than me.

It doesn't take a rocket scientist to work it all out. Connor wasn't my Dad's, he was Terry's. No wonder Terry was round all the time, asking about him. Why not get rid of Dad so him and Mum could be the perfect couple?

And Connor's eyes were blue. Mum's were brown and so were Dad's, but Terry eyes were bright blue. And that's when the biggest bombshell hit.

My eyes are blue too.

I was already as tall as Mum. And I was tall and thin like Terry. I looked nothing like my Dad. Nothing at all. They'd known Terry for years. I knew that. They'd known him way before I'd ever met him. He'd been away or something. Probably been in prison.

All those fights between Mum and Dad over her flirting with other men. He knew didn't he? He knew she was a whore, who'd fuck anyone. She'd done it before. She'd probably done it with dozens of men.

Why not? She didn't give a fuck about anyone. And Dad had never given her another kid in almost 13 years. What if he'd never been able to do it? What if he'd always been firing blanks?

Can you imagine what it's like – growing up feeling like you don't mean shit? That not even your parents want you. Your parents are bad people, the kind of criminals you watch getting put in prison on TV – and you're their kid. That their poison is in your body. That you carry that with you. That you're worthless because you're the cast off of the worst kind of people. And not even they want you. You're even worse than they are.

Imagine finding out you're even worse than that. That your own mother is the sort of woman who could kill your father – and that he might not even be your father, that you were from something even worse. The type of man who looked at a 13 year old girl and eyed her up and talked like he was thinking about fucking her.

I wanted to be sick. I wanted to slit my wrists and let all the poison out. I didn't want to live. The idea of waiting a few years to inherit some money wasn't good enough anymore. I was poisoned. I wouldn't make it. I wasn't worth it. I hated myself more than I could live with. I just snapped.

I didn't know how to do it. I used to hurt myself, but with blunt things. I never used knives to cut myself. And I didn't want to be saved, not by them. I wanted it over and I wanted it over fast.

So I went over the fence again. But I didn't stop and wait for the foxes; I walked through the overgrown grass and weeds and down the bank. I went over the disused rail line and over to the train line that still worked. A chain fence blocked it off. A train went past. I watched it like a zombie. I walked along the fence until I found a place where it was broken enough for me to squeeze through. There was this part near a concrete post that just lifted right up. I could crawl under, if I wanted to.

I stood there shaking. I don't know if I could've done it or not. I don't really remember what was going on in my head. Maybe I was scared. Maybe I was waiting for a train to come.

I heard footsteps and saw the fox boy was standing by me. He was standing as close to me as he was that first day I saw him. He slapped me in the face.

I fell against the fence. It was a complete surprise. I was shocked. He grabbed my hair and pulled me away from the fence. I screamed and I shouted at him. I was being hysterical. He pulled me along for a few metres until I got my balance back and I pulled away from him.

I fell down in the grass. I never was really sure how old he was. Sometimes he looked young, barely older then 10, then other times he seemed closer to 20. Maybe it was just how he needed to be. Small when he needed to be fast, big when he needed to be strong.

He was strong just a minute ago, but now he was smaller. Less big, less threatening. But still angry. He looked furious.

I got up and started shouting random things "What's wrong with you? You hurt me" before I got hysterical again and burst into tears. I was on all fours crying and he just watched me. He said nothing.

Then another voice said, "You have to protect your cubs."

It was the voice of a little black girl. She can't have been more than six or seven years old. She wasn't even as tall as the grass. She wore a tatty dress and no shoes and her hair was a mess.

"There's nothing more important than your cubs. You have to protect them. You have to all of the time." She was a little bossy boots. She had trouble saying all the words, but she had no problem making herself clear.

They were talking about Connor. "He's not my cub. I'm not his mother. He's nothing to do with me."

The fox boy kicked the ground in anger. Bits of mud flew at me.

"He's your responsibility," the little girl said, although she couldn't pronounce it properly. "You've got to look after him because he has no one else to do it."

"I can't do it." I screamed. "I can't carry on." The fox boy ran over to hit me and I screamed. He changed his mind and turned away, kicking at the ground again.

"You're so selfish," the girl said. "Your little brother needs you to look after him. Or else."

"Or else what?" I asked.

She never said. He hissed at me. I'd never imagined him so aggressive or angry. I'd done nothing wrong. I just couldn't take it anymore. I was at the end of my tether. I felt too worthless. Too wrong. Too dirty.

Foxes appeared in the grass. They ran towards her.

"Your brother's crying. You have to go home."

"Why do you care?" I shouted. "Who are you? What are you?"

The fox boy beat his chest and threw his arms around. She knew what he was saying. She was like his translator.

"He says you have to go back home and stop thinking about yourself." She turned around and started to walk away, saying, "Bad things happen to little children who don't get looked after."

241

They left me there in the dark. Or did they? From then on, I felt like they were always watching me.

I walked home. Connor was crying. Mum and Terry were fucking. I went upstairs and changed him and got him back to sleep, but I was crying about as much as he was. I was trapped there. I was trapped there and I saw no future. Not for myself or for him. I felt so worthless.

Terry didn't waste any time moving himself in. He had his stuff over in a week. Nothing was ever said. Mum never talked to me about it. They were always fucking; at first anyway. Mum looked so pleased about it. It's as if she wanted me to be jealous.

I tried not to talk to him, which would wind Mum up. She'd yell at me and I'd ignore her. He'd say I just missed my Dad, like he was standing up for me. She'd say, "Yeah, but you're here now aren't you?" I swore that day that I would never, ever, call him Dad.

Everything was always tense from then on. I was always on edge. Here was this man, a killer, living in my house. And he was unpredictable. I knew my Dad, I knew what made him tick. All I knew about Terry was that he was a bastard and a pervert and a murderer. I hated the way he looked at me. The grin with the big teeth. He acted like an animal on the prowl. Like he was a coiled spring. He could go from calm to angry in the click of your fingers.

I actually started to miss my Dad. Terry was around a lot more. He worked less hours than Dad did, which was no surprise. He probably let Dad do all the work while him and Mum were screwing somewhere behind his back. After a couple of weeks it was as if Dad had never existed. All his things were gone.

Terry kept his work private and I didn't dare ask him about it. He had this way of looking at you so you knew that whatever he was doing was none of your business. He was always on his mobile, a big chunky old one, and took his calls where he thought I couldn't hear. And even when I did listen in, really carefully, he'd never say much. He'd speak in really short sentences. Always just a few short words, so someone listening like me would never get it.

I could barely sleep at night. He had to know about Nan's will. He knew that the house belonged to me. And that if I went, Mum would get it. And then he'd get it. I'd barricade my door at night, and start to panic if I heard him outside.

I couldn't rely on Mum to stop him, why should she? She'd already looked away once. Why would she stop with me? She didn't even like me.

I might've wanted to kill myself, but that's a lot different to wanting someone else to kill you. I was terrified of him and what he might do. There were days when I didn't want to get out of bed, that I cried myself to sleep. I planned my escape route out of my room. How I could get out the window and across the garden if he got through the door.

Only Connor kept me going. He'd done nothing wrong. What had he done to deserve all this? If I wasn't there to look after the little sod, who else would? I felt so guilty about trying to kill myself. I would've left him alone.

His little face was all that kept me going. As much as I hated the poisoned blood we both had, knowing that I could protect him was worth hanging on for. But it was never easy.

I hated it when Terry was with Connor. It was bad enough that he was his real father, but to see him touching him, holding him. That made me sick.

Terry liked to play games with people. This one time, I'd managed to get Connor asleep and I saw Terry watching us. He could do that; sneak up on you without you noticing.

"You're really good with him you are."

I didn't say anything and he just kept staring.

"You should do this full-time you know? Looking after kids. You'd be good at it. Make a nice little job for you."

I was waiting for him to go but he wouldn't. I couldn't stand him watching me. I put Connor in his crib and tried to get out the room. But Terry wouldn't move. I tried to get round him, but he wouldn't shift.

"I want to get past."

"What's the magic word?"

"Can I get past please?"

He moved and stretched out his arm and said "Oh after you your majesty."

He was always doing shit like that. Letting me know he was in control. He didn't care that I hated him; as long as I knew he was in charge.

He leered at me a lot. I was still a child. But he used to look at me and make comments about my clothes and my look. It creeped me out and what's worse is I think Mum knew and would try to rub it in my face that they were together. Like throw herself over him if I came in the room and stare like she wanted to see if I was jealous. It was disgusting.

Terry wasn't a pushover like Dad. Mum couldn't bully or manipulate him. He wouldn't have that. He was even more old fashioned than Dad. He expected dinner on the table and the house to be cleaned up. That was her job, that's why she was at home all day and he was at work. There were rows, but Mum ended up doing what she was told because Terry wasn't going to be told any different.

If she threw a tantrum and tried to get his sympathy, Terry would walk away. If she didn't make dinner, suddenly there'd be less money; she hadn't earned it. If she was whinging about something, he'd leave and go out. Dad used to be worried about the attention Mum was getting from other guys, but now it was the other way around. She was worried he was going to go off and find someone else. I got a bit of fun out of watching her be manipulated.

End of the day, she needed him. She wasn't getting money from anywhere else. And she was still waiting for the big payoff; the one Dad always said was coming. Terry kept saying things were going to pay off and there was big cash starting to come in. But that was just to keep her on the hook.

After getting rid of all Dad's stuff, Terry made himself at home in the attic. He cleaned out all the junk that'd been up there since before Nan died and started to go up there randomly and spend time by himself. He used to call it his office. No one was allowed up there.

I could hear him moving about late at night. I didn't go up and look because there was no way you could get up there without anyone hearing. I was tempted sometimes when they were out, but I figured I was better off not knowing. And I still might get caught then. I couldn't go taking chances. I didn't know what he was capable of. I was afraid all of the time.

When school started again, I had to worry about Mum looking after Connor. I fed him and changed him in the morning and I got home as soon as possible afters school to check he was still ok.

I didn't see or talk to the foxes for the rest of the summer. I was angry with the fox boy. He'd hurt me, been angry with me. I felt betrayed by him. He'd saved my life but it didn't feel like that. He'd stopped me from doing what I thought I had to do. I hated him because he'd stopped me and I hated him because I knew he was right. I'd almost left Connor behind and I hated myself for being so selfish. And I hated the fox boy for making me hate myself.

I was so mixed up. I didn't know what I wanted. He'd not been the hero I wanted him to be, that I thought he was. He was more like an animal. I wasn't sure what to think anymore.

The first day back at school I had to have a private talk with my new form tutor, Mr Summersby. He'd taught me maths in the first year. Lots of the girls fancied him, and to be fair, he looked all right back then. When the class had gone for break he asked me to stay behind and I thought I was in trouble for smoking.

What he really wanted was to say sorry about my dad dying. He could imagine how tough that was and if I ever needed to I could talk to him, any time I wanted.

This was out of the blue – someone taking time to ask how I was. It's amazing how invisible you are if you just keep yourself quiet. Teachers only pay attention to noisy kids. You have to be a pain in the arse before they care about the quiet ones.

I didn't give much away, but I did let slip that Mum was

already shacked up with someone else. That bothered him, but I didn't talk much. Said that I was ok. I spent most of the time looking after my little brother.

I could've told him everything, but I didn't see the point. I didn't think he could help me. And I had more reason to be afraid of my parents – Mum and Terry – than ever before. I'd always been taught to be secretive and not to tell people things. That's probably why all my friends were foxes.

He wasn't very satisfied, but I had classes to go to, so that was the end of that. Problem was that he had a nephew, a little scrawny thing called Guy. He was in my year, and if I looked a bit old for my age, he looked a lot younger. He was really small and innocent.

He had a thing for me. We walked the same way home, and he'd try to catch up with me or wait for me so he could walk with me. He didn't give up for a while. I wasn't very nice to him. But he was pretty harmless.

It all stopped eventually. When it started to get dark early he insisted on walking me all the way home, as if I needed protecting. I said "Whatever, it's your time to waste." Maybe he thought I was playing hard to get.

When we got there, he got a view of what my life was really like. The house was looking a lot worse. The front garden was overgrown and in a mess. Some of the junk Terry had taken out of the attic was there, wet and rotten.

And Terry and Mum were having a shouting match. A proper row you could hear down the road.

He said, "Is that your Mum and Dad shouting?"

"It's my Mum and her boyfriend," I said back. "They do this all the time."

Guy didn't try to walk home with me again after that. He'd been well scared off. He told Mr Summersby all about it though. A few days after he asked me again for a private chat.

He was concerned about my home situation. He said it wasn't because of what his nephew had said, even though it was. He kept mentioning my parents having fights. But he was also talking about lateness, days off, me looking after my baby brother. It didn't help that I'd come in with baby formula on my shirt after Connor had spit on me.

He was asking a lot of questions. No one had really done this to me before. I used to just fob people off about my parents. If they didn't turn up to parent's evening, it was because they were busy. If my school uniform was dirty, it was because the washing machine was still broken. If I had a bruise, it was because I'd fallen over. Perhaps if I'd have had more bruises, a teacher would've asked me before. That would've been big and obvious for them to notice. The cuts I gave myself I made high up on my legs so no one would see them.

But I was starting to crack up. When he kept asking questions, my heart started thumping. The night before I'd gone to the kitchen for something to drink late at night and Terry was sat in there. I didn't even notice until he said, "What are you up to?"

I screamed a little, I was so surprised.

"Calm down, I'm just saying hello," he said.

I poured myself some milk from the fridge and went quickly for the door.

"What's your rush?" he put his leg out to stop me.

"I'm tired."

"Stay. Keep us company for a bit. Your mother's fast asleep."

"No thank you."

"Why not?"

"I'm tired. I just told you."

"You don't like me much do ya?"

I skipped over his leg and went back upstairs. I went to the bathroom a few minutes later and when I came out he was on the landing waiting for me.

"You look nice in your nighty," he said.

I didn't say anything and tried to walk around him.

"You should be nice to me."

I tried to push past, but he shoved me back hard.

"You're a cheeky bitch, aren't you? I work all day and night, pay for your food and your clothes and everything else and you can't even be nice to me."

"What do you want?"

"Maybe you should do some work, for a change? I can think of few folk who'd be interested in your talents."

He tried to grab me, between the legs. I screamed and hit at him until he let me go. I ran to my bedroom and barricaded the door so fast. I could hear him laughing in the hallway.

I was running out of options. It wasn't safe for me there. I was between a rock and a hard place.

I wanted to scream and stay silent. I wanted to stay quiet like I always did, but knew I couldn't keep doing that forever. It was tearing me apart.

I just started blurting things out.

"Mum's not a very good parent. I have to check up on her, make sure Connor's ok."

"But that's not your responsibility, to look after him," Mr Summersby said. "You're only 12. You're at school."

"I'm 13 week after next."

"But you're supposed to be studying."

"That's just how it is, isn't it?"

"And this man, Terry. What is he like?"

I couldn't tell him. I just couldn't. I felt my heart thumping and tears starting up in my eyes.

"He helps sometimes. Makes sure Mum does what's she supposed to."

"Still. I'm very concerned about this."

"It's not your problem."

"It is if it's interrupting your school work."

"It won't. I'll try harder."

"That's not the point."

"I didn't ask for your help." I was trembling. I did want his help. I just daren't ask for it.

"Can I go now?"

Before I left he said, "You can ask for it though. Anytime you want. I'll be here for you. You can trust me."

I didn't answer him. If only he'd known what he was getting himself into.

A day or two later, I got home and I could hear Connor crying. He was on the floor in the living room. He wasn't old enough to crawl, but he kept trying; he'd role over, get stuck and start crying. I didn't know how long he'd been on the floor but he was screaming his eyes out. His nappy was dirty. He could've been there for hours. Mum was on the sofa passed out. Her own child was screaming his head off and she wasn't hearing it.

I yelled at her but she still didn't do anything. I thought maybe something was wrong, so I started to shake her. She groaned and moaned, so she obviously wasn't dead. I shouted at her again and went to clean Connor up. I didn't even know if he'd been fed.

While I was making his formula, she staggered into the kitchen. She looked tired and hungover. But not hungover like she normally was. She was weird, like a zombie. I started yelling at her again. I wondered if she could even hear me.

Finally she shouted back. "Everything's fine. Nothing happened. Get off my back."

She wandered off. And that was not like her. First time in my life she didn't fight for the last word.

I didn't understand right way, not until later when I was taking the bins out. There were syringes in the bin.

Mum and Dad had done drugs; Dad had sold them sometimes. They weren't very secret about it. But they did it just sometimes, not all the time.

I'd seen Mum be a bit spacy before. Terry did a lot of weed, so she did too. I didn't know much about drugs then and what they do to you, but I knew if she was using syringes she was now on something much worse.

It was another great move by Terry. Why row with someone when you can give them something to keep them quiet all day? He was smart, you had to give him that. She'd have to do everything he wanted now if she wanted her fix.

I had plenty of time to work this out. It was hours before I got Connor settled down. If it was like I thought it was, and he was trying to get her hooked on something, then I had a massive problem. I couldn't give a shit if she wanted to kill herself. But she had to look after Connor. I couldn't be there all the time.

Terry came home while I was trying to get him to sleep. I just didn't know what I could say to him. I couldn't tell him I knew what he was doing. I couldn't go accusing him off anything. I didn't know what he might do. But I was fuming. I was so angry and frightened and nearly hysterical. That's probably why Connor wouldn't go to sleep. Because I was like a crazy person about to blow.

When I went downstairs, I had to try and walk normal. If I went down there marching – girl on a mission – he'd get nasty with me. I had to try and be calm.

He was on the sofa smoking with a can of Carling next to him. I walked up to him and froze. I couldn't think what to say.

"What do you want?" He wasn't in a good mood. I had to put my hands behind my back so he wouldn't see me trembling.

"I got home today and Connor was crying. Mum had left him on the floor."

He smoked his cigarette and didn't say anything.

"She was passed out on the sofa. He was crying his head off and she didn't even notice."

"But you sorted it out?"

"Yes, I sorted it out."

"So it's ok then?"

"That's not the point. Connor can't be left on his own. He's not even 6 months old."

"I don't know what you want me to do about it. Talk to your mum."

It was like my heart was pounding in my head. I had fear and anger pulling me in both directions. I felt like I might explode.

"You can't give her that stuff. Not while she's looking after Connor."

"What's that?" He twitched, but that's it.

"I don't know what she's taking. But she can't have it if she has Connor to look after."

"I don't know what you're talking about." He stubbed his cigarette out. I wasn't getting through. My brother's life was in danger but I couldn't get through to him.

250

"She's on drugs and she's supposed to be looking after her son."

He took a swig of lager.

"Don't you understand? He could die. He could get hurt. Anything could happen to him. You can't give her that shit anymore, whatever it is."

"I don't take orders from you."

I just lost it. I screamed "We'll you'd better listen. Because if I come home and she's like that again I'm going to be straight on the phone to social services."

He was off the sofa like lightening. He pushed me across the room until I went smack bang against the wall. His forearm was shoved right up against my neck. I was on my tiptoes. I was choking. I couldn't breathe.

He watched me struggle. "No you won't," he said. "You're gonna behave yourself aren't you?"

I tried to nod.

"This is my house!" he screamed straight in my face. "And you'll do what I tell you. Or else I'll fuck you. I will fuck you up."

He started talking quiet again. "You understand me don't you?" He was sarcastic, but I nodded anyway.

"Good girl. Now get the fuck out of my sight."

He dropped his arm and I got out of there. I landed on all fours in the hallway. Coughing and choking, I crawled to the back door and got myself out.

I ran. I went over the fence for the first time in months and ran through the grass. I didn't go looking for the foxes, not deliberately. But when I couldn't see them, I made my mind up to find them. I ended up walking along the disused rail line. I don't know why I thought that would take me anywhere. I just had to go somewhere.

I walked maybe half a mile. I found an old railway tunnel that went into the side of a steep hill. A road ran above it, over the entrance to the tunnel. The car lights shone some light on us as they drove over. I stood at the opening of the tunnel and dozens of little eyes stared back at me.

The boy walked out of the dark. He looked tall and strong and mature.

Foxes surrounded us. We stood staring at each other for just a moment. Then I threw my arms around him and cried. I let it all out. And he held me and let me get it all out.

I don't know how long I was there, in his arms. It felt like a long time. When I finally let go, it was like something had passed between us. He stared at me and then slowly walked back into the tunnel. Somehow I knew I had to leave him then.

Something in me said that now things were going to be all right. He was there for me and things would be ok. I don't know how I knew. I just knew.

And I was right. Two days later I was walking home when a fox came up to me in the street. He just strolled on up to me as if there was nothing weird about it at all.

It was my friend with the torn ear. He stared at me for a second and then turned around and went walking away. He kept looking back to me to see if I'd follow him. So I did.

He had me walking for miles. I didn't know how long this was going to take. But I knew it had to be important. He took me out to the middle of town where there were factories and offices and warehouses. Did you know foxes can climb trees? Half-ear took me to a brick wall and then, to get over, he went straight up a tree and along a branch to get on top.

I had to jump and pull myself up. It took a couple of goes but I got up there. He didn't warn me about the rows of rusty barbed wire hanging over the other side. I got over, it wasn't sharp anymore, just hard to get around. I was still in my school uniform. I wasn't dressed for any of this.

I landed in a yard. It was a really popular place for fly tipping. There was junk everywhere. Someone had managed to get a whole fridge-freezer over the wall. It's got to be easier to just take it to the tip, surely?

There was a tall factory building there. It was three or four floors high. It looked kind of weird, this big building surrounded by open space. It looked like there might've been other buildings once, because you could still see some foundations.

There weren't any lights on. Most of the windows were boarded up. It was a derelict.

I was going to creep closer. But the yard was lit up by headlights. I ducked down behind the fridge. I heard the old gate being opened. A van drove into the yard. The headlights went off. It was pretty dark but I could see a couple of guys get out. They didn't go to the front doors; they went around the side of the building to some stairs that went down to a basement door. A fat guy came up to meet them.

I had to look hard before I realised they were Terry's mates; I'd seen them hanging around with him and Dad.

I remembered this was his business – security for old buildings, factories and derelicts. Guys started coming up the stairs with boxes and they were loading them into the back of the van. It took them maybe five minutes. They were pretty quick.

When it was all done they said goodbye to the fat guy and drove back out, only turning the headlights on when they were through the gate.

I waited a couple more minutes to come out of hiding. I went to the basement stairs and walked down quietly. There was a heavy door with no handle on the outside. There was a window next to it that was not boarded up, but it had iron bars over it.

I looked in. It was dark and really hard to see anything. There was this sudden flash of light and a man appeared from nowhere. The light disappeared just as fast. I panicked and ran up the stairs, which was stupid because they were made of metal and I made a racket. I must've been lucky because nobody came out after me.

Half-ear had also deserted me by then. I had to drag that fridge-freezer to the wall to climb out. I had a long walk home to help me figure out what had happened. And it took me a while, but I got what the foxes were showing me.

It was a weed farm. Clever Terry. Old factories and empty buildings are great places to grow weed. No one's gonna come looking around, not when you're the security who're there to keep the place safe. You can hook yourselves up to the power and do your growing in private.

I guess buildings with basements are best because you wouldn't want people to see the light. That flash of light I saw was one of those rubber flap doorways you get. Someone had pushed through, and the bright light got out for just a second. Can't grow plants in the dark.

It was a good idea really. Shame a scumbag like Terry came up with it. A lot of weed had come out of that building. I wondered how much money it was making him. I had a feeling I could go up to the attic and find out. That had to be where he was stashing his cash. As well as whatever he was giving Mum.

But he couldn't be in this on his own. He had to have partners, people to work with to get the stuff out. People he might get in trouble with if he upset them.

I was making guesses. But they made sense. The foxes had shown me this place for a reason, so I could take Terry down. Who knew how many weed farms he had. But there had to be a lot of money in this one. And if something happened to all that money, then bad things would probably happen to Terry. Either his partners were going to be upset or the police were going to wonder why this burning building smelt like a giant spliff.

Seemed like the easiest thing to do, set the whole place on fire. I waited until the next night. It was dark by the time I left school. I changed in the toilets into all my best black gear. I had plenty of black clothes; I was starting to go a bit goth.

I'd taken the spare petrol can from Mum's car. It was empty, but I passed a petrol station on my way. Nobody asked any questions. I bought myself a new lighter too.

I went the same way I did the day before. Climbed over the wall in the same place with the petrol can in my backpack.

It was amazingly easy really. All I had to have a think about was how I could get the fire to really take hold. The basement door meant I had a really good place to get it started. There was tons of rubbish I could use for fuel. That stuff would go up a treat. But would it be enough to get the whole building going?

I put bags of rubbish and cardboard down the stairs. I was worried about making too much noise, but I could hear a radio going inside, so I didn't need to be very quiet.

I had to make sure the fire got inside somehow. If I poured petrol around the door, I could be sure some would go under and get in. That was a start, but it wasn't enough. I found an old beer bottle in the rubbish and made myself a petrol bomb with a bit of newspaper.

I filled the space around the door right up to the bottom of the window. I poured out the petrol, some over the rubbish, lots down by the doorway and plenty around the window. I wasn't sure I could get the petrol bomb through the window. So I threw a rock first.

I scored a direct hit, breaking the glass. Then I lit the paper in the bottle and threw that at the window. It didn't get through; it broke on the bars and made this big explosion of flames.

A ring of fire burned around the window and it ran straight onto the rubbish. I had some sacks of rubbish left; I threw them against the window, thinking some of the burning stuff might fall through. I had three bags but I lost my nerve after throwing the first two. There were noises coming from inside.

I hadn't thought about how the people inside were going to get out. I just thought there must be other ways out. I didn't hear about anyone getting hurt.

I ran back over the yard and got up on the wall. I sat on top and watched the fire for a few seconds. I realised there that it didn't matter if the whole thing went up. All I needed was to get the police to notice to cause trouble.

You're probably thinking, why didn't I just call the police in the first place? I don't think I ever really thought about it. I had no reason to trust them. All my parents had ever done was say bad things about them. And I wanted to do this to Terry. I wanted to hurt him myself.

I changed back into my school uniform in a McDonalds toilet on the way back. I didn't know what I was going to come home to. Terry had a mobile, he might know already. He might be at home, he might not be. I hoped he'd just bolt and never

255

come back. But if there was cash in the attic, he'd have to come back for it. As long as he was gone, I didn't really care.

I didn't really know what would happen. In my head some nightmare scenarios were playing out, like Terry deciding to take Connor away with him. Or if he somehow found out it was me; even though there was no reason for him to think it was, there might be some clue I'd left (I almost left the petrol can behind), then I'd end up dead. I don't think I'd really thought the whole thing through. I wanted to save me and Connor. But if I died or got sent to prison, who'd look after him? Who'd make sure he was safe?

There was no point being a hero if Connor wasn't safe. I felt knots tying in my stomach.

I'd been anxious all day. That afternoon before I did it, I was having second thoughts, even though I knew I couldn't pull out. My last lesson at school was with Mr Summersby. I was the last one to leave the class. I went up to him at his desk.

"Sir?"

"Yes Katy."

"Did you mean what you said? About being there if I wanted to ask for help."

"Is something the matter? Katy?"

"Not yet. I just wanted to know."

"I'm happy to help you with anything. All you have to do is ask. Anytime."

I nodded and I left. He called after me, but I left it there. It wasn't much, but I needed to feel like I had some kind of safety net. And someone real who could help me. I just had to hope he meant it.

When I got home, Mum came straight for me. "Have you seen Terry?" she was in a panic. Losing money would do that to her.

"No, why would I?" I said back.

"I need to speak to him, it's important."

"What do you want me to do? I'm not going to see him before you do."

"Don't get smart with me – this is not the fucking time!"

256

She was too nervous to really get on at me. She was pacing around. She kept trying to get him on the phone.

I heard a little squeal from the living room. Connor was still up, playing with his blocks. I knew he was going to be a smart one. He was always building with his blocks.

He'd started speaking a little by then. He used to call me Kay-be. He was saying that ages before he said Mama or Dada.

It was tough to get him to sleep because I think he knew how scared I was. The waiting was the worst part. At least I thought it was. It was all so random. The more I thought about it, the more I realised I didn't know anything and I didn't know what was going to happen.

When Terry got home, it happened with a bang. The front door slammed and I felt my heart stop. Connor had only just fallen asleep. I was still in his room watching him. I heard footsteps stomping up the stairs. I heard Mum shrieking.

"Where the hell have you been?"

Terry wasn't answering her.

"They've been calling me all night, trying to find you. Why didn't you answer?"

I heard the attic steps hit the landing. This is it, I thought. He's going to take his money and run.

I watched through a gap in the doorway.

"What's going on Terry? Why are you ignoring me?"

She started to go up the ladder.

"What's happened? What's – Jesus Christ!"

She slipped down the ladder and fell on the floor. Terry stepped down. He had a sawn-off shotgun. He was pointing it at Mum.

She backed away, up against the wall. He put the end of the gun against her face.

"Stop it Terry. Please, don't point that at me. Stop it. Stop it." He got right up close to her. She was crying.

"What's the golden rule?" he said. His eyes were wild. He looked terrifying.

"What?"

"What's the golden fucking role?"

"Oh – we don't talk about the business."

"We don't talk about the business, that's right. You don't stick your nose in, and you keep your mouth shut.

"So what did you hear on the phone?"

Mum was crying. "Nothing, I heard nothing."

"That's right. You heard nothing."

He lowered the gun.

"I just got worried. Worried about you. And all that money, our money, up in smoke."

"Our money? Our money! That's a fucking laugh isn't it?"

He was poking her in the stomach with the gun.

"When did you fucking do anything, other than moan and complain and fucking nag and go on and on and on. You've never earned a fucking penny in your whole life! Never done a fucking day's work in your whole life!"

Mum was wailing, tears streaming down her face.

"Don't you worry darlin'. Terry's going to take care of it. Terry's gonna look after everything for you, like always."

He went down the stairs. Mum landed on all fours.

"Terry wait," she screamed. "Come back! Come back here."

She got up and ran after him. I heard the front door hit the wall and the sound of her voice screeching outside.

For a little time things were quiet. Connor had slept through the whole thing.

He wasn't going to run. He was going to fight. He was off after someone. Whatever was in the attic, he'd left it behind. Except for the gun. He'd been keeping weapons in the house.

I had to know what was up there. Here was my chance.

I went up the ladder. I thought I was going to see big sacks of cash or bricks of cocaine, but when I got up there, there was hardly anything at all. There was a filing cabinet, with all the drawers locked. There was a chair and a table. There were newspapers on the table, with doodles and scribbles on them. There was an armchair and a box next to it with porn mags in.

Terry couldn't just be going up there for a wank. The filing cabinet must have something in it. But you wouldn't hide something important in a drawer; it was too obvious.

I heard the front door slam. Mum was back. I slid down the ladder and hid myself back in Connor's room. She was crying downstairs, I decided to stay with Connor.

I just had to wait again. Maybe he wouldn't come back. He might get himself shot or picked up by the police.

But he did come back, hours later. I'd fallen asleep on the floor. I wouldn't have thought that was possible, but it takes it out of you, all the stress. I must've drifted off.

I heard him on his phone in the garden. He was trying to talk to someone and be quiet but he kept shouting and getting angry. He swore a lot. I couldn't really hear what he said without opening the window, and he'd probably hear that.

He came upstairs later and went into his and Mum's room. I could hear them talking, but that didn't last long. They were fucking minutes later.

It seemed like whatever was going to happen was over for the night. There was going to be more drama, but it was looking like Terry wasn't going to take off after all.

I got off the floor, checked Connor was ok, and went back to my room to sleep. There'd still be trouble about the factory. I just had to hold on and keep waiting. I'd set fire to more places if I had to. I just had to do what I always did, what I did best: keep my head down and stay quiet.

Turns out that of all the things I'd done, going back to my bedroom to sleep was the worst decision of all. When I woke up in the morning Connor was gone.

I didn't panic, not at first; Mum might've got up early and taken him downstairs. But when I checked there was no one around. That's when I started to lose it. Mum was fast asleep. There was no one in the whole house.

Terry was gone. And I thought he'd taken Connor with him. I'd have to call the police and tell them everything. I didn't care what happened to me. I didn't care. All Connor's things were still there, but Terry was crazy enough not to care about taking them.

Then I saw that the backdoor was open. I went out on to the patio. There was an old cracked plate there. And there was a dummy on it. Connor's dummy.

The foxes had taken Connor in the night. I didn't understand. Why would they do that? They were supposed to be my friends. What had they done? I walked through the overgrown grass in my slippers, wearing my pyjamas, in the freezing cold. It was still dark outside; there was fog everywhere.

I got down to the old rail track and started to run. He was standing in the fog, waiting for me. Connor wasn't with him.

"Where is he?" I yelled. I pushed him. He grabbed my arms. I struggled. He pushed me down onto the track.

We were outside the tunnel. I could hear a baby cry. It was Connor, I was sure. I could tell.

I got to my feet. The boy looked ready to stop me. I looked back at him and into the tunnel. There were shadows there, lots of them. They looked like children. Loads of children.

The little bossy girl appeared out of the weeds and grass. She held a naked baby. I went straight for it. But when I put out my arms, I saw it wasn't Connor. It was a different baby.

"Where is he," I screamed.

"He's safe. We are looking after him."

"But why have you taken him. I was looking after him."

"He was not safe!" the girl shouted. "You are a bad mother."

I was about to say I wasn't his mother. But I was. He had no one else. No one else cared about him. Not really. Not properly.

"I'm looking after him. I'm taking care of him." I was starting to cry.

"He is not safe. There is a predator in his home. We told you if you could not look after him, we would take him."

"I tried. I thought I was doing what you wanted!"

"He will not be safe until the predator is gone."

From nowhere the boy pulled out a knife and I nearly screamed.

"You have to kill the predator," she said. "Then it will be safe."

I looked at her and I looked at him. He held a bread knife. It was old and rusty.

"Who are you?" I shouted. "What are you?"

"We're the lost children. And we look after our own."

The little baby cried a little. The little girl, who was barely big enough to carry him, started to rock him side to side.

The boy dropped the knife. The two of them walked back into the tunnel. Foxes ran through the grass after them.

I watched them and looked down at the knife. I picked it up with my hands shaking. Any knife would probably have been better for killing, but this was what they'd given me.

I walked back wanting to be sick. I wanted Terry dead, Christ I did. But kill someone? And get away with it... He was bigger than me. Stronger than me. Better than me.

But I had to do it. And plan it. And get away with it. Not for me, for Connor. To save him from whatever it was that they'd do to him. Turn him into a fox. Eat him. I didn't know. I didn't understand. It didn't make sense, but I didn't have any time to think about it.

Connor was my responsibility. I was his mother. I had to do it. I had to get rid of Terry once and for all. I had to be strong. I had to be smart. I had to be clever.

I was so cold it was hurting me. I went over the fence and back into the garden. I moved the plate and the dummy. I had some time to plan. It was only eight in the morning.

I couldn't kill Terry in the house. I could get hurt and I had to get rid of the body. I thought about the land outside the house, where the foxes were. The body could go down there. Nobody went down there. I could hide him in the bushes. The foxes could eat him for all I cared. But how could I get him down there?

I had another problem – Mum. What was she going to do? I wouldn't have minded killing her too. But I needed her. I couldn't raise Connor on my own, not legally. She had to stay around. But she wanted Terry and more than that she wanted his money.

She could be up any time. What was I going to tell her about Connor? I was going to skip school. That was obvious. But what I could do with Connor?

261

My mind was all over the place – and then there was a knock at the door.

I looked into the hallway. Through the frosted glass I could see people outside. It was the police.

They knocked a second time. Mum wouldn't get up, I was sure. Even if she was awake, she was used to hiding from the pigs.

I saw one go look through the living room window. They went after a few minutes. I didn't need them on my back too. I already had enough on my plate.

I moved fast. Even though Connor was gone, I got his pushchair ready and all the things I needed to take him out. I went to Mum's room and woke her up.

"I'm taking Connor for his doctor's appointment."

"What appointment?"

"His check-up."

"What check-up?"

"I knew you'd forget."

"You never said anything about an appointment."

"Yes I did. I knew you'd forget. I'm taking the day off school to do it."

Best thing I could do was get myself out of there and she wouldn't realise Connor was gone. It was totally surreal. I was walking for hours with an empty pushchair. I had to bulk it up to make it look like he was in there.

I was worried the police were watching. But no one followed me down the street. I called school from a payphone to say Mum was ill so I was looking after Connor.

It was freezing and I'd almost no money. I bought a McDonald's breakfast, but was too worried to sit down all day. My plan – which I was still working out – depended on Mum getting off her face and putting herself out of action. I figured if she was on her own for hours, she'd have no reason not to get stoned.

I also needed it to get dark. I couldn't take care of Terry in the daylight. And I had to find out where his money was.

I spent hours walking around in circles. I drifted back to my house at about 1 o'clock. I was scared I was being watched.

If the police were watching, they wouldn't do it from a cop car. They'd use a normal one. But they didn't know what I looked like so I went up and down the street to see if anyone was watching.

Stupid thing was that if I got back and Mum was still up and about, I'd have to go away and come back again.

I checked the cars were all empty then risked going to the front door. I listened in. I couldn't hear anything but the radio in the kitchen. The living room looked empty. I had to chance it.

I unlocked the door so quietly and once I was in I checked out the downstairs and then headed upstairs. She was in her room, in her dressing gown. She was lying face up on the bed – gone to the world.

I'd been lucky. It looked like she'd got out the shower, thought, fuck it, and got high. Her dressing gown was open; she was flashing the world, stoned off her face.

I could've just done her in there and then. And believe me, I thought about it. But it was too messy. And there'd be a body. And the police would know she'd been murdered, so I decided against it.

What I needed to do was go back up to the attic. I hadn't heard Terry go up in morning, so I guessed what I was looking for was still there. I could break open the filing cabinet, but what was the point? He wouldn't put his money somewhere so obvious. He'd have to hide it. But there was nothing else in there. I checked the seat cushions in the chairs, rummaged through his porn, but I knew I'd never find it there.

I thought about the floorboards, but that'd be too noisy. He wasn't going to go hammering around at night. And then I just had this idea to look up at the roof.

It all snapped into place. I could see a little join in the roof insulation. I just reached up and pulled. I stripped it off and down fell the money. Wads of cash tied up with elastic bands. It was almost fun. I tore off the insulation and made it rain cash.

I had the bait for my trap.

There was so much money; I didn't have time to count it. It was all in £50s and £20s. I filled up this sports bag and had to fill all the pockets and I still couldn't fit it all in. I had a dozen wads of cash leftover. I stashed them in my room just in case.

Terry had filled almost a whole side of the roof. It was incredible. I couldn't believe he'd hoarded all this money. What was he going to do with it all?

I didn't waste time thinking about it. I went back to Mum's room and slowly, quietly, I turned the whole place over. I opened up and tipped out draws, messed up her closet, scattered her shoes, emptied storage boxes and her jewellery boxes. I made it look like someone had gone through the place to find her valuables and steal them.

After I'd made a load of mess, I closed the door and found something to wedge under the handle. A little bookcase from Connor's room did the job. No matter how long she was high, she couldn't get out now.

I trashed the whole house. Turned the whole place upside down. I wrecked the kitchen – threw things out of draws and emptied out the cupboards. I pulled up the carpet in the dinning room, turned over potted plants. I tore open seat covers in the living room, wrecked the telly, and tipped over this big display cabinet. If I hadn't been so tensed up I would've had fun.

When I was done, I took a shovel from the shed and went to the wasteland and dug myself a hole. I did it down behind some young trees and bushes just to be sure I wouldn't be spotted. I didn't need the hole to be deep, just to cover the bag of money.

I buried it and went back to the house. I had to wait till it started to get dark. It was winter so it only took an hour or two.

When the sun was almost gone, I got on the phone. It went straight to his answerphone.

"Terry, some guys have been over. They've wrecked the place. Turned every room upside down. Get over here now."

I hung up and waited. Again. The seconds just got more unbearable and unbearable. You know, this was it. My life on the life. Connor's life on the line. Life and death and waiting for it to happen.

I sat on the stairs with my heart pumping watching for his car to appear out front. I got to my feet when it did. I saw his shape appear in the glass, coming to the door. Longest few seconds of my life. He threw it open and came right up to me.

"What's happened!" he shouted.

"Two guys were here, they were smashing the place up when I got home."

He pushed past and started up to the attic and saw the ladder on the landing.

"Yeah, they went up there. But they didn't find your money. No need to panic." He spun round. He had that look on his face again.

"You were lucky," I shouted. I had to get his attention and stop him from seeing Mum's room blocked up. "All they had to do was look up and spot the roof was all messed up and out of shape. Took me about 30 seconds to find it."

He went to grab me and I pushed him away but slipped and fell down the last few stairs.

I was back on my feet again before he could touch me.

"I saved your money. Don't worry. I thought they might be back. They ran out when I got home."

He was sizing me up. Deciding whether to listen or rip my head off.

"I hid your money in case they came back. I didn't think they'd be scared off long by a girl."

He tried to grab me by my shirt. When I stopped him, he got hold of my hair instead.

"You show me where my fucking money is. You show me right now!"

"Let go and I'll show you," I pushed him and he let his grip slip.

"It's this way," I shoved him for a change and led him to the garden. "Mum and Connor are ok by they way," I said, but he didn't care. I took him to the fence: "It's on the other side, I hid it where no one would look."

"You go first."

I needed him to get ahead of me. I went over and waited for him to climb after me. When he landed his jacket dragged

265

on the top of the fence. I saw the shotgun stuffed into the back of his trousers. I was breathless, speechless for a second.

"Where now?"

I pointed with my arm shaking. "Over there, by those trees and bushes."

He started off and I followed him. I couldn't do it straight away. I had to wait till I was a bit further away from the houses and windows and risk of people watching. This was it. This was the time to do it.

I had the fox's knife with me. Why I didn't swap it for a better one I don't know. He was walking in front of me. I was staring at his back. All I had to do was raise my arm and push it in. Just push it forward and push it in.

I held the knife out and I could see it shake. He was walking fast and I had to skip to catch up. And then I slipped and he looked around at me and saw it.

"What the fuck is this?" he said. Suddenly he was smiling at me. He started to laugh.

"Well, well, what do we have here?"

I stepped back. "Well go on then?" he shouted.

I looked at him. I looked at the knife. He hit me. I fell down and I lost the knife. He jumped on me. He grabbed my hair and punched me in the face.

"Where the fuck is my money?"

I thought this was it. He's going to kill me. He raised his fist again. I turned to look away when I saw the foxes come.

One ran up his back and put his teeth through his ear. Terry bolted up and the fox fell, taking half his ear with him.

They were jumping up and scratching. Clawing his legs and scratching at his back and at his belly. Some were running and butting him in the stomach.

He was swearing and shouting and stumbling about. But he was still on both feet and I saw him reach for the shotgun.

I found a rotting tree branch in the grass. I couldn't let him shoot them.

Terry couldn't aim the gun; the foxes were close and all over and butting him and scratching at him. He wasn't looking at me and only just saw me the second before I smacked him.

The end of the branch broke off when I whacked him on the forehead. It was so satisfying.

He fell down and the foxes surrounded him. But instead of tearing at him they looked to me to give him the fatal blow.

He tried to roll on his side. He was reaching around for his shotgun in the grass. I gave him another smack in the head. I kept smacking him until there was nothing left of that rotten branch.

He was face down in the grass. He'd stopped moving. I could see blood in his hair. The foxes moved in. They took hold of Terry with their teeth. They pulled and struggled and dragged him through the grass. I followed them. I should've helped really.

I knew where he was going. We went over one rail line and on to the next. To the same spot in the chain link fence where I went when I thought I couldn't take it anymore. I held up the broken part so they could drag Terry through.

I watched them pull him onto the tracks and then run for safety.

There was a train coming. I watched Terry to see if he would move; I didn't know if I'd killed him or not.

The train lights were bright. The driver saw him but the train was going too fast. There was the shrieking sound of the brakes. I watched Terry as the train wheels crunched him up. I saw his feet and legs spin around as the wheels went over him.

For a minute I felt nothing. I was frozen to the spot. I only went to hide when I saw the driver's door open.

I crawled through the grass and I went back to the old train track. I walked down the track almost calmly. My heartbeat went steady. It was done. He was gone. I'd done what they'd asked for. I felt strong. I didn't feel one ounce of guilt for Terry. Not one bit.

I didn't run. I walked slowly. I knew they'd be waiting for me.

He was guarding the tunnel entrance again when I got there. He stared at me and I stared back at him.

"Where's my brother?" I shouted.

He did nothing. He just kept looking at me.

I pulled out the knife, the one he'd given me. I pointed it at his chest, not even an inch away, and said, "Give me back my brother."

He smiled and stepped back. The little girl came along and she had Connor with him. He was wrapped up in one of his blankets and he seemed happy.

I started crying when I saw him. I was so happy he was ok. I held him so tight. My little brother.

The two of them watched me. And there were others too. More children, more foxes. Eyes staring at me in the dark.

A little fox cub curled itself around the little girl's feet, like a cat trying to get her attention.

"Are they all children?" I asked them. "Are all the foxes children?"

"Not every fox. We're very special, because we got a second chance to be alive. Now we're one big happy family."

I saw the boy smile at her. It was the only time I ever saw him smile.

They held hands and I watched them walk away into the dark.

I took Connor home. One last walk along the rail track. I wasn't scared any more. The most amazing thing had happened. I felt strong. I felt unstoppable. I felt like I deserved to be a mother, his mother.

I felt strong enough to do one last thing to make our lives better. I was going to take one last risk, because I felt like I could do anything now.

When I got back home I could hear Mum struggling upstairs. I didn't rush to her. I put Connor in his pushchair for now. He was as calm and chilled out as he'd ever been.

I went upstairs and moved the bookcase. Mum was through the door before I said a word. "What the fuck is going on?" She looked up at the attic and then back at me.

"Come downstairs and I'll tell you all about it."

I went and sat myself down by the kitchen table and waited for her to get there. She was going through all the rooms and flipping out over all the damage.

"What the fuck's happened Katy?"

268

"Sit yourself down and we'll talk."

"Don't play games with me. Who did this?"

"Just sit down and let me tell you."

She picked up a chair and slammed it down by the table.

"Terry's gone Mum."

"What are you talking about? Who the fuck did this to our house?"

"Terry flipped out. He upset a few people. They had to take care of him. Look outside if you don't believe me. See all those lights." I pointed out the kitchen window. "Those are ambulances and police cars. They did him in and threw him under a train."

She stood and stared out the window.

"You're lying. Don't you fucking lie to me. This isn't the time for fucking games."

"You're not very lucky are you? One husband dies in a car accident, your next boyfriend goes under a train. Better tell the next guy you suck off not to get on an aeroplane. "

She went for me, but I just lent back on my chair and took Terry's shotgun out from under the table. She was so shocked she backed right off.

"You can't point that at me. I'm your mother. Put it down!"

"Money's gone Mum. I helped them find it. I didn't want it. I've already got money waiting for me.

"This is all that's left." I threw a Tesco bag on the table with everything left from Terry's haul in it.

"Take it and go. I'll look after Connor, like always. The police will be here soon. They'll want to know about the money. And even if they don't throw you in jail, Terry's friends will probably want to keep you quiet."

"You fucking little bitch."

"It's better than you deserve," I got up and put the gun to her head. "You remember Dad? What you did to him? You let him die like he was nothing. There's your fucking money. There's your fucking payday. You've got five minutes to grab your shit and go. I'm going to tell the cops all about you. And that's only if Terry's mates don't come and get you first."

269

She wasn't moving. So I screamed "Go" at her, jabbed her with the gun and she got the message. She grabbed the carrier bag and went upstairs. I lit up a cigarette and waited for her to get going. She packed a suitcase pretty quick.

She came downstairs and took one last look at me as if I was going to do something to suddenly save her. I stared back at her.

"Aren't you proud of me? Admit it, you couldn't have done better yourself."

She just turned and went. I got the last word after all. When I saw her car go by I knew it was over. It was finally all over.

Nothing that was going to happen next was ever going to be so bad. My life, I knew, was never going to be as bad again.

I did some more waiting. I wanted to give my mum a head start, before I called the police. I wiped my fingerprints off the shotgun and put it behind the filing cabinet upstairs. I phoned the police after a couple of hours and said I knew who it was who'd gone under the train.

When they came over, I let them in and told them my Mum was gone. Then I told them I wasn't going to tell them anything. Not unless I had it in writing that they were never ever going to take Connor away from me. I had leverage. If they wanted to know what happened, I needed to know that Connor was never going to go anywhere.

I waited while they called in a social worker. She told me that because I was 13 I wasn't legally allowed to look after a child but they'd do everything they could to keep us together.

I told her I'd already been looking after Connor and I didn't give a stuff about her rules and the law. I looked after Connor, and if they ever wanted to know what had happened at the house they were going to have to try harder.

After they'd talked it around, they asked if there was anyone they could call, a friend of the family or someone who could take responsibility for us both. I told them they could call Mr Summersby. There wasn't anyone else.

He came around at about 9 o'clock looking pretty shocked. He asked me what was going on. I said I needed to ask for his help now. And I needed him not to ask too many questions, not yet. I said that I knew I was asking a lot, but I needed his help and there was no one else to turn to.

Eventually they agreed – him and the police and the social worker – that me and Connor could stay with him. I went and got all of Connor's things together. He just slept through all of this. It was good one of us was calm about everything.

I hadn't really thought about Mr Summersby's family. He had a wife who was seven months pregnant. She'd wanted a family. This wasn't what she was expecting.

I said I was sorry to them both. He said he was going to help me out of this mess. But I needed to trust him. I said I'd tell him everything. But not now. I needed to sleep and rest.

I had all night to think about what I was going to say to the police. That was good and bad because it meant I got to work on my story, but it also meant I spent so much time worrying over details and not getting any rest. Like how come no one had tried to open the filing cabinet? I suppose they found the money first and didn't need to, officer.

I took Connor with me to the police station the next day. Mrs Summersby – Jill – she went with me. In my version of events my Mum knew everything. She and Terry talked about the money all the time. I'd been suspicious that she knew about my Dad's death because I'd heard her on the phone with Terry that same night, before the police had called. Of course they'd been having an affair. I'd suspected for years. But I didn't want to say anything because I was afraid of them and I was young and I hated the police because that's what I'd been taught.

I'd come home and caught two guys trashing the house. They'd blocked Mum in her room upstairs. When they couldn't find the money, they made me phone Terry. When he got home one watched me in the house while the other took Terry outside and over the fence. When he came back he said Terry had "gone under the train."

I described them as looking like the two people I saw at the factory. But I left it pretty vague. They had masks on,

271

obviously. They told me and Mum we should leave town and never come back. I told Mum I didn't want to go with her and she said that was fine and left.

It was hearing the whole story that won Jill over to helping me. She hadn't known what to think before. But now she really wanted to help me.

It's funny, I don't feel bad about anything I did, but I do feel bad about lying to Jill.

I didn't worry about them finding Mum and her telling a different story, because mine was much better and made more sense. After all, how was I going to have killed Terry?

They asked me a lot of questions. I don't think the story tied together as well as they wanted it to. But it didn't matter. They interviewed me about three times over the next few weeks. The crime was never solved. And that was fine. I didn't really care.

Mum never did show up again. I always thought I'd get a visit one day and find out she'd died of an overdose in some shit hole. But for all I know she's still out there. I reckon she went on to the continent. A woman can get away with almost anything if she's always up for it. And Mum was always up for it. If there was something she could get out of it.

Things worked out pretty well after it was all over. Eventually I was properly adopted. Jill and Bradley turned out to be really good people. And it was nice to know that there were really good people out there. They looked after me and Connor and they did it well. And we have a sister too. Their little girl Emma was born and her and Connor get on, most of the time.

He's done well in school. He's at university now. We sold Nan's house. I didn't really want to go back there. I sold that and split the money with Connor and with Emma, because I owe my new family a lot. They're the parents I wished I'd had growing up. Connor – he's pretty normal. He doesn't remember anything about those old days.

I used to think about us being poisoned. But there's nothing but goodness in Connor. He's grown up to be pretty special.

I've still had problems. Too many to go through. I'm doing ok. It's never been as tough as it was back then. It casts a long shadow over your life. I'm so glad Connor isn't damaged like I am. He gets along really well.

Things really have turned out ok. Much better than I had any right to expect. There's actually been some perks – I've never had to worry about money. And I'm not just talking about the money I got from the house.

About two weeks after I moved in with the Summersby's I happened to just look into their garden. Theirs doesn't back onto any wasteland. It's a pretty, looked-after garden; Jill's really into it. But there was a really muddy sports bag waiting for me there one day. One last present from my faithful friends.

There are still foxes where I live now. But they're not the same. They don't work together. They're like normal. There's nothing special or magic about them. But I still leave them food sometimes. I've never told anyone why.

I don't know what I saw back there in that tunnel and in Nan's garden. I don't know how a lost child can live again as a fox. But there are plenty of foxes and plenty of children who suffer. Maybe there's something good about them being saved and living again in some way. But I'd sooner be properly alive and be sort of normal. And to have saved my brother.

I owe them so much. I'm so grateful to them. They made me strong. They taught me how to fight. How to protect what's important to me.

And I've been fighting ever since. That's the one thing that's never really changed. I just keep my head down and stay quiet. No one expects anything or suspects anything, when you keep your head down and you stay quiet.

THE END